Julian Symons is primarily remembered as a master of the art of crime writing. However, in his eighty-two years he produced an enormously varied body of work. Social and military history, biography and criticism were all subjects he touched upon with remarkable success, and he held a distinguished reputation in each field.

His novels were consistently highly individual and expertly crafted, raising him above other crime writers of his day. It is for this that he was awarded various prizes, and, in 1982, named as Grand Master of the Mystery Writers of America – an honour accorded to only three other English writers before him: Graham Greene, Eric Ambler and Daphne du Maurier. He succeeded Agatha Christie as the president of Britain's Detection Club, a position he held from 1976 to 1985, and in 1990 he was awarded the Cartier Diamond Dagger from the British Crime Writers' Association for his lifetime's achievement in crime fiction.

Symons died in 1994.

BY THE SAME AUTHOR
ALL PUBLISHED BY HOUSE OF STRATUS

CRIME/SUSPENSE

THE 31ST OF FEBRUARY
THE BELTING INHERITANCE
BLAND BEGINNINGS
THE BROKEN PENNY
THE COLOUR OF MURDER
THE END OF SOLOMON GRUNDY
THE GIGANTIC SHADOW
THE IMMATERIAL MURDER CASE
THE KILLING OF FRANCIE LAKE
THE MAN WHO KILLED HIMSELF
THE MAN WHO LOST HIS WIFE
THE MAN WHOSE DREAMS CAME TRUE
THE NARROWING CIRCLE
THE PAPER CHASE
THE PLAYERS AND THE GAME
THE PLOT AGAINST ROGER RIDER
THE PROGRESS OF A CRIME
A THREE-PIPE PROBLEM

HISTORY/CRITICISM

BULLER'S CAMPAIGN
THE TELL-TALE HEART: THE LIFE AND
    WORKS OF EDGAR ALLEN POE
ENGLAND'S PRIDE
THE GENERAL STRIKE
HORATIO BOTTOMLEY
THE THIRTIES
THOMAS CARLYLE

A Man
Called Jones

Julian Symons

HOUSE OF
STRATUS

For My Mother

INTRODUCTION

The French call a typewriter *une machine á ècrire*. It is a description that could well be applied to Julian Symons, except the writing he produced had nothing about it smelling of the mechanical. The greater part of his life was devoted to putting pen to paper. Appearing in 1938, his first book was a volume of poetry, *Confusions About X*. In 1996, after his death, there came his final crime novel, *A Sort of Virtue* (written even though he knew he was under sentence from an inoperable cancer) beautifully embodying the painful come-by lesson that it is possible to achieve at least a degree of good in life.

His crime fiction put him most noticeably into the public eye, but he wrote in many forms: biographies, a memorable piece of autobiography (*Notes from Another Country*), poetry, social history, literary criticism coupled with year-on-year reviewing and two volumes of military history, and one string thread runs through it all. Everywhere there is a hatred of hypocrisy, hatred even when it aroused the delighted fascination with which he chronicled the siren schemes of that notorious jingoist swindler, Horatio Bottomley, both in his biography of the man and fictionally in *The Paper Chase* and *The Killing of Francie Lake*.

That hatred, however, was not a spew but a well-spring. It lay behind what he wrote and gave it force, yet it was always tempered by a need to speak the truth. Whether he was writing about people as fiction or as fact, if he had a low opinion of them he simply told the truth as he saw it, no more and no less.

This adherence to truth fills his novels with images of the mask. Often it is the mask of hypocrisy. When, as in *Death's Darkest Face* or *Something Like a Love Affair*, he chose to use a plot of dazzling legerdemain, the masks of cunning are startlingly ripped away.

The masks he ripped off most effectively were perhaps those which people put on their true faces when sex was in the air or under the exterior. 'Lift the stone, and sex crawls out from under,' says a character in that relentless hunt for truth, *The Progress of a Crime*, a book that achieved the rare feat for a British author, winning Symons the US Edgar Allen Poe Award.

Julian was indeed something of a pioneer in the fifties and sixties bringing into the almost sexless world of the detective story the truths of sexual situations. 'To exclude realism of description and language from the crime novel' he writes in *Critical Occasions*, 'is almost to prevent its practitioners from attempting any serious work.' And then the need to unmask deep-hidden secrecies of every sort was almost as necessary at the end of his crime-writing life as it had been at the beginning. Not for nothing was his last book subtitled *A Political Thriller.*

H R F Keating
London, 2001

CHARACTERS IN THE STORY

In the Hargreaves Advertising Agency

EDWARD HARGREAVES	*Founder of the Agency*
LIONEL HARGREAVES	*His elder son*
RICHARD HARGREAVES	*His younger son*
GEORGE TRACY	*Creative Director*
JACK BOND	*Production Manager*
CHARLES SINCLAIR	*Copy Chief*
JEAN ROGERS	*Copywriter*
ONSLOW	*Another copywriter*
MUDGE	*Studio artist*
MISS PEACHEY	*Receptionist*
MISS BERRY	*Her friend*

Outside the Agency

MR JONES	*A mystery*
MRS LACEY	*A landlady*
EVE MARCHANT	*An actress*
MYRTLE MONTAGUE	*Another actress*
JOSEPH VAN DIEREN	*An art agent*
POLLY LINES	*His secretary*
ARNOLD CARRUTHERS	*A freelance artist, cousin of*
	Lionel and Richard Hargreaves
WILLIAM WESTON	*Lawyer to the Hargreaves family*
EDGAR SINCLAIR	*Brother of Charles*
JULIA BOND	*Wife of Jack Bond*
JACKSON	*Servants in the Hargreaves*
WILLIAMS	*family*
DETECTIVE-INSPECTOR BLAND	*Of Scotland Yard*
DETECTIVE-SERGEANT FILBY	

WEDNESDAY, JANUARY 15

Chapter One *6.15 to 6.45 p.m.*

Charles Sinclair paused for a moment on the steps of the house in Redfern Square, and looked at his watch. A fine mist of rain blurred the dial, and he had to hold it close to his face before he saw that the time was *6.15.* He shivered involuntarily as he hesitated, for some reason that he could not have named, before the open door of the house; as he turned, with a second decisive shiver, to go in he heard his name called and the figure of Jack Bond, jaunty and overdressed, appeared through the drizzling rain. Bond's dark face was rich with malice, and he tapped the steps with the silver-headed cane which he used, a little unnecessarily Sinclair thought, to conceal a slight limp. His voice, like his manner, was unsympathetic, harsh and grating and curiously unfriendly.

'I hope you feel it an honour to enter these portals, Sinclair? To step upon rich carpets that have been trod by all the advertising talents of Great Britain?' Sinclair grunted. 'As our American friends say, a pretty nifty joint.' Bond bent down to examine with comical carefulness the plain red hair carpet. 'But the old man's been practising economy in the hall. The pile carpets are kept for the places where they matter.'

Sinclair found himself annoyed, as he frequently found himself annoyed, by Bond's facetiousness. 'What sort of carpet do you expect to find in a hall?'

'My dear chap,' Bond protested, 'here I expect flunkeys on every side, bearing salvers of beaten gold on which we shall drop the cards we haven't got, so that we may be announced suitably. And here comes the flunkey. But no salver. Very disappointing. My hat, certainly,' he said, giving to the man a hat with a small red feather in it, 'and my stick and case.' He passed over a small brown leather attaché-case. 'And here we are,' he said, as another servant opened a large white panelled door, 'entering the scene of revelry. How delightful – by which I mean, of course, how dull – to see the old familiar faces we saw an hour ago.'

The scene was hardly one of revelry. The room they entered was fully forty feet long, and some sixty people were standing in it, looking rather depressed than gay. In front of a pair of folding doors there was an improvised bar, with two bartenders. An enormous iced birthday cake with twenty-five candles stood on a buhl table: this cake commemorated the twenty-fifth birthday of the nationally-famous Hargreaves Advertising Agency. And when people thought of this Agency with admiration, distaste or envy, they did not think of it as Hargreaves & Hargreaves, which was its established name now that Edward Hargreaves had taken his eldest son into partnership; they thought of the Agency in terms of the initials EH, which stood for Edward Hargreaves.

Among these thousands EH was in a small way a legend. He never spoke of his past life, but it was known, or at least said with all the familiarity of truth, that he had been a newspaper-boy, an invoice clerk, a gravedigger's mate and a maker of model aeroplanes, before he was twenty-one: and he had not merely held those jobs, but had been dismissed from all of them. The steps by which he had started his climb to wealth and success were hidden: but when at the age of forty he came from America to his native country he brought a few thousand pounds and some unexpected ideas with him. It was said that these ideas were not always what the conventional might call respectable; that Edward Hargreaves, in those early days, was not only a little smarter than any of his competitors, but that his smartness might, in any more tediously ethical occupation, have put him

4

in some very awkward situations. But those st/
the past and lent, in a way, a flavour of romance to u..
Edward Hargreaves. Nobody could deny that now, at sixty-fiv.,
EH had become conservative, traditional, a Grand Old Man of
advertising. His knighthood was expected yearly by his staff. He
had married twice; the first thin, faded woman who had borne
him two sons, and whose presence in the household had become
less and less noticeable until at last she seemed less to have died
than simply to have vanished from a scene where her presence
was no longer required. A year after her death, when he was
sixty-two years of age, EH had married a girl of twenty-two,
who met her death in a yachting accident within six months of
their marriage. Such was Edward Hargreaves, the owner of the
Hargreaves Agency. On the Agency's twenty-fifth birthday a
party was being given, a cake was being cut, and a speech was
being made; dancing was to follow the speech.

All the members of the staff had been invited, from the other
directors down to the girls in the Accounts Department, who
giggled whenever anyone over the age of thirty spoke to them;
only the messenger-boys had been given a pound note each, and
told to go out and enjoy themselves. The invitation was an
order: but there would in any event have been little inclination
to refuse, since all the women on the staff were anxious to show
how delightful they looked away from the office and in evening
dress, and almost all the men thought it might improve their
standing if it were known that they had been to a party at the
old man's house in Redfern Square. 'Evening Dress – Optional'
had been marked clearly on the cards which, in order to give the
occasion importance, had been sent by post to each member of
the staff: but very few, Sinclair saw, had decided to avail
themselves of the option. He got a glass of sherry and a biscuit,
and sipped the sherry reflectively, while he looked round.

The party, he thought, could hardly be called a success at the
moment. Little departmental groups had gathered together, and
were talking almost in whispers. The four Accounts girls, quite

overcome by the occasion, were giggling together over their gin and grapefruit. Onslow and Mudge, two young copywriters, were standing firmly together in front of the buffet, and drinking hard and fast. Mrs Rodgers, who looked after copy from what everyone except Sinclair, who had charge of the Copy Department, called the woman's angle, was talking to Tracy, the Creative Director, and Bond. Lionel, the other Hargreaves in the name, was standing at the side of the room, near the windows, fiddling with a small box on a table. There was no sign of EH or his youngest son, Richard. Sinclair was debating which of the several little groups he should join, when Lionel Hargreaves beckoned to him. Lionel was a well-built, fair man of thirty-five, with a weakly handsome, sensual face, an amiably supercilious manner, and, Sinclair had always thought, very little aptitude for advertising. He greeted Sinclair with the friendly condescension of a duke who is being pleasant to a baronet.

'Looking lost over there, Sinclair. Devilish bore these things, aren't they?' The question was almost rhetorical, and Sinclair did not answer it. 'You know what the old man's like, though – loves that touch of ceremonial.'

'Oh, yes,' Sinclair said. EH couldn't do without the ceremonial.'

Lionel ran a finger round his collar. He was wearing a dinner-jacket. 'I could do without it myself, and without these damned monkey jackets, too.' There was a particularly loud giggle from one of the Account girls, and Lionel's eye strayed towards them. 'That girl – what's her name – Miss Gardner. Got a fine figure, hasn't she? Pity she giggles so much.'

Sinclair was rather short. 'She's engaged to be married.'

'Is she now. Hell of a thing, marriage – can land you in a devil of a mess. Certainly has me.' Lionel suddenly looked alarmed, as if he had said something he had not intended. 'This buhl furniture and these Aubusson carpets now – I don't like that kind of thing, do you? Ornate.'

'It helps with the ceremonial – and it must have cost ⟨ of money.'

'Money, oh ah, yes.' Lionel's attention had wandered. With an almost visible effort he pulled it back to Sinclair and laid his hand on the box which stood on the table by his side. 'Never been here before, have you?' he asked, and although it could not be said that his tone was offensive, it was too noticeably that of the lord of the manor congratulating one of his retainers on a step up in the world to be agreeable to Sinclair, whose 'No' was rather stiff. 'You won't have seen any of the old man's musical-boxes, then.' He lifted the rosewood lid of the box on the table, and Sinclair saw a long brass cylinder with small spikes sticking out of it, which impinged on a steel comb. At the back of the box sat three little figures with drumsticks in their hands and drums in front of them. Sinclair, although he was annoyed by Lionel's manner, was too interested to be sulky. He bent close to look at the box and said, 'Charming.' Lionel moved a switch at one side of the box, and stood back with a slightly self-satisfied smile. The cylinder revolved, the figures beat on their drums, and the box gave a pleasant. tinkling rendering of 'The Blue Bells of Scotland.' Heads in the room turned towards them, talking stopped for the necessary and polite few seconds and then recommenced. Bond left Tracy and Mrs Rogers, and joined them in looking at the musical-box. 'My word,' he said. 'That's a fine box – one of the best forte-pianos I've seen. I didn't know the old man went in for such things.'

Lionel affected a faint surprise. 'You know about these things, do you, Bond? Shouldn't have thought they were your line of country.'

Bond's laugh was loud. 'Precious few things that *aren't* my line of country. Always been interested in mechanical devices, and these musical-boxes are damned ingenious things. Does the old man collect them?' Lionel did not answer, and it was plain that his abstraction was such that he really had not heard what was said. 'Where is the old man, by the way?'

'He'll be along,' Lionel said vaguely. 'Had to go to some meeting or other. But he wouldn't miss this for worlds – gives him a chance to perform you know.'

'My word,' Bond said, 'look at Tracy and Mrs Rogers over there – they are going it, aren't they? I left them because I thought they'd like to be al-o-o-ne.' He exaggerated the last word comically. Sinclair looked across the room and saw that Tracy and Mrs Rogers were certainly engaged in what seemed to be earnest conversation.

'Don't know what you're damned well talking about,' Lionel said.

'Well, I do think it's a bit scandalous. Jean Rogers is all very well, but, after all, Tracy is supposed to hold a certain position in the firm. I don't know what EH would say if he knew about it.'

Sinclair did not much like Lionel, but he liked Bond less, and he could not help feeling pleased when Lionel said shortly, 'Should keep that sort of gossip to yourself if I were you, Bond. Ah – there's Dick. You're a bit late, Dick, old man. Haven't seen you since lunch.'

Richard Hargreaves was two years younger than his brother, but he looked less than his age. His face was smooth and unlined; it showed, like Lionel's, marks of weakness round the mouth and chin, but he had willowy handsomeness emphasised by his choice of clothes. He was one of the few men not in evening dress. He was wearing a dark double-breasted lounge suit slightly tapered at the waist, with a red carnation in his buttonhole, and dark brogue shoes. He said in a gentle, rather high-pitched voice, 'I'm sorry. I got held up. Haven't even had time to change yet. I'll slip upstairs in a minute or two.'

'Been hitting the highspots?'

Richard Hargreaves said in the friendliest possible tone, 'I think you can give me lessons on that, Lionel. I've been out with Eve – Marchant – we went back and had coffee in her flat.'

'Eve Marchant!' A flush mounted slowly from Lionel's neck to his face. "You're a bloody fool if you mix yourself up with Eve – she's poison.'

Richard took a cigarette from a thin silver case, and tapped it deliberately, and a little theatrically, before he said with a faint smile, 'Didn't I hear something once about one man's meat…?'

Lionel's face was alarmingly red as he said, 'My God, Dick, you're a bloody fool. I must talk to you about this.' It was at this point that Sinclair pressed Bond's arm gently, and led him away. Bond went unwillingly, and with a slight leer on his face. 'What do you know about that?' he said.

'I know it's time I had another sherry, and I know if some of us don't fraternise a bit with the juniors this party's going to be a flop.'

'Damn the party. They shouldn't wash their dirty linen in public if they don't want anyone to watch them doing it.'

Sinclair had had enough of Bond. 'I should put on a false beard and do some eavesdropping, since you're so interested. I'm going to liven up the lads from the Studio.' He made his way over to where half a dozen young men and women were talking in whispers and looking rather gloomily at the floor.

"Look, George,'…Rogers said, 'there's Sinclair gone over to talk to the Studio boys. You should go and cheer them up – they do look pathetic. After all, they are your department, aren't they?'

'Hell with the Studio,' George Tracy said, 'and to hell with it all, and to hell with this party. I've had enough. I've a good mind to throw in my hand altogether.' He made an eloquent gesture, a throwing out of his hand as it were, in the air. He was full of eloquent gestures.

Jean Rogers sighed. 'Yes, George.'

'God preserve me from advertising men,' Tracy said, by no means in an undertone, 'but God preserve me most from top-class advertising men. If there's a lower species of life, I don't know it.' He made another eloquent gesture in the direction of

Lionel and Richard Hargreaves. 'One of them without the faintest knowledge of advertising or, indeed, of any other subject that requires the application of intelligence, the other a stuffed, tailor-made dummy who should be in the window of a multiple clothes store as an example of natty dressing.'

'George, I think we've been standing and talking long enough. We agreed it wasn't a good thing. I think I should – '

'A good advertising man, Jean, is nothing less than a creative artist. He has a soul. You and I have souls – and souls are delicate things. The treatment they get from these insensitive idiots is enough to drive any creative man mad.' He ran his hand through the black hair that stood up like pins on his head. Jean Rogers, looking at him, thought again that he was one of the most handsome men she had ever seen. She said placatingly, 'Richard's not bad. He's rather sweet in a way. I think I – '

'Rather sweet?' Tracy snorted, and made no further comment on Richard. 'And as for EH – you know what I think of EH.'

She sighed again. 'Yes, darling.' Then: 'Here he is.'

Onslow and Mudge from the Copy Department had arrived early. They had each drunk six cocktails and eaten three biscuits, and they were feeling cheerful. Onslow was in his late twenties, and Mudge was a year or two younger. Both of them had taken advantage of the option on dress; they were wearing corduroy trousers and sports jackets and knitted woollen ties. Their opinions of their seniors were not more favourable than the views Tracy had expressed on the Hargreaves family.

'Do you know what I think of advertising agencies, old boy?' Onslow said. 'I think they stink.'

'Right you are,' said Mudge.

'But what stinks worst in them is the executive class – the managerial class.' Onslow tapped Mudge's chest with one finger and enunciated clearly. 'An advertising agency can only exist in full perfection in a capitalist system which is showing the – the iridescence of decay. It thrives in an atmosphere of commercial competition – '

'Right you are,' said Mudge.

' – and exists to sell people goods they don't want at prices higher than they can afford to pay. Its owners are sharks and its personnel are rats.'

'I say, old boy.'

'Yes?'

'What about us? After all, we're personnel of an advertising agency, aren't we?'

'Until the overthow of the capitalist system,' said Onslow, scoring points rapidly on Mudge's chest. 'After that we shan't be. In the meantime, what do you want us to do, starve? But if you ask me what I think of EH and his bloody birthday cake, I think he's a – '

'He's here,' said Mudge.

Edward Hargreaves was standing in the doorway.

Chapter Two *4.00 to 4.15 p.m.*

The person who used the name of Jones put down a book called *The Abbotsford Murders* and crossed to the window. The clock outside the optician's shop opposite said two minutes past four. There was plenty of time. Mr Jones (that was the name given when the room was booked) thought back again over the things already done, and the things that were still to do. Up to the present, at any rate, there had been no mistakes. 'And there won't be any mistakes,' Mr Jones said to himself. 'There won't be any mistakes.' From a battered suitcase Mr Jones took out a Smith and Wesson revolver, rather clumsily because he was wearing a pair of lemon-yellow gloves. Mr Jones put the revolver in his overcoat pocket, relocked the suitcase, and opened the door of the first-floor room. On the ground floor, down a flight of narrow dark stairs, was a telephone. Mr Jones called down the stairs in a curiously deep and harsh voice, 'Mrs Lacey.' The landlady's head, in a mob cap, appeared at the foot of the stairs, peering up into the shadows where her lodger was standing.

'What is it you're wanting?'

Mr Jones said in the same harsh voice, 'I have to go out in a few minutes Mrs Lacey, and I am not sure when I shall return. May I make a telephone call before I go?'

'Sure you can, Mr Jones. Just so long as you put in your two-pence, otherwise you won't get your number.' She laughed at her joke, but there was no answering laugh from the lodger. 'Thank you,' Mr Jones said – and then, instead of coming down to telephone, returned to the room and closed the door.

Chapter Three *6.45 to 7.30 p.m.*

Edward Hargreaves was rather above medium height; he had a florid complexion and a fine head of white hair, and although he was now in his middle sixties, his walk was as brisk and his back as upright as it had been twenty years ago. There was a weight and portentousness about his words and gestures which fitted well with the part of Grand Old Man of advertising which he constantly played ('EH passes you the salt,' a friend had said, 'as if he were giving you a five-pound note.') Sometimes the pomp spilled over into geniality: but the heavy brows, the flaring nostrils and the downward curve of the thin mouth, told a story easily read. One did not have to know Edward Hargreaves well to know that beneath the surface of pomp and geniality lay a ruthlessness which was not the more pleasant because it was concealed. His first sight of that mouth convinced Sinclair that most of the stories he had heard about Edward Hargreaves' early life had not been exaggerated. At the present time, however, the corners of the mouth were curved upwards into a smile of palpable falsity. There was hardly a person in the room at that moment, including his sons, who liked EH or would have felt any sorrow if they had been told of his death; and yet such is the power of money and convention that when he smiled and said, 'Good evening. I am very sorry to be late,' every one of the faces that greeted him smiled in return.

With the smile fixed firmly in place EH walked round among his staff, giving them words of welcome. A dispassionate observer, if one had been present, would have noticed that although all the words he spoke to his staff were in appearance friendly, most of them looked more relieved than happy when he had passed on: and the conversation, which had been flowing a little more easily, was checked again to whispers. He stopped before Tracy and Mrs Rogers, and said amiably to Tracy, 'I'm so glad you're looking after Mrs Rogers, George. But we can't have any conspiracies between copywriters and artists tonight. Time off from business this evening, you know, time off from business.' If Bond had been within earshot he might not have said so confidently that EH knew nothing of an affair between Tracy and Mrs Rogers.

Tracy was foolish to rise to this palpable bait. 'We weren't talking business.'

EH was almost arch in reply. "I thought you looked so much as if you were – I *do* apologise.'

By the time EH had sympathised with Onslow and Mudge on their lack of dinner-jackets, congratulated Bond on his wit in making the Accounts girls giggle, asked Sinclair anxiously whether he thought the boys in his department could stand so much strong drink, and made similar observations to the heads of the Research and Space Departments, he was looking almost benign in his cheerfulness. But as he walked across the room to where his two sons were standing the smile was cut quite suddenly and sharply off his face. The mouth turned down and the heavy brows contracted: the effect was not pleasant. Lionel and Richard awaited him with the air of two soldiers who are about to be inspected by their Commanding Officer, and are guiltily aware of spots on their tunics. They said in unison, 'good evening, EH' EH looked at a point somewhere between them and said, 'Good evening. Lionel, I shall want to talk to you for a few minutes after the dancing has begun. I hope you can find it convenient to make yourself available. Richard, I shall be glad if you can make arrangements to change into appropriate clothing as soon as possible.' He turned, a Commanding Officer who had found the inspection even less satisfactory than he had expected, and marched away leaving Richard looking dejected and Lionel looking alarmed.

Chapter Four *4.15 to 4.25 p.m.*

Mr Jones opened the door of his room. Feet clattered uneasily on the uncarpeted stairs. At the bottom of the stairs stood the telephone; the door of the room down the passage that Mrs Lacey called her parlour was slightly open, and a thin gleam of electric light shone through to the hall. Mr Jones carefully placed his old suitcase on the floor, and took out from his pocket two pennies which he regarded for a moment with a purposeful look. He picked up the telephone receiver, inserted the two pennies, and dialled a number. The shaft of light coming through into the hall grew almost imperceptibly wider as the two pennies dropped to the bottom of the box. Mr Jones had pressed Button A.

He spoke for a couple of minutes and then hung up the receiver with an inaudible exclamation of annoyance. He called out suddenly, 'Good-bye, Mrs Lacey,' picked up his suitcase, turned the round knob of the Yale lock and was out in the street. He was still wearing the lemon-yellow gloves.

Outside in the street Mr Jones' shoulders were raised and lowered almost imperceptibly in a sigh. 'Well, thank God *that's* over,' he thought, and began to walk briskly towards the main road, which led to the Elephant and Castle. Just once he patted the left pocket of the big raglan overcoat he was wearing, and the corners of his mouth moved in the ghost of a smile.

Chapter Five *8.10 to 8.30 p.m.*

EH had been speaking for twenty minutes, and had the appearance of a batsman who after a shaky start is settling down to a good solid knock, when his serene expression changed suddenly to a look of lowering concentration. His eyes searched among the audience as though he were looking for someone, and he noticeably quickened the pace of his speech. He slowed down, however, as he came to the crucial point:

'I hope,' he said, 'that this brief history of the Agency's past activities and successes will have been of some interest to you. H'rm. All of you have shared in these successes, I do not hesitate to say that you have been in large part responsible for them. On this silver anniversary of the Agency's birth I propose to show some concrete appreciation of the long service rendered by you all. This appreciation will take the practical form of a 10 per cent rise in salary for the whole of the staff present here tonight, from our valued directors, to the stenographers, receptionist and switchboard operator whose work is equally valuable in its own sphere' (here there was a slight rustle among the audience). 'I hope that this step will meet with your approval. And now, without making any further call on your interest or time, I propose to cut this cake.' And EH was as good as his word: but he cut the cake with a look which showed that his mind was on other things. Suddenly he called on his son Richard, who, now wearing full evening dress, was standing looking rather moodily at his feet.

'Where is Lionel?'

'Eh? Isn't he here? I suppose he must have slipped out.'

EH's look of concentration became converted to a frown. It was obvious that he did not approve of people slipping out while he was talking. He cut several slices of cake in a perfunctory manner, and then said, 'Look after things for me, my boy. I'm going to find Lionel.' Richard Hargreaves shrugged his shoulders as his father strode out of the door from the dining-room to the hall. Then he made a faintly comic deprecatory gesture to the assembled members of the staff, and they all crowded round the cake. There were mixed feelings about the 10 per cent rise. What would happen, Bond asked Sinclair, when next they asked for a rise in the usual way? They would be told they had had one recently. 'And, my lad,' Bond finished up with the dogmatic tone which many people found offensive, 'it so happens that a rise is just about due to me. Now – I've had it.'

'There may be something in what you say. I wonder where Lionel's got to. I haven't seen him for some time.'

'Here he is. No he isn't – it's EH alone. I say, he looks as if he'd picked up sixpence and lost a ten-bob note, doesn't he?'

EH's face was mottled, and his cheeks were puffed out with anger. 'Richard,' he said, 'I insist on knowing where Lionel is. Jackson who is on the door, says he went outside at about half-past seven. If that's so, he wasn't in here while I was talking.'

Richard Hargreaves shrugged his shoulders again. 'It's no use asking *me*. Maybe he's gone out.'

'Nonsense. He knew that I wished to speak to him.'

'Maybe he's in the – ' Richard made a gesture, and EH seemed momentarily disconcerted. 'Oh.' His cheeks puffed out again. 'Well, let's see.' He slammed the door as he went out. Richard went on cutting slices of cake.

'When the old man gets on the warpath, the sparks certainly fly,' Bond said with a grin. He seemed to be enjoying himself. Sinclair was about to take another piece of cake when the door to the hall opened again. EH was standing there, an expression on his face was one of such shocked ferocity as no one in that room had ever seen. He looked from face to face and then, without speaking to anyone, crossed the room to the telephone, and dialled a number. They were all staring at him openly now.

'Scotland Yard,' EH said. His voice had a thick, choked quality. 'My name is Edward Hargreaves. I wish to report a murder.'

Chapter Six *8.50 to 10.00 p.m.*

The cake lay untouched on the plates, the drinks stood half-empty on the tables. Nobody spoke. One of the girls from Accounts had hysterics and was taken outside by the bartenders. No one else left the room. Richard Hargreaves sat well away from his father, turning over idly in his hands the knife with which he had been cutting the cake. Tracy leaned against the wall and stared at the door: he did not look at Mrs Rogers. Other people sat uncomfortably on the edge of their chairs. Occasionally somebody coughed. EH himself sat on a stiff chair near the single door in the room, that led out into the hall, rather as if he were on guard. He had not spoken to anyone since making the telephone call. It was a relief to all of them when the police arrived.

They came in the person of a man of middle height, about thirty-five years old, wearing a light fawn raincoat spotted with rain, and a snap-brimmed trilby hat which he held in his hand. He had a fresh complexion, well-brushed fair hair and a round, smooth face; the curious innocence of his expression was contradicted by the watchful look in a pair of blue eyes which were not unfriendly but impersonal. He paused in the doorway and looked at them, and probably there was nobody in the room who did not feel a little disturbed by that look. It was not unsympathetic, but it was detached: it seemed to say, 'I can well understand that you are all upset, and that you may behave oddly. At the same time I am bearing in mind the fact that you

21

may be behaving oddly because you have recently committed a murder. I am here to understand everything, but what I am most concerned to understand is a murderer's mind.'

As he stepped into the room the man said in a voice which was pleasant enough, but was curiously flat and expressionless, 'Mr Hargreaves, Mr Edward Hargreaves? I am Detective-Inspector Bland from Scotland Yard.'

EH said 'Yes,' in a hoarse voice. 'My son Lionel has been killed. This is my house. His body is in the library.'

Bland looked at his watch. 'Were these ladies and gentlemen present when he was killed?'

'They were all here. It – happened some time between half-past seven and half-past eight.'

'Oh.' Bland looked again at the rest of the people in the room. 'I shall be glad if you will remain here. I may have some questions to ask you.' As EH and Bland moved towards the door Richard Hargreaves said to his father, 'May I come too, sir? I may be able to help.' EH merely inclined his head.

They walked out of the large drawing-room into the hall, where the two footmen who had received the guests were standing together. 'These men say my son left the drawing-room – God knows why – about half-past seven. They also say nobody came out after ten to eight.'

'That was about the time when you started speaking,' Richard said. In answer to Bland's unasked question he said, 'It was a special occasion, and my father made a short speech.'

Bland looked at the elder of the two servants. His voice was hard as he said, 'What's your name?'

'Jackson, sir,' the man said. He was a man of about fifty, with grey hair and a hooked nose. He looked rather like the popular conception of an Ambassador, but his voice was soft with years of deference. 'And this is Williams.' He indicated a young and perky man with bright black eyes who stood beside him.

'Were both of you on duty here in the hall?'

'That's right sir. We were on duty all evening. We haven't had very much to do so far, but we were to be on hand all the evening to give any assistance required.'

'Have you been here long?'

There was a touch of reproachful dignity in Jackson's voice. 'Ten years, sir. And Williams has been with us for five.'

'And you were on duty here in the hall, both of you, after Mr Lionel Hargreaves left the drawing-room? Neither of you left the hall for any reason?'

'That is correct, sir. As a matter of fact, neither of us left the hall during the whole evening, from six o'clock onwards, for more than two or three minutes.' There was almost a touch of acidity in Jackson's gentle voice as he said, 'This is our place of duty, sir!'

'And you are absolutely sure of the time when Mr Lionel Hargreaves came out of the drawing-room?'

'Within a minute or two, sir,' Jackson said, and Williams nodded agreement.

'What makes you so sure?'

Jackson coughed. 'A moment or two before, sir, Williams had looked at the clock and remarked that it was nearly half-past seven, and we should be late for our supper. It had been tentatively arranged that the dancing should start at eight and that we should go off for supper in turn after that time. Very soon after that, Mr Lionel came out of the drawing-room and walked down that passage.' He indicated a passage that ran along the side of the drawing-room.

'Do you confirm all this, Williams?'

'All absolutely right, sir,' Williams said emphatically. Both of them, Bland thought, looked more curious than distressed. 'The passage leads to the lavatories and through the library out into the garden. And it leads to the dining-room, too.'

'Did you see which way Mr Hargreaves went? Which door he entered?'

23

'Oh, no sir. You can't see that from the hall. Of course, we thought he'd gone to the lavatory.'

'And did you notice that he had not returned?'

Jackson spoke again. 'We noticed it, sir, but we did not remark it specially. We thought that perhaps Mr Lionel had gone to smoke a cigar in the library. And of course, sir, it was not for us to enquire into Mr Lionel's actions.'

'I realise that. Now, think carefully, before you answer this. Are you able to remember who came out *after* Mr Lionel Hargreaves – that is between the time Mr Lionel Hargreaves came out and his father went to look for him?'

Jackson bowed his head slightly. The gesture was impressive. 'Williams and I have discussed that point already, sir. We realised that it might be important. And the most we can say' – Jackson included Williams with a wave of the hand – 'is that we think we could pick them out. We knew Mr Lionel. We don't know most of the other gentlemen here, and so we couldn't be absolutely sure of identifying them.' He hesitated, and Richard said quickly, 'I came out for a couple of minutes. Don't be afraid to mention that Jackson.' Jackson did not reply, but merely bowed his head again.

Bland's face showed neither pleasure nor annoyance. 'You mentioned gentlemen. What about the ladies?'

'On that point, sir, Williams and I are positive. No lady came out of the drawing-room between the time Mr Lionel went down the passage and Mr Hargreaves came out to look for him.'

EH had listened to this dialogue with growing impatience. 'I can't see the point of all this.'

'It has a point,' Bland assured him. 'One of my men will come along and ask you both some questions about the people who came out of the drawing-room. Answer them as fully as you can. You've been very clear so far. Thank you.' They walked down the corridor, and came to two doors on the left-hand side, and two on the right. Richard acted as guide. He pointed to the two doors on the left. 'Men's washroom and lavatory, ladies' washroom and lavatory. On the right, dining-room and then library, with an interconnecting door between them.'

Bland nodded. They were standing outside the library door. He said to EH, 'You turned the handle of this door, I suppose?'

'Why, yes, man. It was closed.'

'Did you enter the dining-room?

EH seemed a little taken aback. 'No, I didn't. I didn't suppose Lionel would be in the dining-room. As Jackson said, he might have gone into the library to smoke a cigar.' Bland said nothing, but turned the handle of the door.

The library was a large square room. A glass-fronted bookcase over eight feet tall ran along the wall to the left of the three men; in the wall in which the door was placed stood another bookcase, and a bureau with a writing desk; in the wall opposite to the door curtains were flapping in front of a pair of french windows. Almost in the centre of the room the body of Lionel Hargreaves lay on the floor. The dead man was lying on his face with one arm flung out above his head. Bland knelt beside him. 'Shot through the back,' he said, and sniffed. 'From close range. Powderburns on the jacket.' He made a gesture towards the curtains. 'Was the window open when you came in?'

'Yes. I've touched nothing. The window leads out into the garden.'

Bland walked across the room and looked out into the darkness. Three steps led down from the french windows into a garden. He spoke from the window. 'I'm right in thinking, am I not, that there's no possible exit from that drawing-room where your party took place?'

'Yes. Normally the folding-doors provide another exit which leads into the dining-room, but we had the buffet arranged in front of them, and they were locked.'

'And your guests are?'

EH said harshly. 'I am an advertising agent. You may have heard of me. The people here are members of my staff.'

Richard Hargreaves had been staring at the body on the floor with no particular expression. Now he looked up and said, 'Perhaps we'd better explain some details to the Inspector. This was a little party to celebrate the silver jubilee of the Hargreaves Advertising Agency, Inspector, and all the members of the staff are in the drawing-room.'

'Where does this garden lead to? Is it easily reached from the drawing-room?'

Again it was Richard who spoke. 'Anyone coming out of the drawing-room could reach the garden by coming down the passage and into the library as we have done. Otherwise he would have to go out of the front door, walk round the back of the house, and come in through a door in the wall, which leads into the garden.'

'And if Jackson and Williams are telling the truth, nobody came that way. Do you think they are telling the truth? Are they absolutely reliable?'

EH exploded wrathfully. 'Good God, yes. There can't be any doubt about that. They'd have no reason to lie.'

'This door in the garden wall. Is it kept locked?'

As a matter of fact,' Richard said apologetically, 'it isn't. The lock went wrong a couple of years ago, and it's never been put right.' Bland raised his eyebrows. 'I know it sounds careless, but really the wall's so low – only about six feet – and anyone could get over it in a few seconds if they wanted to come in that way.'

'So,' Bland said. He came in from the window. 'Do either of you recognise these? They were on the steps outside the french windows.' He held up a pair of yellow-lemon gloves. The two men looked at them curiously and shook their heads. Bland examined the right-hand glove carefully, and smelt it. 'Faint powder-marks and a distinct smell. The murderer has left us a present,' he said gravely. He put down the gloves and spoke to EH 'Was the light on or off when you came into the room, Mr Hargreaves?'

'Off. I snapped on the switch and saw – '

'Yes. Now correct me if I'm wrong. Next door to this room is the dining-room, and next door to that is the drawing-room which you were using at the party.'

'That's right.'

Two lines of worry creased Bland's smooth forehead. 'And you didn't hear a shot? Nobody heard a shot.' He said in a gently deprecatory tone, 'That seems to me very odd.'

Richard Hargreaves clicked his fingers. 'Not so odd. The walls of this room are soundproof.'

'Soundproof?' Bland's eyebrows went up.

EH said curtly, 'This is my library. When I come here to read or work I don't want to be disturbed by Richard's damned gramophone playing jazz tunes or by giggling servants. These walls and doors are lined with asbestos to exclude sound.'

'So that's why the shot wasn't heard. But in that case – ' Bland checked himself and nodded towards the french windows. 'How large is your garden?'

Richard Hargreaves answered. 'It's really hardly a garden – just a back yard. It's about twenty-five yards long by thirteen or fourteen wide. It leads on to Labriole Street.' He said tentatively, 'Of course the man must have come that way.'

Bland's chubby face was grave. 'There's no of course about it. There are two obvious possibilities. First, that Lionel Hargreaves was killed by one of your guests, who came in after him, shot him, opened the french windows and left a pair of gloves outside for us to find, and then returned to the party. In that case he's one of the people who left the party after half-past seven, to go to the wash-room. Or he may have been killed by someone from outside who did all those things, and who came in and out through the garden door. If the murder was done by a guest, it's easy to see why the gloves were left – they'd be highly compromising. So would the revolver. If one of your guests is guilty we can expect to find the revolver – indeed we're bound to find it, since none of them has left the house.'

'Oh, but really,' Richard said, 'this is preposterous.' He took a blue silk handkerchief from his coat sleeve, and wiped his forehead.

'Is it? Can you tell me any reason why your son should have been killed, Mr Hargreaves?' Bland spoke impersonally, and looked at EH, but Richard was included in the question. There was silence before either man spoke.

EH said harshly, 'I know of nothing. Every man makes enemies. I've made them myself in the way of business. Lionel made as many enemies as most men. But I know of nothing that would have caused anyone to kill him.'

'What about the servants?'

'Ridiculous. They had very little to do with Lionel.'

'In any event, surely they cancel each other out, as they were both on duty?' Richard said.

'Unless they were both concerned,' Bland said coolly. 'Very well. My men will go over this room for fingerprints, and they will search the garden. It will also be necessary to conduct a search of the house and everyone in it, for the revolver. And – '

The door from the passage opened, and a woman stood in the doorway. She said, 'They told me I should find him here. Where is he?' She saw the body on the floor, put her hand over her eyes, and looked for a moment as if she were about to fall. Then she groped for a chair and sat down. EH and his son spoke at the same time. EH said in a voice more savage than Bland had yet heard him use, 'Young lady, are you accustomed to entering houses to which are not invited?' Richard said in a quiet moan in which astonishment and some other emotion were equally mixed, 'Eve, what are you doing here?'

The woman took her hand away from her eyes, and stayed perfectly still for a few seconds. Bland, who was not particularly impressionable, thought that she was one of the most beautiful women he had ever seen. She was perhaps twenty-three years old, rather below medium height, with a slim figure: but it was her face that made Bland catch his breath. Beneath thick, black, shining hair dark eyebrows were outlined decisively against a rich creamy skin; below the eyebrows two magnificent dark eyes shone with an emotion that might have been anger, sorrow or fear. Her nose was short and straight above a small, rosebud mouth and a determined chin. She was wearing a white chiffon dress, that was very simple but obviously expensive. It revealed very clearly that she had a beautiful figure.

All this Bland noted while she was sitting in the chair, and such was the power of her beauty that when she raised her eyes to his he looked away for a moment.

EH, however, was unmoved by her appearance – or if he was moved, it was merely to rage. He walked over and stood in front of her, apparently almost incoherent with anger. 'Who are you? What are you doing here?' She said simply, 'I am Lionel's wife,' and the words brought Bland out of his spell; for to his pained astonishment her voice was brassy and hard, with a Cockney accent overlaid by a thin Kensington veneer. The voice was so incongruous with the passionate and strange beauty of her face that for a moment Bland thought someone else had spoken.

The effect of her statement was curious. It seemed rather to calm EH, who stared at her for a moment, and then turned his back on her abruptly. But Richard's face went very white. 'It's a lie,' he screamed. His voice had a feminine shrillness. 'I don't believe it. Eve, you couldn't be such a bitch. You – ' He lapsed into obscenity, and his father turned on him. 'Be quiet, sir,' he said, in the tone men generally use for speaking to dogs. Like a dog that had been struck, Richard shrank to silence.

'Have you any proof of this remarkable statement?' EH asked. 'My son passed as a single man. Perhaps you can explain why he was reluctant to acknowledge you as his wife?'

'Oh, really, this is the end,' the girl said. 'I come here and find Lionel dead, and then I'm asked all these damned questions by his stuffed-up, pompous ass of a father. If you really want to know, he said he couldn't acknowledge me as his wife because his father was such a damned awful snob. He also said his father wanted him to marry to improve the family position.' She put a good deal of brassy malice into the last three words. 'He might have added the family manners.' EH was about to retort when Bland said, 'Excuse me.' He moved into the centre of the room, and there was an edge to his manner that made all three of them look at him. 'We've had enough of this. In future, Mr Hargreaves, remember that I'm in charge, and I ask the questions. I should like you to come next door, while I ask some now.' The girl shrugged her shoulders, but went with them into the dining-room next door.

A long, dark oak refectory-table ran down the middle of the vast dining-room, with chairs on either side of it. Bland set down his hat carefully upon the table, took off his fawn raincoat and laid it with the hat, and sat down on one side of the table, indicating by a gesture that they should sit on the other. They sat facing him with chairs conspicuously far apart, EH on the left with his hands on his knees. Richard in the centre not looking at his father, and the girl on the right. Light from a ceiling fitting gleamed on the girl's white face and blazing dark eyes, and on Bland's innocent expression and fair hair. It was very quiet in the room. Bland sat back and tapped his teeth with a pencil. He said, 'Mrs Hargreaves – ' She raised both hands in a curiously theatrical and unconvincing gesture, and said in her shrill voice, 'don't call me that. My name's Eve Marchant – my stage name. I'm an actress. If you want me to answer any of your questions don't call me Mrs Hargreaves.' EH snorted and Richard looked wounded. Bland leaned forward, and his voice was soft and sympathetic. 'Do you want to talk about your husband now and get it over, or do you want to answer questions? I'd like you to tell me all about it you met him, why you married, how many people know you're married – the whole thing. It would be easier for you to talk to me, I think, and I should get a clearer story. But I can ask questions and you can answer them, if you'd prefer that.'

The girl looked down at her hands. 'They told me Lionel had been shot. Is that right?'

'Yes. Somebody killed him.'

She gave a short bark of laughter. 'You don't have to tell me Lionel didn't kill himself – he wasn't the suicidal type.' She stared at Bland for a few seconds, and this time his gaze did not drop. Then she smiled. 'I like you. I think you're a nice policeman. But I don't have to talk in front of them, do I?'

'Certainly not, if you don't want to.'

'Eve, darling,' Richard said, 'I think I ought to know anything – ' Both Eve Marchant and his father looked at him, and his voice trailed off. Then she frowned, with a curious air of indecision. 'Of course you're perfectly right, Dick. I know I've behaved terribly badly, but it's been so difficult. Oh well, really I couldn't care less. Let them both hear it – it may do the old bore good to hear what one of his sons was like.' EH shifted in his chair and Richard moaned. She said with no perceptible change in her voice, 'What the hell, Dick, I can't help it.' She ran a red tongue over her small mouth, and began to talk.

'Really, we're making all this to-do and you might think I had a great story to tell, but I haven't. Lionel and I met four months ago. I'm in a show at the Splendid – third chorus-girl from the left sort of thing. Of course it's not what I want to do, but there you are. I know some people think being a chorus-girl is the end, but maybe they'd change their minds if they had a living to earn. Anyway, Lionel sent round his card one night after the show, and we met. I thought he seemed nice enough, and he took me out to dinner.

'After that, if I do say it that shouldn't, he made a dead set at me, as dead a set as I've ever seen a man make at any girl. He used to come to the theatre every night, he sent me masses of flowers morning and evening, and we went out to dinners and dances almost every night. He was a wonderful dancer. Then he – '

'Just a moment. Did you know about this pursuit of Miss Marchant by your son, Mr Hargreaves?'

'I have never heard of Miss Marchant. And with regard to her statement that she has a living to earn, I suggest – '

'And you?' Richard did not reply, but Eve gestured impatiently. 'Oh, Richard didn't know anything. That all came later on. Except that he knew I went out with Lionel, didn't you, darling?' Richard still did not say anything, and a spot of colour showed on the girl's cheek. She went on talking.

'Within a week Lionel asked me to marry him. I refused. He asked me every day, rang up after I'd gone to bed at night and before I got up in the morning. He was mad to get married. But then I asked if I could meet his family, and he said his father wanted him to marry into society, and he thought it would be better if I didn't meet him just yet. He introduced me to Dick, but nothing was said about getting married in front of him. For a long time I stuck out that I should meet his father, and we should do it all properly. If I'd known what his father was like, I wouldn't have bothered. Then we had a row and I told him I couldn't care less whether I met his father or not, if he was too snobby to introduce me. And then we patched the row up – and one day we got married.' If there was a certain inconsequence in Eve Marchant's narration, Bland did not seem to be aware of it. He listened attentively, and made an occasional note. Richard was looking down at the floor, and his face was not visible. EH seemed to be bottling up something resembling a thunderstorm.

Bland said, 'How long ago did you get married?'

She looked down at her left hand on which there was no ring. 'Two months ago, at Paddington Registry Office.'

EH sneered. 'So you held out for two months. Remarkable endurance!'

She turned to Bland, with her fists clenched and her fine eyes sparkling. 'My God, I won't put up with being insulted by this filthy old snob. If you want me to talk, make him keep his mouth shut. Christ, this really is the end.'

Bland's voice was suddenly warm with feeling. 'Mr. Hargreaves, if you interrupt Miss Marchant again I shall have to ask you to leave this room.' He turned to her again. 'What happened after you were married?'

Her beautiful dark eyes met his frankly. 'What didn't happen? I found out inside about a week just what kind of rat I'd got married to. I married Lionel because I thought I loved him, and because I thought he'd give me a good home.' She repeated the words slowly. 'That's what I wanted, a good home. Lionel married me because he wanted me.'

EH thrust his head forward. He looked like a fine white-headed bull. 'I knew Lionel was a fool, but I didn't know he was that much of a fool – to marry a girl because she played hard to get. You married him because you found out that he was my son. You knew he was pretty well fixed. You – ' The girl jumped to her feet, and moved past Richard with the speed and grace of an animal. The anger in her face made her look more beautiful than ever. She slapped EH's face with her hand, twice, hard. The second time EH caught hold of her wrist and twisted it, so that she cried with pain. Richard rose to his feet and stood irresolutely before them. From the other side of the refectory-table Bland said, without getting up, 'Mr Hargreaves, I think no good purpose is served by your remaining during Miss Marchant's interrogation. Let us have a talk later.'

EH let go of the girl's wrist and she began to rub it. He stood up. His eyes were like small blue marbles. He measured his words carefully, not looking at any of them particularly. 'If this story is true – and I can believe that Lionel would be fool enough for anything where a woman was concerned – I cannot stop you from obtaining what little money my son may have in his banking account. I doubt if there is very much, because he was in the habit of spending it all on women like you. I advise you, Richard, to, give up your curious association with this woman who claims to be your murdered brother's wife. If you persist in it, the consequences will be unfortunate. Inspector, if you wish to ask me any questions I shall be available at my office tomorrow. No doubt, however, you will be able to draw your own conclusions from the information given you in the last few minutes.'

Bland tilted back his chair and stared at EH with something that looked like amusement. He said, 'How much money would you reckon your son Lionel had in the bank, Mr Hargreaves?'

EH seemed a little taken aback, but he replied without reluctance. 'I should be surprised if it were more than a few hundred pounds.'

'Not very much to provide a motive for murder.' His faint smile grew broader. 'That is what you're suggesting, isn't it – that Miss Marchant murdered him for his money?'

EH's small blue eyes did not leave Bland's face. 'Crimes have been committed for as many shillings.' He turned on his heels and made an impressive exit, spoiled only slightly by the fact that at the door he almost collided with a tall, lean man with a narrow head, who looked down from his great height and addressed Bland. 'Are you ready for us next door, sir?'

'Yes, Filby. I want the room and the body photographed. Check the room for finger-prints. Pay special attention to the french windows. Check the steps leading out to the garden for footprints, and put two men on to a search of the garden. They're looking for a revolver, and for anything else of interest they can find. If they don't find anything we shall have to make a search of the guests, and then of the whole house. Post a man on the front door. Ask the guests which of them went outside the drawing-room after 7.25 and before the discovery of the body. Then check their statements by those two servants, Jackson and Williams, who were on duty all the time. Make a note of any discrepancies – anyone who stayed out a long time, anyone who went out a bit before Lionel Hargreaves went out at 7.30, and didn't come back. Let me know the full result. If you have any trouble with the guests, let me know and I'll come and talk to them myself. And ask Dr McCullen to make an examination as soon as he arrives. All clear, Filby?'

'All clear, sir.' The narrow head disappeared.

'Well,' Bland said with a sigh. He turned to Richard Hargreaves and Eve Marchant, and gave them a smile so friendly that it transformed his face, and made him look almost boyish. 'One of the most disagreeable duties of a policeman is that he has to pretend to an inhumanity and callousness he doesn't feel. Believe me, I know you've both gone through a bad time, although officially I'm not permitted to allow that to have any influence on me. But I'd like you to finish your story, Miss Marchant, if you feel able to do so. Then I've got a couple of questions, and then your ordeal will be over.'

Eve Marchant smiled back at him, with a good deal of effect. 'You're very sweet. There really isn't a lot more to tell. After we married Lionel was as beastly to me as he could be. He paid the rent of my flat, but apart from that we might as well not have been married. I saw him about once a week. We never even had a honeymoon. He didn't so much as buy me a frock, and the ring was the cheapest he could get.' Her voice was brassily acquisitive, vibrant with desire for money. Bland glanced at Richard. He was gazing at her with his lips slightly parted and an expression of yearning in his eyes. 'There's no use pretending – inside a month Lionel was going about with other women, and wishing he hadn't got married.'

'And what did you think about it?'

Her voice softened as much as her voice could soften. 'Why, I'd met Dick. And I guess that was just a case of the old, old story – love at first sight, on both sides. Isn't that so, Dick?'

He wriggled uncomfortably. 'I don't like to – in front of the Inspector – '

She snapped at him, and Bland had the feeling that a tigress was showing her claws. 'Oh hell, darling, don't be tiresome.

35

You'll be lucky if you don't get asked anything worse than that.'

Richard's elegant toe moved on the carpet. 'Well, it's true, yes. Eve is so beautiful and understands me so well. But of course I didn't know – ' He stopped, apparently overcome by embarrassment.

'You did know she was married to your brother.'

She broke in, speaking excitedly, with quick gestures, and Bland had the fancy that the claws were being fairly clearly shown now. 'But you must see I *couldn't* say anything to you, Dick darling. I'd told Lionel I'd keep our marriage a secret and not tell *anyone* – and then I knew if I told you, Dick, I should have to stop seeing you. And I asked Lionel for a divorce.'

'But that would have meant publicity.'

'Exactly what Lionel said. He wouldn't agree to it because of the publicity. He thought his father would cut him off with the good old penny.' She laughed, not very pleasantly.

'You could have obtained a divorce, if he was unfaithful.'

She wagged a finger at him. 'My dear man, exactly what I was going to do. But I hadn't taken any steps about it – of course he was very unwilling – and now – ' she spread out her hands.

'So the position is that Lionel knew nothing of Richard, and Richard knew nothing of Lionel?'

She flushed. 'You're being perfectly beastly, but – yes.'

'And you confirm that, Mr Hargreaves?'

'Oh yes – yes. It was a terrible shock to me to learn this evening – ' Richard's voice died away, and he waved a thin white hand.

'All right. Now, one or two questions to you both, just for the record. You were out of the drawing-room after 7.30, weren't you, Mr Hargreaves?'

Richard Hargreaves took a cigarette from his silver case and tapped it reflectively. A certain alertness was apparent behind his languor. 'Yes, I was. Not for more than five minutes, though. Jackson and Williams can confirm that.'

'You didn't notice Lionel go out?'

'No. But there's no reason why I should have done.'

'No reason at all. Were you fond of your brother?'

Richard's air of alertness was a shade more noticeable, but he answered the question readily enough. 'I couldn't say that. In fact, we didn't get on well. Lionel was always the practical, hearty type, and I was always more artistic or aesthetic. At school he played Rugger, while I was secretary of the Dramatic Society. You know the kind of thing. And it went deeper than that.' He gestured faintly. 'I don't think Lionel was fundamentally a pleasant or generous person. He had an amiable manner, but he was really rather vicious. God knows, all the Hargreaves family are pretty vicious, but I think Lionel was the worst of us. But I know one shouldn't speak ill of the dead. You can put it that we were irreconcilable types.'

'Thank you.' Bland leaned back in his chair. 'Miss Marchant, where were you between 7.30 and 8.30 tonight?'

She said with some composure, 'I was in my flat in Catherine Street, Westminster.'

'Alone?'

'Yes.' She smiled and showed white, even teeth. 'I was reading a book. I'm afraid I've failed to provide myself with an alibi. But a funny thing happened this evening. Someone rang up about a quarter to six. They said they were speaking for Lionel, and that he wanted me to meet him here at half-past nine. So I got a taxi and came along.'

'Wasn't that a very unusual request?'

'Yes, it *was* unusual – because, of course, I'd never been here before – and I wondered what it was all about – but he rang off before I could ask any questions.'

'You don't know who telephoned you. You said "he." Are you sure it was a man?'

She looked doubtful, and for the first time a little frightened. 'You've got me there. I was bathing Binkie – my Peke, you know, such a sweet boy – and so I didn't pay all that much attention, until I came to think about it afterwards. And then it's easy to disguise a voice, isn't it? This voice sounded very deep and husky – it sounded like a man's voice. But why should anyone want to bring me down here? Do you think it was – the murderer?'

'Your guess is as good as mine. What's certain is that it's somebody who knows you were married. How many people knew that?'

'Nobody, I didn't tell *anyone*. I don't know if Lionel did – he always swore he hadn't.'

Bland had been making notes. His voice had a slight edge to it as he said, 'Thank you both for being so helpful. Will you leave me your address and telephone number, Miss Marchant, so that I can get in touch with you if necessary. I shall have to ask you to stay a few minutes, until we decide if a search of the guests is necessary, but I'll try to make it as quick as possible. No doubt you're feeling tired. And Mr Hargreaves, no doubt you're anxious to see Miss Marchant home.' Richard looked at Bland sharply, but his face might have been made of wood.

When they had gone out Bland stood up and stretched. He was walking towards the door when it opened and Filby came in. The tall detective was carrying a cloth-covered bundle rather as if it were a baby, but the jerk of his finger and the rolling of his eye clearly had reference to Eve Marchant. 'What a girl,' he said. 'Sex, and no mistake. Plenty of sex.'

'Oozing with it. And very effective it seems to be. She claims to have married one brother, and now he's dead she wants to marry the other, and finally she's got you under her thumb.'

'Take more than her,' Filby said indignantly, and pulled down the lower lid of his eye. 'See any green?'

Bland examined the eye. 'No green, but it looks very bloodshot. You should see an oculist.'

'I'd need my head examined if I fell for one like her,' Filby said. 'A dangerous woman. But I got something you'll like.' He laid the bundle on the refectory-table, and unwrapped it carefully to show a Smith and Wesson revolver. 'There's the revolver all right. No prints on it.'

Bland picked it up, broke it, sniffed and grunted. 'One shot fired. Where'd you find it?'

'In the garden. About ten yards from the library window. Foot or two off the path. Ground's hard. No footprints.'

'Good work. Any luck with the french windows?'

'Dozens of fingerprints. Can't get anything out of 'em. Nice, clean crime this one, if you ask me.' Filby always tried to make every crime a kind of sporting event, and he liked the criminal to have a fair chance. 'I've got that list of people who went outside, too. All went down the corridor, of course – they were going to the lavatory, or so they say. The two servants check it as OK. Nobody went upstairs or out the front door.'

'How many of them?'

'Five – six if you count young Hargreaves, the one who just went out – seven if you count the chap who was knocked off. All men. I've got 'em more or less in the order they went, too. Thought that might be important. Here we are. Half-past seven the chap who was murdered went out. Next was a chap called Bond, about five minutes afterwards, he was. Then a squint-eyed one named Tracy. Then young Hargreaves. Then two young lads who went out together, and last someone named Sinclair, who must have come out just before the old man's speech started at ten to eight. Nobody dared to go out while that was going on'.

'Sinclair,' Bland said softly. 'Yes, of course, Sinclair. I was trying to remember.' He became conscious of Filby's startled gaze and said, 'Sorry, day dreaming. None of them tried to deny they'd been outside?'

Filby pulled at a protruding underlip. 'Bond didn't say he'd been out, but when the servant's pointed him out he said he thought it was before 7.30. Nothing to it, probably.'

'Very likely not. All right, Filby. You can let the rest of them go home now. I've seen young Hargreaves, but I shall want to see these five.'

'You mean we can narrow it down to them already?' Filby breathed admiration.

'Not at all. Anyone may have come in from outside, and it may be nothing to do with any of these people. But it certainly can't have anything to do with those who didn't leave the drawing-room.'

'So we send them all home.' Filby leered, and the effect was cheerfully obscene. 'That girl with plenty of sex wouldn't be wanting an escort, I suppose?'

'She's got one already – Richard Hargreaves.' Filby raised his shoulders in a comic, exaggerated gesture of disappointment. 'But I've got a couple of jobs for you, in the way of checking up on her. Her name's Eve Marchant and she claims she was married to Lionel Hargreaves about three months ago at Paddington Registry Office. Check on it and get all the details you can. I have a feeling there's something fishy about it, from the way she told her story. And she says someone telephoned her about a quarter to six tonight at her flat in Catherine Street, Westminster, asked her to come along here, and that she took a taxi from her home at about a quarter to nine to come here. Check on those things too.'

'So she's in it, is she? She looked too good to be true to anybody.' He laughed at his own joke. Bland gave it a blank stare. 'No, this is just a routine check-up. Then you can go home. And now I'd better see these people. I'll take them in the order they went out – Bond, Tracy, then the two lads, and Sinclair last.'

'Oh ah,' Filby said. 'There's a woman called Mrs Rogers who's asking to see you. Quite a piece in a sly little way. Said something about information. Might be worried about something.'

'All right. Keep her waiting. Let's have Mr Bond.'

Chapter Seven *10.20 p.m. Wednesday to 12.35 a.m. Thursday, January 16*

The room was dim, with patches of light round the refectory-table. Bland tilted back the dark oak chair in which he had been sitting and stifled a yawn. He said, 'So you went outside just about 7.30, Mr Bond?' He considered the man in front of him with impersonal distaste. His eye was offended by the smartness and newness of Bond's double-breasted dinner-jacket with its padded shoulders, and by the thin dark hair that was too smoothly sleek; his ear was offended by the strident assurance of Bond's voice. Thirty-five, he thought, or perhaps a young forty, working-class come up in the world and proud of it, strident perhaps to conceal an inferiority complex. The kind of man who is much too kind to his mother.

'Absolutely, old boy. One of those natural needs, you know. Wasn't out there more than three or four minutes. Didn't see a soul except those two chaps hanging about in the hall, and then I met old Tracy coming out of the drawing-room just as I went back to, join the happy throng.'

'You didn't see Lionel Hargreaves leave the drawing-room or any sign of him outside it?'

'Not a thing, old boy. Sorry.'

On the table lay the revolver and the gloves, covered by the cloth in which Filby had wrapped the revolver. Bland removed the cloth. 'Do you recognise either of these?' Bond shrugged. 'Not the revolver. The gloves might belong to anybody. Dick

41

Hargreaves sometimes wears lemon-coloured gloves. So do I, for that matter.'

Bland made a note. 'What is your position with the Hargreaves Agency?'

'Production Manager. Look after blocks, make sure advertisements get in the papers to time and that the right ad goes in, generally act as head cook and bottle-washer looking after the production end.'

'How long have you been with them?'

'Nearly a year.'

'Have you any idea why Mr Hargreaves might have been killed?'

Bond rubbed the side of his face thoughtfully with his hand. His upper lip twisted in a grin, and his dark handsome face looked both malicious and sly. 'Well, there you have me. I don't want to tell tales out of school, wash dirty linen, all that sort of thing. But it's an open secret that Lionel was one for the ladies, and that he made a pass at Jean Rogers.'

'Jean Rogers?'

'Mrs Rogers – she's one of our copywriters. Women's angle, that sort of thing. Well, as I was saying, Lionel made a pass at her – quite unsuccessful, I gather. Nothing unusual in that – Lionel made a pass at anything in a skirt. *But* there was something special this time, because it's an open secret that Jean Rogers and Tracy, our Art Director, are – like that.' He twined two fingers. 'There you are. I don't say there's anything in it. If it's not that, though, you'll find it was something to do with a woman. There must be a hell of a lot of husbands in London who won't be wearing black because Lionel's dead.'

'You're implying that Tracy and Mrs Rogers are lovers?'

Bond laughed. 'Don't let's be technical. It's an open – '

'An open secret, yes. But if Tracy has been successful, would he have any motive in murdering an unsuccessful lover?'

Bond shrugged his padded shoulders. He clearly thought that Bland was too finicky. 'Maybe Lionel made another pass at her

– he made at least two at most women. Maybe he had better luck the second time, and Tracy found out. I don't know. That's your business.'

Bland's face was blank. 'One more question. How well do you know the geography of this place?'

'Don't know it at all. Never been here before.'

Bland nodded. 'All right, Mr Bond. I can get in touch with you at the agency if I want you?'

'Any day. Do I take it that I'm now free to depart?'

'Perfectly free. Ask Mr Tracy to come in, will you?' As Bond went out Bland noticed that he had a slight, but perceptible limp.

When Bland looked at George Tracy he saw a very small man, with broad shoulders, an erect stance, and with dark hair standing up straight on his head. Vain, Bland thought, looking at the self-conscious handsomeness, the boldness of his strongly-marked features, the squint in the dark eyes that rather added to his attractiveness. Probably arrogant, he added after a moment's thought; and a strong personality. Tracy sat down in the chair on the other side of the table, and at once began to talk.

'Let me put my cards on the table, Inspector. I didn't like Lionel Hargreaves.' Tracy paused to give emphasis to the admission. 'And yet – life and death are astonishing things. Now that he's gone I feel as violent a shock as if I'd lost someone who was dear to me. When I think that less than three hours ago we were standing together next door, eating, drinking, talking – ' Tracy shook his head solemnly. An indifferent dramatic performance, Bland thought. 'I'm telling you this because I want to say here and now that, little though I liked Lionel, if there's anything I can do to send his murderer to the gallows – by God, I will.'

'The word gallows is obsolete,' Bland said rather coldly, 'but it will be helpful if you will answer some questions.' The balloon of Tracy's eloquence seemed to be a little deflated. 'You went out of the drawing-room about half-past seven tonight.'

'Certainly I did.' Tracy's squint became alarming. 'Are you suggesting – '

Bland's voice was weary. 'Lionel Hargreaves went out of the drawing-room just before half-past seven. He didn't come back. Therefore the movements of anyone who left the drawing-room after that time are a matter of interest to me. Is that clear? Now, how long were you out of the room?'

'I – ' Tracy was looking alarmed, and his speech now had no ornamental flourish. 'About ten minutes.'

'What were you doing?'

'I went to the washroom. Then I walked up and down the passage, and came out once or twice into the hall. Jackson and that other fellow must have seen me.'

'How do you know Jackson's name?'

'Well, really,' Tracy said, and laughed. 'I've been here a good many times to dinners and parties. What's the purpose of all these questions?'

'Did anyone pass you while you were walking up and down?'

'Yes. First of all Dick Hargreaves, and then those two young copywriters, Onslow and Mudge. They all went into the washroom and came out again.'

'They didn't go into the library?'

Tracy hesitated. 'I couldn't swear that one or other of them didn't open the library door and slip inside – they might have done so while my back was turned. But then they'd have had to slip out again while my back was turned, too. I should think it very unlikely.'

'You saw or heard nothing of Lionel Hargreaves? You didn't hear a shot?'

'No.' Tracy looked triumphant. 'But then I shouldn't. The library's pretty well soundproof, you know.'

Bland made no comment. 'You said you didn't like Lionel Hargreaves. How well did you know him?'

'Not very well. I'm Art Director of the Agency, and we were on the Board together. I might see him for an hour or so perhaps three days a week. But I was never intimate with him.' Tracy said it as though he had missed a chance of winning a sweepstake.

'Do you know of any reason why he should have been killed?'

Tracy's generous mouth tightened, and his manner became again that of a ham actor approaching a purple passage in Shakespeare. 'Perhaps I can tell you that, Inspector, if you'll tell me one thing. Do you think Lionel was killed by someone at the party tonight?'

'You do me too much honour. I've been here an hour and a half. I don't think anything yet.'

Tracy leaned back in his chair. His voice lost its tone of drama, and became deep, melodious, pleasant, and yet still not altogether natural. He might have been acting an altogether different part – that of the mature man-of-the-world delivering carefully his judgement on life. 'I think the most I should say is this – and I say it as one who, for his sins, has twenty years' acquaintance with the Hargreaves family. I came to this Agency twenty years ago as a junior copywriter, and I've known them, senior and juniors, ever since that time. God forbid that I should speak ill of them, and especially of the one who's dead.' Tracy's fine dark eyes looked hard into Bland's blue ones. 'But there are a lot of mysteries in that family, and I think you'll find the secret of Lionel Hargreaves' death in them. Look into the past, Inspector. Look into family history.'

Bland did not seem much impressed. 'I understand you are the creative Director. What does that imply?'

'It means that I organise all the creative work that goes out of the Agency, all the drawings, layouts, the whole of the Studio.'

Without any change in tone Bland said, 'You didn't like Lionel Hargreaves. Did your dislike of him have anything to do with his relations with Mrs Rogers?'

The man-of-the-world vanished, and was replaced by a furious John Bull, as Tracy's face became very pink and he thumped the refectory-table with a surprisingly large fist. The cast in his left eye was strikingly obvious. He got up from the chair and said with a deep bull's bellow, 'I refuse to have her name brought into this.'

'Just as you please. Have you ever seen these?' Bland whipped the cloth off the revolver and gloves, but the effect was disappointing. Tracy merely shook his head, with no sign of discomposure. 'All right, Mr Tracy. I'll bear your suggestion in mind.' After Tracy had gone out Bland stepped to the door and called 'Filby.' A square-headed man appeared. 'Filby said you'd asked him to make some enquiries. Anything I can do, sir?'

'Yes. Ask Mrs Rogers to come in.'

Bland looked attentively at Jean Rogers. She was, as Filby had said, quite a piece: but it was true that she could not be called a beauty, and he noticed with some distaste the black and green sequins at the neck and hem of her evening dress. He said, 'You wanted to see me, Mrs Rogers.'

'Yes.' She was obviously ill-at-ease. 'It's not *certain* that some-one here at the party had anything to do with this thing is it? I mean, it could just as well have been someone from outside?'

'Why not?' Bland's voice was not encouraging, but Jean Rogers went on talking. She was turning and twisting an artificial flower in her hands. 'Then there's something I think you ought to know. There's a man named Carruthers who had a grudge against Lionel. He's a cousin of the family – the Hargreaves family, I mean their only relation or something like that. He's a commercial artist who does work as a freelance. A lot of different firms call on him when they have something which is in his particular line. He's rather good on doing nice, decorative stuff for fashion books, and things like that. Well, about eighteen months ago, he did a lot of work for us on an account for women's clothes – I know about it, because I wrote the copy on that account. Lionel Hargreaves was the director in charge of it, and he was very rude about the work Carruthers had done. Carruthers is rather a nice little man, very meek and mild generally, but he was really upset about this. They had an awful row, and Carruthers wasn't asked to do any more work for us for over a year.'

'That means he has done some recently?'

'Yes,' she said rather unwillingly. 'It's been patched up a bit in the past six months, because Tracy and Sinclair both know Carruthers is a useful man, and want to use his work. But he's not spoken to Lionel since they had their row.'

'I see.' Bland was playing with his pencil. 'And you think he may have murdered Hargreaves because of their feud?' There was only the faintest hint of irony in his voice, but Jean Rogers flushed.

'I'm not saying anything of the sort. I thought you would be interested to have information about someone who disliked Lionel. Apparently I'm mistaken, and the police aren't interested in things like that. I'm sorry to have wasted your time.' She tugged at her artificial flower and got up.

'Sit down, Mrs Rogers.' Bland said. His voice was not loud, but it was compelling. 'It is evident that you are an intelligent woman, and that you had a purpose in telling me this story. Are you seriously suggesting that Lionel Hargreaves was murdered because eighteen months ago he quarrelled with a man about some drawings – a quarrel which has since been patched up?'

'I'm not suggesting anything,' she said violently. She was nearly in tears.

'Or are you anxious that enquiry should be diverted from somebody else who had a quarrel with Hargreaves recently – and about you?'

She put down the flower, and, surprisingly enough, spoke in a tone of some composure, mixed with contempt. 'You don't waste time in digging for scandal, do you?'

'One doesn't need to dig when there are willing scandal-bearers.' His innocent blue eyes were sympathetic. 'And I'm here to listen to all kinds of stories – even stories like the one you've just told me. I try to deal with all those that involve emotional relationships as tactfully as I can, but all sorts of people are likely to be hurt in a case of murder. That's unavoidable. Try not to blame the police too much – they're only doing a job.'

Her eyes were wet. 'I know. I'm sorry. I'd better go.'

He leaned forward and spoke earnestly. 'If you like to answer some questions you may help me, and help yourself too. Let me tell you what's been told to me. I've been told that you and Tracy are in love, that Lionel Hargreaves made advances to you and that Tracy resented them. Is that true?'

'Yes, that's all true, but it doesn't really mean anything. George has a violent temper, and he simply told Lionel what he thought of him. It was all awfully foolish, because, of course, a lot of people in the firm heard about it – but it didn't really mean anything.'

'How long ago did this quarrel take place?'

She sighed and said, 'I think I'd better tell you the whole thing, though it's going to sound much more important than it was. About a fortnight ago I was in Lionel's office and he put his arm round me and kissed me. I told him not to be silly. He didn't take any notice, but just kept on kissing me and trying to make love to me. Then George came in and – lost his temper. He knocked Lionel down, and told him a few home-truths about himself. It was all over in five minutes, and half an hour later Lionel apologised to me. Needless to say George, like a fool, left the office door open, and the receptionist, Miss Peachey, passed by while the row was going on. No doubt Miss Peachey told her best friend, Miss Berry, and the whole thing was ridiculously exaggerated.'

'Did Edward Hargreaves know about it?'

She looked startled. 'Why, no. At least I hope not. He'd be dreadfully angry, because Lionel was the apple of his eye.' She chuckled. 'I think he'd have taken the view that absolute obedience should have been my role in obeying the instructions of a director.'

'Did Lionel repeat his attempt to make love to you?'

'Why certainly not. Did someone say he had?'

'It's been suggested.' Bland paused, and then said without emphasis, 'Now, Mrs Rogers – please believe that I don't ask this without a reason – what are your relations with Mr Tracy?'

Her gaze met his quite frankly. 'We're in love with each other, and if it were possible we'd get married.'

'Why isn't it possible?'

She sighed again. 'I married five years ago, when I was twenty-five. I left my husband after six months. He was a rat – a mental pervert. He was never unfaithful to me, but he had a mean, perverted mind. He thought up the most outrageous explanations for the simplest actions. If I bought some clothes he would make up a tremendous fantasy about my reasons for buying them – he'd say I wanted to attract men, and make all sorts of awful insinuations.' She drew a deep breath. 'I'm not telling you all this because I like it – simply to show that it would be terribly difficult for me to divorce him. I've asked him to divorce me, but he won't even consider it – he's a strict Catholic. When I left Alan, I had to get a job, and after knocking about for a bit I got one with Hargreaves as a copywriter. I don't like any of the family much except Dick, but they pay fairly well, and Sinclair, who runs the Copy Department, is very nice.'

'And then you met Mr Tracy?'

'That's right. It's vitally necessary for both our sakes that EH shouldn't know about us. He may have been a rake in his youth – everyone says he was – but he's a puritanical, cold-blooded old devil now.' She spoke with some warmth.

'And what do you hope to do in the future?'

'God knows.' She got up and walked about the room. 'I've often wondered. I hope that one day Alan will divorce me, but I really don't know –' She stopped suddenly, and looked at him almost with hostility. 'I can't see that my private troubles have anything to do with you.'

'I hope you're right. Have you ever seen these before?' Bland showed her the revolver and the gloves, but she shook her head. 'Have they got something to do with it all?'

'Rather more to do with it, I think, than the story you told me when you first came in. But thank you for what you told me afterwards – it may be very helpful. Good night, Mrs Rogers.'

She stood with her hand on the door and a frown on her forehead, as if she were about to ask a question. Then she said 'Goodnight,' and closed the door.

Onslow and Mudge had heard nothing, seen nothing, and said that they had gone to the washroom together and returned together. They showed a purely malicious interest in the murder ('To me,' Onslow said loftily, 'it's simply one exploiter the less, though not such a dirty one as EH'), and by the time he had finished with them that slight edge of exasperation had returned to Bland's voice. He was smiling, however, when he said to one of the detectives in the hall, 'Ask Mr Sinclair to come in,' and he was smiling still when he made a gesture for Sinclair to take a seat. The chief of the Copy Department was a tall man in his middle thirties. He had a mass of curly fair hair, a big straight nose, and a firm mouth and chin, and his face, as he looked across the table, was puzzled. Bland said, 'You don't remember me?'

'Why, yes.' Sinclair was hesitant. 'But I don't just place – '

'Charles Sinclair, isn't it? And you were at Beldham Grammar. Captain of the School, leading light in the Dramatic Society, captain of the cricket team. Remember the boy who went in number nine and tried to bowl slow leg-breaks?'

'Good *Lord*,' Sinclair said. The firm mouth broke up into a laugh, and the effect was charming. 'Wily Bland. Remember we always used to call you that because you were always convinced of your cunning even when you'd been hit for four fours in an over. You always thought you should have been kept on for one more over. I remember you were always a wily lad at school, but I never expected – ' He checked himself.

'Go on, go on, don't mind me. I know nobody regards a policeman as a human being, and I'm inclined to agree with them. I'll tell you one day how I happened to become one. It isn't a bad story. Do you still play cricket?'

'I turn out occasionally for the Banks. And you?'

'Haven't tried a leg-break in fifteen years. And I used to think I was England's answer to Clarrie Grimmett. Smoke?' He pushed across a packet.

'Thanks.' Sinclair busied himself with a lighter. Bland puffed reflectively for a moment, and then spoke in a voice that was less official and carefully controlled than usual.

'I recognised you when I arrived, and that's why I kept you until last. I've asked everyone here the routine questions about motive and opportunity, and in most cases I've got routine answers. There are one or two things that may lead somewhere, but it's very clear to me that I shan't get to know anything about these people personally unless I know something about the general set-up. How well do you know these people and this place?'

'Place – I've never been here before. Lionel was being rather catty about that earlier this evening. People – well, I joined the Agency about three years ago as chief of the Copy Department. Been in Advertising since I was twenty-one. I know them all reasonably well, and naturally I know the way an advertising agency works.'

'Fine. How would you like to lend a hand by giving me an insight into the way in which these people are related to one another, both personally and in the Agency? It might help me a lot – and at the same time you'd see a murder investigation going on from inside. Enlarge your experience as an advertising man.' He grinned.

Sinclair's answering grin was enthusiastic. 'Nothing I'd like more. just tell me where and how to start.' He blew a perfect smoke-ring.

'First of all, the routine questions. Did you see anyone else when you went outside at about a quarter to eight?'

'I saw a couple of servants hanging about in the hall. Went into the washroom and came straight back into the drawing-room.'

'You didn't hear anything while you were outside? Any noise that might have come from the library?'

'Sorry, I didn't. Should I have done?'

'It would help if you had – though, as the library walls were lined with asbestos, it's not likely anyone will have heard anything. Have you ever seen this before?' Bland took the cloth off the revolver once more, and it gleamed in the lamplight. Sinclair looked at it in apparent fascination. 'The weapon? No, I've never seen it.'

'We can't be sure it's the weapon yet, but someone left it lying about in the garden. Nor these gloves?' Sinclair shrugged his shoulders. 'Impossible to say. Two or three people in the firm wear gloves like these. Bond, our Production Manager, for instance.'

'All right, It's disappointing, but I didn't expect anything better. Nobody recognises the gloves or the revolver. Now, the question of motive.' Bland made a faint gesture of irritation. 'In the last hour some of the least adequate motives for murder I've ever heard have been suggested to me. What do you know about Tracy, for instance?'

'He's a good chap, and a damned good advertising man – too good for the other directors. Damned rash and tactless, though – always bashing his head against a wall.'

'And about Mrs Rogers?'

'Oh, I see.' Sinclair looked for a moment as if he had tasted some unpleasant medicine, and then grinned again. The grin, Bland thought, made him look very much like the Captain of the

School. 'I hadn't realised the kind of things you might want to know. But you've obviously been told about them already. It's all a pretty open secret – I should think half a dozen people in the firm must know. I believe they can't get married. It's a damned shame.'

'Did you know that Lionel Hargreaves had made a pass at her, and had a row with Tracy about it?'

'I'd heard some rumours flying about. But I'm not a bit surprised. Lionel would make a pass at any woman.'

'Well, that situation has been suggested to me as a motive for murder. A singularly stupid one, I must say, since Mrs Rogers powerfully repulsed the attack. It's also been suggested that he may have been murdered by a man named Carruthers, who was annoyed because Hargreaves had a row with him eighteen months ago about some drawings.'

'Oh, I say.' Sinclair laughed aloud. 'They have been picking out some corny ones for you. That's too ridiculous – though it's true that Carruthers doesn't like – didn't like – Lionel very much. Carruthers is a cousin of the family, you know.'

'So I've been told. What kind of man is he?'

'Mild, inoffensive, rather slimily pleasant. Not at all my idea of a murderer. He'll probably be in the office tomorrow, if you want to see him.'

'It's also been suggested to me, vaguely, that the secret of the case lies in the past.' Bland held up his hand as Sinclair began to speak. 'There's a résumé of what has been suggested to me in the way of motive. Now, if you can add anything to it, I'll be very glad. If you feel you know of any *possible* motive, don't hesitate to tell me – I'm grateful even for the things that have already been suggested, improbable though they are. I'm fishing in deep waters of the infinite at the moment, and I'll be grateful for any bait. And if you can give me a sketch of the principals, that will help too.'

In the dim light of the dining-room Sinclair's strong face looked oddly irresolute. 'I can hardly know where to begin. That suggestion about the past – who told you about the past?' There was the faintest pause before Bland replied, 'Tracy.'

'EH's second wife died two years ago.' Sinclair said slowly. 'At the time there were rumours that her death was not accidental.' Bland snapped his fingers and said with uncharacteristic excitement, 'Of course – I remember. A yacht. Possible suicide. Not that I had anything to do with the case.'

'Perhaps I'd better tell you the tale the way I heard it. When I joined the Agency I knew that EH had a reputation for being hard as nails, and tough to get along with. I soon found out that he was a mean, hard, vicious old autocrat who won't be told when he's in the wrong. And although his publicity sense is pretty good, he frequently is wrong, or a bit old-fashioned, in his approach nowadays. But all that's by the way. I was saying that EH is tough – and he prides himself particularly on his toughness in personal matters. I don't believe he's got a spark of feeling in him for anyone but Lionel. He's certainly fond – *was*, I should say – of Lionel, although he hasn't much use for Dick. And that's odd when you think of it, because although Dick's a pansyfied type he's really not a bad chap, whereas there was something pretty nasty about Lionel. But perhaps it was the vicious element that appealed to ER – sort of case of Lionel doing all the things he'd repressed in himself, getting tight, chasing after all sort of women, particularly other men's wives. Yes, EH was fond of Lionel. And of course he was in love with Lily – that was his second wife – as far as he could be in love with anybody. But I'm rambling. Sorry.'

'You're doing very well. Don't worry about rambling.' Bland lighted another cigarette. 'How many of the people who came out of the drawing-room tonight after Lionel came out were with the firm then?'

'Bond wasn't, nor Mudge, nor Onslow. Tracy was there, Creative Director was a much better advertising brain than Lionel or Dick, always having rows with them, and EH always backing them up. Well, to get back to this story. One day after

I'd been there six months EH came in and said he was going to get married. It took us right back, I can tell you. And when we heard that she was only twenty-two, and when she came up to the office and we saw her – well, that took us back even more. She'd been a nurse-companion at the house of some friend of EH, and she was pretty and unsophisticated – very unsophisticated, I should say. EH treated her with a kind of kindly courtesy that he has always on tap, and that she obviously found very fetching. And of course he had money. I suppose that was why she married him.

'They were married at St Margaret's, Westminster – I remember that I got awfully tight at the reception – and went away for a month on the honeymoon on a yacht EH had hired. They decided to stay on, and Lionel and Dick joined them, and a chap named Weston, EH's solicitor. After they'd been out a week at sea, it happened. She went out on deck one night and never came back. The accepted explanation was that she had fallen overboard.'

'Was EH upset?'

'Very much upset. I wouldn't have believed that anything external to himself could upset him so much. Lionel was upset too, curiously enough – it took a lot to upset Lionel. And so was old Weston, I believe. He's the chap who could tell you anything there is to know, if he liked to open his mouth. He was very fond of Lily. In fact, I think everyone liked her. She was a nice, simple girl.'

There was silence in the room for a moment after Sinclair finished his story, a dead, heavy silence in which the two men sat in their chairs, with the table separating them, and looked at each other. Then Bland said, 'Do you play chess?'

Sinclair was startled. 'A little.'

'I have an uncomfortable feeling that the death of Lionel Hargreaves is the opening gambit, as it were, in a game of chess. Consider, for instance, the revolver and the gloves. No attempt is made to conceal the revolver – it is thrown in the bushes, as though the murderer had disposed of it in fright or hurry. But the gloves were placed carefully on the steps outside the french window, and the person who coolly took off those gloves and placed them for us to find was not suddenly overcome with fright about the revolver. That's assuming, of course, as I think we can that the same person left both. It seems to me that everything that has happened this evening has happened to plan. Everything has proceeded logically and clearly, according to somebody's intention, and it doesn't seem to me that any end has yet been achieved. Then there are several minor queries. For instance, what was Lionel's appointment?'

'Appointment?' Sinclair stared.

'Certainly an appointment, or why did he go into the library? Everything shows that the murder was premeditated – the revolver, the gloves, the fact that it took place in the library, where a shot wouldn't be heard. Clearly, Lionel had an appointment with somebody in the library. Who was it? Did someone come up to him at the party and say "Can I have a few words with you about such-and-such?" That seems very improbable, or they'd have walked out of the room together. Surely Hargreaves would have been surprised and suspicious if this someone had said, "You go out and I'll follow you in a few minutes." The only person he might possibly make an arrangement like that with is his father.'

Sinclair shook his head. 'No, EH came in looking pretty angry, and told Lionel in ringing tones that he wanted to see him later.'

'In any event, he didn't leave the room until he went out to look for Lionel. Now, let's put that problem in another way. Suppose someone said earlier in the day, "I must talk to you this evening. Step out from the party at about half-past seven, and I'll slip out after you.' That would imply that this problematic person – let's call them X – and Hargreaves were on pretty intimate terms. Now, is there anyone, except his brother Richard, who's on sufficiently close terms to say something like that?'

'No. But it might be that this X had a piece of news or information so confidential it transformed the whole situation, and made Lionel treat him as an intimate. Isn't that so?'

Bland nodded. 'Surely. But we haven't any indication at present that such a piece of news existed. Until something like that turns up – something it was important for Lionel Hargreaves to know or to keep secret – we can hardly theorise on it. If there *was* anything, it's a fair bet that it had something to do with his wife.'

'Lionel's *wife?*' Sinclair looked astonished. 'I didn't know he was married.'

'Neither did anyone else, but she turned up here this evening saying somebody had telephoned her at home and told her that Lionel wanted her to come here. Since their marriage was supposed to be secret, either somebody else knew about, or she's telling lies. There's something fishy about her. She says now that she's in love with Richard Hargreaves, and he certainly seems to be in love with her.'

'What a wonderful woman. What's she like?'

'Enough sex and beauty to sink a battleship, common as copper and hard as stone. First sight of her bowled me over, I must say. Now – if we suppose that Hargreaves had arranged to meet her in the library – '

'But why should he do that when the marriage was secret?'

'God knows.' Bland passed his hand across his forehead. 'It's too late for my brain to function properly. Let's have a talk tomorrow – I mean, at some more decent hour today. Will you be at your office in the morning – say ten o'clock? Good. I'd like to have a look round.' He gripped Sinclair's hand firmly.

'Are you coming away now?'

Bland's fresh-complexioned face looked tired. 'Not just yet. I've got a few notes to make and things to think about.' When Sinclair went out the detective was tapping his teeth with a pencil and looking abstractedly at the wall.

THURSDAY, JANUARY 16

Chapter One *12.30 to 1.30 a.m.*

EH moved restlessly under the linen sheet. His eyes wide open, stared into the darkness patterned by vague shapes never quite revealed as bookcase and dressing-table. He thought about his son Lionel and about his other son Richard, and his thoughts were not pleasant. He thought about the early days of his life, of the towns he had left in a hurry because of his skill with cards, of the cheap chisellers' tricks played on old women. These were thoughts that rarely oppressed him. He thought about other women, the women he had met and used and sometimes slept with in his twenties and thirties, the wife who had borne him children and to whom he had been coldly and monotonously unfaithful, and the second wife whom he had come as near to loving as it was in his nature to love anyone. These, too, were not comfortable thoughts.

He belched suddenly, and switched on the bedside light. 'Indigestion,' he said. 'Indigestion, on a night like this.' He felt vaguely aggrieved as he walked over to the dressing-table to get the tablets.

Richard Hargreaves' bedroom was decorated in green and silver. The ceiling was green, the low divan bed was green, the carpet was green, and the walls were dull silver. The curtains were silver edged with green. A light-green chest of drawers with silver handles stood in one corner of the room. A green telephone stood on a silver-lacquer bedside-table. Richard Hargreaves sat on the bed and pulled off his dark shoes. His

61

mind was still stunned by the thoughts of Eve's marriage to Lionel. How could she do it, he thought, how could she do it? Her marriage appeared in his thoughts as a move directed against him, a move taken by the hostile brother who was part of a hostile world. He had a feeling of injury that Eve should have joined the conspiracy against him. His thoughts flickered vaguely over the other events of the evening, the police Inspector whose name he could not for the moment remember, and the loathsomeness of his father. He thought again about Eve, and then suddenly remembered the look of Lionel's body on the floor. He shivered, got into a pair of Cossack style green pyjamas, walked over to the mirror, and began rather half-heartedly, to dab cold cream on his face.

When Bond returned to his house in Highgate his wife was waiting up. She was a big-boned, morose woman, and she did not greet him cheerfully. 'You're late,' she said. 'I wondered what had become of you. The baby's got spots on his forehead – I think it's chickenpox.' Bond left his leather attaché-case in the hall, and went into the sitting-room. He let his wife go on talking for a few seconds, and then cut brutally across her words. 'Lionel Hargreaves was murdered tonight,' he said. 'Shot. At that stupid party of the old man's.' She stood with her mouth open, looking at him. 'Mr Lionel?' she said. 'The old man's son?'

'Did you think it was his daughter? So now you know why I was late – and it's the first evening in a week I've been late – I don't know what you're moaning about. I want my slippers.' She got his slippers from under the sofa and gave them to him without a word. 'I shan't be coming up to bed yet, and I've got more important things to think about than chickenpox. So if you want to stay down here keep your mouth shut.' She went upstairs without saying anything. For half an hour Bond sat staring into the dying fire.

Eve Marchant sat at her dressing-table and looked at herself in the triple mirror, with critical approval. She began to talk to herself aloud, which was one of her bad habits when she was alone. 'No wonder you bowled over that Inspector, my pet. He certainly fell like a load of bricks.' She wagged her finger at the mirror. 'But he's not such a fool as he looks. Rather sweet, I must say. My God, what an evening.' She sighed and took out of the top drawer of the dressing-table a big book, bound in red morocco tooled in gold. She headed a page 'Wed. Jan. 15' and began to write in it, in a round, sprawling hand:

My God, what an evening. Mysterious telephone call, taxi to see Lionel, and then I find him murdered. And then a grilling from a rather nice police Inspector. But before I put it all down, let's be quite honest, I'm not sorry Lionel's dead I'm glad, glad, GLAD!! And I simply couldn't help hinting as much to the policeman. Was that foolish? If it was, I just couldn't help it.

Poor old Dick, I'm afraid it was all an awful shock for him. He was very cold and deeply injured at first, but, after he brought home I got the fluence to work, and it was all right again. Dear Dick – he really is a pet – I couldn't ask for anyone sweeter.

I feel quite shattered. But before I get into bed I simply must put down an account of the whole awful day. It started badly – the water in the bath was half-cold because the geyser went wrong –

Her pen scratched on the thick paper.

Sinclair let himself into the flat which he shared with his brother. I shall never be able to sleep, he thought. He took off his clothes, put on pyjamas, got into bed, and began to read *Why*

Was Lincoln Murdered? a biography of John Wilkes Booth. Within five minutes he was asleep.

Jean Rogers found Tracy waiting for her when she came out of the house in Redfern Square. They were silent all the way back to Hampstead in his Morris car. The tyres crackled on gravel as Tracy turned in the drive. When he cut off the engine they sat there a moment. He said, 'This is a terrible thing about Lionel, Jean. Terrible. I don't mind telling you that it's really shaken me.'

'Yes,' Jean Rogers said in a flat voice. 'It's a terrible thing, George. You're quite right.' She got out of the car. Still in the same flat voice she said, 'I shall go home tonight. I have rather a bad headache. Don't bother to come with me.' The flat which she had rented, but rarely stayed in, was a few doors up the road. Watching her walk slowly away, with her shoulders sagging a little, Tracy felt quick desire for her. He walked after her to the end of the drive, and placed his hands upon her shoulders. She turned with a little start. 'No,' she said, with a kind of horror in her face. 'Not tonight. My headache is too bad. Please.' Something in her expression made him let her go.

Mudge was staying the night with Onslow in his unfurnished room in Camden Town. They brewed some strong tea and after Onslow had given Mudge a brief lecture on the reactionary nature of advertising agencies, they began to discuss the murder.

'Who, d'you think it was?' Mudge asked. 'All joking apart, who was it? Who d'you think, Jack?'

Onslow turned his lean, handsome, supercilious face towards his friend. 'I'm not much interested in the private reasons for which a member of the boss class gets knocked off. I'm more interested in the system which permits so transparently worthless, stupid and lecherous a specimen of humanity as Lionel Hargreaves to lord it over you and me. But if you want my opinion' – here he paused, and Mudge leaned forward to show by the urgency of his attention how much he *did* want it – I should say that two most likely candidates would be the people nearest to him, who had most opportunity of knowing what a rat he really was – his father and his brother.'

Chapter Two *9.30 to 9.45 a.m.*

In a small room with bare walls distempered an unpleasing shade of brown a man sat behind a desk on which were placed neatly two inkwells, a blotting-pad and a paperweight shaped like a monkey. The place was Scotland Yard, and the man was Inspector Bland; he was looking at a file of newspaper clippings. The door in the room was opposite his desk, and he did not look up when he said 'Come in' to a knock. Filby's narrow head looked round the door. The tall detective was excited.

'Beginning to look as if he's slipped up somewhere. We've traced the weapon.' Filby repeated with ghoulish satisfaction, 'The murder weapon.'

'Well,' Bland said. His voice was noticeably sharper in this congenial air.

'Man bought it second-hand four days ago in a shop off the New Cut,' Filby said. 'We checked it through the number. God knows why he didn't file it off. And when I say a man bought it, I mean a man. And what a man. Flaming red hair, bushy eyebrows, rasping voice. Wouldn't take it away – asked to have it sent to him – gave the name of Jones. Do you know what I think?' Filby leaned across the desk.

'You think he was disguised.'

Filby was disappointed. 'How did you guess?'

'I'm gifted that way. It's not the disguise that impresses me as odd, though, but the fact that he should buy a revolver at all.'

Filby stayed. 'If he was going to shoot the man, wouldn't he want a revolver?'

'Yes.' But would he buy it in an obvious disguise just four days before he decided to murder somebody, ask to have it sent to him, and then forget to file off the number? There's no doubt this is the revolver?'

'It's the one all right. Ballistics checked on the bullet. Anyway, we've got the address of this chap Jones. Probably a phoney, but shall I go down and check on it?'

Bland hesitated, and then said, 'I'll go myself. You can send back these cuttings on Lily Hargreaves to Records. Reading between the lines, and looking at the report Chappell, who worked on the case, sent in at the time, there doesn't seem much doubt that she committed suicide, although nothing could be proved.'

Filby sat on the desk and swung his leg. 'I've not had time to check on the vamp's marriage lines, but I have checked on the phone call she received, and it's okay. Made at a quarter to six from a public box in Piccadilly. We're looking for the taxi-man who picked her up, too. I think that's all.'

'Let me have that address, will you?' Bland said. He took the slip of paper Filby rather unwillingly gave him, and read 114 Willington Street, Borough, SE1. He said thoughtfully, 'It's a very special sort of murderer that has red hair and bushy eyebrows and leaves his address in the shop where he buys a revolver. Do you know what sort of murderer?'

Filby's mouth was slightly open. He closed it with a snap. 'What sort?'

'A murderer with an alibi,' Bland said. He closed the door.

Chapter Three *10.00 to 10.30 a.m.*

A large beautifully-polished brass plate on the outer pillars said 'Hargreaves & Hargreaves. Ground Floor.' Bland pushed open the swing doors and stepped into a hall that breathed money. A commissionaire in uniform said, 'The lift, sir?' and looked critically at Bland's raincoat. The detective shook his head and walked through more swing doors straight in front of him. Inside these doors was another hall, and a reception desk, which was unattended. A door to the left said PRODUCTION, another said STUDIO. The air was warm and heavy. To the right ran a long corridor with doors opening off on either side. Bland's cough broke into air that was padded with quiet. The door of the Studio opened and Onslow and Mudge came out. They seemed not to have changed their corduroy trousers, sports jackets and knitted ties of the previous evening. They were deep in conversation.

'Something quite simple,' Onslow said, 'perfectly functional, to express their character as architects.'

'Quite,' said Mudge.

'The name alone surrounded by a thick rule would be enough. No copy. But what chance is there of doing anything simple – anything good – ' He broke off and stared superciliously at Bland, seeming to see him for the first time. 'The sleuth on the track. Good morning.'

'Good morning. Is Mr Sinclair in?'

'I'll take you along to, him.' They walked down the corridor. 'I've always felt rather sorry for murderers,' Onslow said. 'Not that I approve of murder – but in the stinking capitalist world we live in it seems very hard that one man, who probably had some good reason for killing another, should be chased around by a lot of people who haven't the first idea of all the psychological subtleties involved, the whole complex of motives that drive people to commit crime.'

'Speaking as a policeman, I'd say that most murders aren't committed from a subtle motive. The chief motives for murder are two – money and sex. Anything else, believe me, is rare.'

Onslow raised his eyebrows. 'Is there anything subtler than sex?' he asked, and before Bland had time to think of a reply said 'Here's Sinclair's room,' and walked away. Bland knocked and went in. The room was panelled in oak, Sinclair's desk was a lighter shade of oak and the carpet was green. Sinclair looked pale and worn this morning, but his greeting, as he got up from behind the desk with hand outstretched, was warm. Bland accepted the cigarette he was offered, and sat down in an easy-chair.

'You seem to have something about Lily Hargreaves' death,' Bland said. 'Our man on the case had suspicions of suicide at the time, but we were never able to trace anything definite. I'll take your tip, I think, about seeing Weston. Where shall I find him?'

'It'll get his address for you. He's by way of being a personal friend of EH – known him for some years, anyway. Handles any legal work we have here.' Sinclair dialled a number on a house telephone and said, 'Let me know Mr Weston's address, will you? 27 Lexington Square, EC4. Thank you.' He made a note on a piece of paper and pushed it across the desk. 'That's his office – they haven't got his home address. Anything fresh on the case?'

'We think we've traced the purchase of the gun. And the purchaser.'

'No!' Sinclair breathed admiration. 'Quick work. How the devil did you manage it?'

'It wasn't difficult. The number was left on the gun, and it was bought only four days ago. The man who bought it kindly left his name and address. The name was Jones, and the man had flaming red hair and a husky voice. I'm going down now to check up on the story, and see if I can find Mr Jones. Would you like to come along? Or am I taking you away from something important?'

Sinclair waved his hand at two papers that lay on the desk. 'There's nothing that can't wait – and I'd certainly like to see you in operation. I thought you wanted to have a look round here?'

'I do – and I want to see Edward Hargreaves. But I think those things will have to wait on this.'

Sinclair opened the door of the adjacent room and said, 'Hang on to anything that turns up, Onslow. I'm going out with the Inspector. He's a bright lad is Onslow,' Sinclair said as they walked along the corridor. 'Damned good young copywriter. Red, of course, as they all are.'

'He seemed anxious to, impress me with his sympathy towards the murderer.'

Sinclair laughed. 'He never knows when to stop talking – though you'll have gathered that nobody liked Lionel. What you make of the case?'

Bland smiled broadly. 'I may be able to tell you after we've been to 114 Willington Street, Borough. Do you remember that day when Towser put carbide in the inkwell, and old Squiffy said – '

The swing doors closed behind them.

Chapter Four *11.00 to 11.30 a.m.*

A dirty lace curtain hung at the small ground-floor window. Outside an optician's shop opposite a dog was chasing its tail. A small boy sat in the gutter throwing fivestones with one hand and picking his nose with the other. Bland's knock was answered by a small woman with hard black eyes and a dirty face. 'It's a pint today,' she said, and then stopped and said accusingly, 'You're not the milkman.'

'Not the milkman,' Bland said gently. 'The police.'

The woman did not show surprise or any other emotion. Her black eyes grew a little harder, and she ran her hand quickly across her nose. 'You've come to the wrong shop, then. This is a respectable place, there's nothing wrong goes on here. And how do I know you are a copper, anyway?'

Bland showed his card. 'You've got a lodger named Jones, I believe?'

'Then you believe wrong. He left yesterday.'

'Perhaps you'd be good enough to answer a few questions about him.'

'P'raps I would and p'raps I wouldn't. I don't like narks, not even when they're dressed respectable. Why should I answer your questions?'

'It's a case of murder,' Bland said mildly, and her self-possession left her. 'My Gawd, murder. All right, you'd better come in.' She led them into the room with the lace curtain. Almost all the available space on the walls was filled with plates in wire frames, and brownish reproductions of Victorian paintings. The leather chairs squeaked protestingly as they sat down. 'Mrs Lacey, my name is,' the woman said, 'and ten years I've been here and never a word of complaint from anyone. You can ask all of 'em up the street,' she added triumphantly.

'What about Mr Jones?'

She ran her hand across her nose again. 'I thought he was an odd one. But it's not my business, you know, to pry into my lodgers' doings.' Her black eyes looked hard at Bland, and he leaned forward and said persuasively, 'It's just Mr Jones that interests me, Mrs Lacey. What did he look like?'

Quite unexpectedly Mrs Lacey hooted shrilly with laughter. '*Look* like – he looked like a bloody scarecrow, that's what. I've never seen a man with such real tomato-red hair. Real flaming red, not just carroty. And thick eyebrows and a big red nose – yes, he certainly looked a scarecrow. And gloves.'

'Gloves?'

'*Always* wore gloves. Yes, he was a funny customer altogether – only came 'ere half a dozen times all told, and never stayed the night. Booked up for a month, paid his rent in advance, left after a fortnight – yes, he certainly was a funny customer. I never saw him but he was wearing a pair of yellow gloves, and he wore 'em inside and out of his room. I know that because once I 'ad to go up there for one thing or another, and he opened the door with the gloves on.' Mrs Lacey's little eyes sparkled, and she lowered her voice. 'It's my belief that there was something wrong with 'is 'ands, and 'e wore the gloves to hide it.'

'Any idea of his height? Do you think you'd recognise him again?'

'I'd know that 'ead of 'air anywhere,' Mrs Lacey said. She was becoming quite gay. ' 'Eight – well, I don't know, didn't notice it specially. But I'd know 'is voice – it was sort of deep and thick, if you know what I mean.'

Bland sighed. 'Yes, I think I do know. Now is there anything special you associate with Mr Jones? Did he ever say or do anything that you particularly remember?'

Mrs Lacey pondered, and drew her hand across her nose again. 'You must excuse me,' she said. 'No, there was nothing. 'E just came one day with a suitcase that 'e kept locked all the time – not that I tried to look inside,' she added hastily. 'And then 'e went a fortnight later – I don't suppose 'e spoke half a dozen words to me all told.' She paused and then said slowly, 'But there was something else. I've just remembered it. A telephone call. Yesterday, just before 'e left 'e made a telephone call.'

'Did you hear what he said?'

'I never listen,' Mrs Lacey said with dignity. 'Though the phone's in the hall, and generally you can't 'elp 'earing. But as it so happens he spoke very soft.'

'I noticed the telephone as we came in,' Bland said. 'Excuse me.' He went out into the hall. Mrs Lacey fixed Sinclair with a nasty look. 'I don't want to get into any trouble over this.'

'No, of course not,' Sinclair replied politely. He was feeling rather uncomfortable.

'Because I 'ad nothing to do with any of it. Does 'e think this Jones did it?'

'I wouldn't say that. These are just routine enquiries.'

'What are you – a sergeant? You don't look like a copper to me.' Sinclair was glad when Bland came back and said that he would like to see Mr Jones' room. Mrs Lacey nodded, although she muttered under her breath as she led them up the stairs. The room contained an iron bedstead, a wash basin, a cupboard, and very little else. Bland gave it a not very thorough examination. He opened the cupboard, looked at the bed, walked over to the window, stood there a moment, and nodded. Within five minutes they were out in the street again. The small boy was still throwing five-stones and picking his nose. He stopped for a moment to stare at them, and then resumed both activities with increased concentration. 'A citizen of the future,' Bland said gravely as they walked past him, and Sinclair could not tell whether or not he spoke ironically.

Chapter Five *11.30 a.m. to 12.15 p.m.*

'It's Blackfriars we want,' Bland said, 'and this tram will just do us. What could be better?' He seemed almost gay as they mounted to the upper deck. 'Have you ever heard of Joseph van Dieren, Art Agent, 183 Old Bridge Street, Blackfriars?' Sinclair shook his head. 'Because that's where we're going now. What exactly is an art agent, by the way?'

'Roughly speaking, someone who has a number of advertising artists on his books, and handles their work. He may have one artist who's good at figure work, another who specialises in whimsical drawings, and so on. He sells their services to advertising agents like ourselves, and sometimes to advertisers direct, and gets his commission. Perfectly legitimate and often profitable business. We know most of the big agents, but Joseph van Dieran is a new one on me. Why are you interested in him?'

'Because the telephone call made by Mr Jones was to van Dieren's number. Don't the activities of Mr Jones strike you as very curious?'

Sinclair hesitated. 'He certainly seems a remarkable figure. That touch about wearing yellow gloves all the time sent a bit of a chill up my spine.'

'I didn't mean quite that. I meant the way in which Mr Jones advertised his actions.'

Sinclair seemed momentarily fogged. 'I don't get you.'

'Just consider his activities. Let's assume that Mr Jones equals X – that is, the murderer. For some reason unknown to us he takes a room with Mrs Lacey and adopts what would appear to be disguise. But what sort of disguise does he use? A self-evident one – a disguise which *calls attention to him*. Nobody would be likely to forget that red hair and the deep voice. And then the gloves. It shows very praiseworthy caution to wear gloves continually so that you will leave no fingerprints – but why *yellow* gloves? It's possible that Mrs Lacey might not have noticed a pair of dark brown or grey gloves, but she couldn't fail to notice yellow. And then calmly to leave what were presumably the very same yellow gloves outside the french windows last night. And why leave the number on the revolver? We should have traced it eventually, but he certainly made things easy for us. If our ballistics expert hadn't said quite definitely that the bullet that killed Hargreaves *did* come from that revolver I should suspect that we were being led up the garden path.'

'I see what you mean. And what do you think about this telephone call?'

'God knows. I'm inclined to think that in some obscure way Mr Jones and the telephone call are being used to provide an alibi. But what sort of alibi is it that you establish four hours before a crime?'

A frown creased Sinclair's brow. Suddenly he grinned. 'It would be funny, wouldn't it, if after all this there were a real red-headed man named Jones who'd killed Lionel just because he disliked him?'

'Very funny.' Bland agreed without enthusiasm.

The building was a small office block, decayed and worn. A small wooden board outside said 'Joseph van Dieren, Art Agent – Down Corridor.' Inside the door it was darkish, and there was a smell of cats. They walked down the corridor past a flight of stairs until they saw a door which said in black lettering 'Van

Dieren – Art Agent. Knock and Enter.' They knocked and entered, and found themselves in a kind of cupboard, with another door to the left and in front of them a hatchway and a bell with a note above it, 'Please ring.' The hatchway shot open before they had time to ring the bell, and a voice said 'Yes.'

Framed in the hatchway was a woman's head, small and round. Beneath hair taken up in tight golden curls, her face looked like a doll's face. There were two patches of colour on her cheeks, and her mouth was shaped with lipstick into a perfect Cupid's bow. She wore large bracelets on her arms, with silver coins on them and they jangled when she moved. She said in a shrill voice, 'If you want Mr van Dieren, he's out.' Her eyes, large, round and blue, with very black lashes, looked suspiciously at Bland but meltingly at Sinclair. 'If there's anything I can do – ' she said, and simpered.

'I am a police officer,' Bland said, 'and I should like to see Mr van Dieren.'

'Perlice,' the girl said. She looked at Bland with unconcealed dismay for a moment, and then said, 'But I've told you he's out.' Her voice had gone up a tone in shrillness. 'He won't be in till after lunch.'

'Perhaps you can help me. I'm trying to trace a call that was made to this office yesterday, between 4.15 and 4.30. Do you take the incoming calls?'

She seemed suddenly more composed. 'Course I do. There's no one else here.'

'And was there a call about 4.15 and 4.30?'

'As a matter of fact,' she said, 'there was. Though I don't know that I can tell you much about it. What d'you want to know for?' She looked down at her red-stained fingernails, up at Sinclair, and said with no very obvious relevance, 'My name is Polly Lines.'

Bland gave the impression of someone with an immense store of time and patience. His round face smooth and untroubled, he said earnestly, 'I'm afraid I can't tell you that, Miss Lines. But if you can tell us anything about the telephone call I shall appreciate it very much.'

She considered the question with some care, and after a few seconds she decided to smile. The smile revealed very small, white, even teeth. 'Won't you come in – both of you.' She flashed another smile to include Sinclair, got up and opened the door they had seen to the left. When they went through this door they saw that what had looked like a block of offices was really two rooms. One of them bore the name 'Mr van Dieren,' and the other, 'Secretary.' This room was about ten feet square and contained a small kneehole desk, a typewriter, a telephone and a wall switchboard, a small electric fire and two chairs. Miss Lines tapped across the room on high heels, sat on one of the chairs and crossed her legs with a rustle of silk. Bland sat on the other chair and Sinclair leaned against the wall in an attitude which he hoped was appropriate to a plain-clothes policeman. Miss Lines started to talk.

'Really, there isn't much to tell. A call came through about twenty past four, and I thought it might be Mr van Dieren himself – he'd been out since before lunch, and I thought he might have phoned to say he'd been detained. When I took off the receiver someone said, "Is Mr van Dieren there?" It was a deep, gruff sort of voice, and there was a sort of excitement about it. I said he wasn't and the voice gave a – well, sort of sigh, it might have been relief.' She broke off suddenly, and looked at them both coyly, with her head on one side. 'But d'you *really* want to know all this? I'm not just being silly, am I?'

Bland assured her gravely that she was not being silly. She giggled. 'Well then, I said, "Who is that speaking?" or something, like that, and *he* said, "My name is Jones." So I asked if there was any message I could take, or if it was any particular Mr Jones – because, after all, Jones is a common name, isn't?' She appealed to Sinclair, and he said, 'It certainly is.'

'*Then* he said, very quietly but still in that deep husky sort of voice, "He'll know who I am. Just say Mr Jones called, and that

I'll be getting in touch with him – and pretty soon too." I wouldn't swear to the exact words, but that was more or less what he said, and he spoke in a rather nasty way, if you understand what I mean.'

Bland and Sinclair both nodded encouragingly. 'And did Mr van Dieren come back?'

The black lashes fluttered over Miss Lines' blue eyes like two tiny machines. 'That's the funny thing. Mr van Dieren *did* come back, soon after five o'clock, and he didn't know anything about this Mr Jones. We have a Mr Jones on our books, an artist, but I should know *his* voice. So, Mr van Dieren said it must be a practical joke of some sort, and not to take any notice of it.' She finished triumphantly on a high note, and her two listeners nodded approval again, with a slightly comic unanimity.

'And when are you expecting Mr van Dieren?'

Miss Lines became confidential. 'There you have me. Sometimes he doesn't come in till after lunch, but usually he telephones in the morning. He hasn't been in touch today so far. It's been a dead-and-alive morning – until you gentlemen came.' Her eyes fluttered again at Sinclair, and Bland noticed suddenly that Sinclair was looking fixedly at something on the wall. Bland turned round and saw that a whimsical sketch of two children playing with a ball much bigger than themselves hung there, and at the same moment Sinclair spoke.

'I wonder if you can tell me who made that sketch?'

Miss Lines looked astonished, but not displeased. 'Yes, it's one of the artists we have on our books. His name's Carruthers.'

Sinclair nodded to Bland. 'That's the man I was telling you about. You remember, the cousin. It's odd that he should be on the books of – ' His voice melted away.

Miss Lines looked warmly and invitingly at Sinclair. 'I didn't know policemen were interested in art,' she said.

Bland stood up. 'Will you give Mr van Dieren this card and tell him that I'll call round here at 2.30 and that I'd like to see him.' They were at the door when he said, 'just one other thing, Miss Lines. How long have you been here?'

She considered, looking at her fingernails. 'Just on a year now. Soon after Mr van Dieren opened business.'

Chapter Six *12.35 to 2.15 p.m.*

It was half-past twelve when they got back to the Hargreaves office. Sinclair had accepted an invitation to lunch from Bland, but even the chief of the Copy Department, he explained, must make a pretence of doing some work, or at least of seeing what work had been done. In the reception office they met Richard Hargreaves and Eve Marchant. Richard was dressed with some care in perfectly plain dark clothes, with a cream shirt, red tie and handkerchief, and black suede shoes. Eve Marchant, wearing a bottlegreen man-cut suit, greeted the detective with the enthusiasm of an old friend.

'Don't you think I'm brave, Inspector, to invade the holy of holies? It's the first time I've been here, and I'm terrified the old man's going to jump out at me from behind a corner. Is there any news? Or is that something I shouldn't ask in a flippant tone? Dick's great on tones – he's always telling me I'm using the wrong one.' Before Bland could reply Richard Hargreaves said, 'Did you want to see me? Eve and I are just going out to lunch, but that can wait if there's anything you want me for.'

'Just one question. I expect it's wasting my breath, but – have you ever heard of an art agent named van Dieren?'

'Van Dieren?' Hargreaves teetered nervously from one foot to the other. 'No, I don't know that I have. But Tracy's really the man to ask – I don't have much to do with our artists. Is he something to do with the case?' He suddenly turned to Sinclair.

'Been the most damnawful row going on this morning. Just as well you were out, so that you didn't get involved in it.'

Sinclair raised his eyebrows. 'The old man on the warpath again?' Richard Hargreaves nodded. 'My God, yes. All about money this time. Production costs too heavy, art costs too heavy. Poor old Tracy's been in with him for the last half-hour, and I had a lecture for an hour on the errors of my ways.' With a curiously girlish gesture he waved goodbye to them. Eve placed her hand in his arm and they went out through the swinging doors.

As Bland followed Sinclair down the corridor, a door to their left suddenly shot open, and Tracy was in the doorway with his back to them. EH's voice, heavy with power, came through to them. 'Understand, Tracy, I will not tolerate this kind of waste. An advertising agency is not an art gallery, it is a commercial concern, and its purpose is to make money, not to support unsuccessful artists. Do I make myself clear?'

'Perfectly clear.' Tracy slammed the door and turned round. His face was red with anger. He said, more, as it seemed, to himself than to Bland or Sinclair, 'I hope that bastard dies,' and walked across the corridor to a room opposite Hargreaves'. Sinclair looked after him unhappily. 'He takes it too hard. This sort of thing happens once a week and Tracy certainly gets his fare share of kicks. But it's a mistake to – '

The door of Tracy's room opened again suddenly, and his head was framed in the doorway. 'Could I see you for a minute, Inspector?' Sinclair waved a hand and moved on down the corridor. 'Pick me up in the Copy Department when you're ready. No hurry.'

There was plenty of fake panelling in Tracy's room; Bland reflected that it acted as a kind of keynote for these offices. A cigarette was offered and accepted, and he sat waiting for Tracy to begin talking. The Art Director was not looking well this morning. His colour was bad, and he had apparently cut his face while shaving. He seemed to find the silence uncomfortable, and yet to be at a loss for words. He said at last, in a tone of reluctant apology: 'Blew off the handle last night I'm afraid – about Jean Rogers. Sorry. But frankly, I find this whole damned thing a strain. I'm a sensitive man, and I hate anything to do with violence.' Bland merely inclined his head. There was another silence. 'Is there anything fresh?' Tracy asked, in what seemed a kind of desperation.

'One or two things. But you had something you wanted to say to me?'

Tracy ran his hand quickly through his thick hair. 'Well, damn it, yes I have. You know what I told you last night that I thought you'd find the key to all this in the family history. Have you followed up that line?'

'I'm thinking about it. An art agent named van Dieren wouldn't have anything to do with the family history, would he?'

'Don't know the name,' Tracy said irritably. 'I was thinking about the death of Lily, EH's wife, two years ago. Know anything about that?'

'Suppose you tell me.' Bland was looking at his fingernails. 'I know she was drowned in an accident.'

'Accident, hell. She committed suicide.' Tracy wagged a finger. 'I met the captain of the yacht afterwards, and he told me. A sea like glass, a part of the ship where there wasn't the remotest chance of her going overboard. No doubt in the captain's mind about it. And I'll tell you another man who knew more about it than he said, and that's old Weston, EH's lawyer. He's a closemouthed old devil, but he can tell you a lot – if you get him to talk.' The Art Director thumped the desk in front of him. He was impressively earnest. 'Find the reason for Lily Hargreaves' suicide, and you'll find Lionel Hargreaves' murderer.'

'What was Lily Hargreaves like?'

'Charming,' Tracy said emphatically. 'Young, fresh, pure. Innocent – you might almost say ignorant. God knows why she married EH. But the Hargreaves family have always had fascination for women.' There was another silence. Tracy sat in a revolving chair with his face to the light, and the cast in his eye was distinct and disturbing. Bland said, 'And that's all you have to tell me?' His eye was caught by a picture on the wall opposite, an oil painting of two fishermen in reds and greens, the paint laid on thick. Tracy noticed the direction of his look, and smiled. 'A genuine Tracy. And don't tell me you like it, because I know it's bad. I used to think I might be an artist twenty years ago, but I became an advertising man instead. That's the trouble with creative advertising work – it takes the energy out of you for anything else.'

Bland said again, 'That's all you have to tell me?'

'I thought you should know that,' Tracy answered absently. When Bland went out he was still standing looking a little wistfully at the painting. His large, firm hand was tugging at his hair.

Bland stepped across the corridor to EH's door, knocked, and went in without waiting for an answer. He said while he walked across the room. 'I called on Joseph van Dieren this morning.' EH stared at him from behind a desk that was noticeably bigger in a room that was noticeably bigger than Tracy's. 'Should I know that name?' he asked. He looked genuinely perplexed.

'I don't know. I'm trying to find out where he fits in the picture.' Bland sat down without being asked, and held his hat on his knees. 'He's an art agent. He was telephoned by the man who bought the gun with which your son was shot.' EH bent forward eagerly, and Bland said, 'No, we've not found the man. He took a room for a few days in the name of Jones, and the two things we know about him are that he bought the gun and that he telephoned this man van Dieren. Van Dieren was out, so he didn't talk to him.'

'You think you're on the track of something?'

Bland shrugged. 'It could be that Jones is the murderer, and then again it could be all a sideline.' He paused and added carefully, 'We might be doing better if you were quite frank with us yourself.'

'What do you mean?'

Bland said, still speaking carefully, 'What happened to your second wife, Mr Hargreaves? You know as well as I do that her death wasn't an accident.'

The red face turned purple and then the blue eyes bulged. Then EH said, with a restraint that was at the same time dignified and reproachful, 'Somebody has been telling you lies, Inspector. My wife's death was an accident.'

'Oh, come now, Mr Hargreaves,' Bland said, in a tone that was not less than insulting. 'When the sea was like glass, and when she was in a part of the ship where she couldn't possibly have fallen overboard? Of course nothing could be proved, but the captain had no doubts, and neither had our man on the case. Don't think that we're *too* simple, Mr Hargreaves.' He waited for the explosion, but it did not come. With a wounded dignity that was not less than admirable, EH said, 'I can only repeat what I said, sir. My wife's death was an accident. If you will not believe that, you must disbelieve it. The subject is too painful for discussion.' Bland was rising to go when EH said, 'Stay a moment.' Behind the big desk EH's gaze was sincere and appealing. When he began to talk, phrases rolled from his mouth easily, and with a curious falsity.

'I am anxious to make my position clear, Inspector, Lionel's death is a serious blow, both to me personally and to the business. Personally, because he was my eldest, and my favourite, son. In the business, because he was a man who it will not be possible to replace. So that both as father and as a businessman I shall not rest until I see his murderer apprehended.' He paused for a moment. Bland was looking at his hat. 'I say this partly because – very wrongly, I fear – I failed to pass on to you last night what may be an important piece of evidence.' He pushed over the desk a letter and an envelope. 'This arrived by post yesterday morning. I was going to speak with Lionel about it last night. I held it back after his death, thinking – God knows why – that I might be able to do something with it myself. But it should be in your hands. I must have been almost insane with rage ever to think anything else.' Perhaps it was because EH's general appearance was so coldly calculating, Bland reflected, that the things he said sounded so improbable. He looked at the letter and the envelope.

The envelope was addressed in amateurish typing to, E. Hargraves, Esq., The Hargreaves Agency, 18, Boxeter St., WC. The letter was also amateurishly typed, on flimsy paper. It read:

Your son Lionel is married to a girl named Eve Marchant, a tart who shows herself off every night half naked in the chorus of the Splendid. Go and have a look at her and see how you like your daughter-in-law. Not quite a society marriage, is it, Mr Snotty Hargreaves?

'It is true that you wanted a society marriage for your son?'

EH said calmly, 'It would have been for the advancement of the family.'

'Was it generally known that you wanted a society marriage for him?' EH nodded. Bland put the letter and envelope in his pocket. 'I'll keep these. Anything else?'

'Nothing else,' EH said. 'I'm glad to have got that off my chest. It was worrying me.' He gave a sudden, dramatic picture of an executive type looking worried, and shot out a hand. 'Let me know of any progress, Inspector. My thoughts are with you.' He stood up, and Bland stood up too. EH said with every appearance of sincerity, 'I shan't rest until Lionel's murderer is found.'

When Bland returned to Sinclair's room he found the Copy Chief talking earnestly to a dapper, baldish man with a soft voice and a ready smile. He gave Bland a limp handshake. Everything about him, indeed, was a little limp, the defeated droop of his shoulders, the casual drabness of his suit and tie, the handkerchief dropping from his coat sleeve, and the rather down-at-heel shoes he wore. Sinclair was beaming. 'This is Carruthers – you know, I was telling you about him, Lionel's cousin – I've just been asking him about van Dieren. I told him that I'd spotted one of his things on the wall of that office.'

Carruthers uttered a deprecatory cough. 'I hope there's nothing criminal in that, Charles. Really, all this questioning terrifies me.' He spoke with an uneasy jocosity.

Bland introduced himself and said, 'Tell me, what do you know about van Dieren?'

'I don't know him well at all, not really, at all.' Carruthers seemed for some reason very nervous. 'You know, of course, that he's my art agent. Not that he's ever done anything much for me – a pretty poor art agent. I only stay with him because I'm too lazy to change.'

'What does he look like?'

'I suppose he's about fifty – might be a little more. He's got a lot of grey hair and shouts a bit. But there's something else about him.' Carruthers seemed to reach in the air for a word, and finally brought it down out of space. 'Something – funny. He doesn't ring true, somehow. It's as if he had a secret past in which he'd been quite a different person from the man he is today. That's as near as I can get.' He looked solemnly at Bland.

'How long have you known him?' asked the Inspector.

'About a year. He hasn't been in business much longer than that.' He wriggled again, and blew his nose. 'But I really – ah – hardly know him at all, in the real sense of the word. I doubt if I've seen him more than a dozen times.'

There was a little silence. Carruthers consulted an enormous turnip-shaped watch. 'I'm sorry to be so little helpful. I've got an engagement for lunch. Is there anything else you wanted to ask, Inspector?'

Bland said slowly, 'Not just at the moment. I'd like to have your own address, though. Just in case I need to get in touch about van Dieren,' he added, seeing Carruthers' look of alarm.

Carruthers gave him an address in Balham. 'I have a little flat there. And now if there's nothing else – I must fly.' He smiled uneasily, and wriggled himself out of the room. Sinclair stared after him in unaffected surprise. 'I wonder what's the matter with him. He seems to have got the wind up about something. This van Dieren sounds an odd fish.'

'Perhaps when I see him I shall find out what's worrying friend Carruthers so much. In the meantime even a policeman must eat – and frankly, I'm very hungry. Shall we see what Soho has to offer?'

At lunch Sinclair chatted easily and rather maliciously about all the people in the case. He contrasted EH's determination to appear unaffected by Lionel's death, which must have hurt him badly, with Richard's attempt to simulate a sorrow he did not feel. It would be pathetic if it weren't comic, or comic if it weren't pathetic, Sinclair said, to watch the two of them together. Indeed the whole place was like a Freudian study-circle of psychopathogical cases, from Tracy mooning away after Mrs Rogers, whom he could never marry, to Richard steering himself into the arms of somebody who would serve as a substitute for his mother – or would it be his father? Or look at Carruthers. A nice quiet little chap, who had sex on his mind because he could never get off with girls.

'Bond?' Bland suggested.

'Bond,' Sinclair said. A glance at him showed that he was a mass of frustrations, and probably perversions. Frustrated ambition chiefly, leading to malice, envy and all uncharitableness.

'What do you know about the office boys?' Bland asked, and Sinclair gave his dazzling smile.

'Now you're having fun, and you're quite right not to mind my chatter. After all, aren't we all psychopathological cases? I'm sure all policemen must be.'

'And you?' Bland asked, and Sinclair smiled again.

They had paid the bill and were just outside the door when Bland felt suddenly a pain in his eye. He put his hand to it, and pulled down the lid.

'What's the matter?'

'Something in my right eye.' Sinclair clucked with concern. They stood in the street, and poked about with handkerchiefs ineffectively. The eye was watering, and when Bland tried to look out of it he was blinded by a mist of tears. 'A chemist, or better still, a doctor,' Sinclair said, but Bland, handkerchief to eye, was looking at his watch. 'I'm late now, and I don't want to miss this man. I'll call in at a chemist afterwards, if I don't get it out in the taxi.' He hailed one, and it swerved to the kerb. With the handkerchief to eye Bland called 'Goodbye'. In the taxi he pulled the eyelid down and dabbed at the eye with a corner of his handkerchief. He succeeded in shifting what he took to be the piece of grit so that if he kept his eye half-closed it did not water.

Chapter Seven *2.30 to 3.00 p.m.*

The hatchway opened and Miss Lines' head appeared. 'Oh, it's you.' She seemed disappointed. 'Where's your friend?' without waiting for a reply, she added, 'Mr van Dieren's in now. I'll tell him you're here.' Her head popped out of the hatchway for a moment, and then back. 'Go in, will you.' Bland turned the handle of the door which said 'Mr van Dieren.'

Mr. Joseph van Dieran was a surprising, and indeed theatrical, figure. He gave an impression of extreme size and extreme disorderliness, and yet he was neither very big nor, really, very disorderly. Through his half-closed eyes Bland saw that his hair was grey and extremely thick, his eyebrows bushy and his face florid. He had a large handlebar moustache, of a kind that Bland had thought to be long extinct, and he wore a rather shabby suit of rich, ginger-coloured Harris tweed. There was a great deal of this suit; it billowed around him like a wave, and was the most conspicuous thing about him as he stood up and waved Bland to a chair. His voice was a deep and manly roar, varied occasionally by a querulous higher note, as he said that he was sorry to have been out, and asked what he could for the Inspector.

'Do for me,' Bland said vaguely. He looked round the room, and as he did so his right eye gave a twinge, and he was obliged to use his handkerchief. In his brief look he noted the general air of disorder and decay, the files bursting with papers and covered with dust, the empty inkwells and the extraordinary mass of oddments on the desk. He saw on the desk a litter of papers, a quarter-full bottle of port, a mass of cigarette-butts, an empty bottle labelled 'Phosferine', a torch battery, an old black shoelace, half a sandwich, a watch key, and a number of books on art. He noticed also that Mr van Dieren, no doubt a reader of detective stories, had given him a seat in the light, while his own chair and face remained half in shadow. Bland turned his chair so that the light did not fall on his eye, and said, 'What can you tell me about Mr Jones?'

'That telephone call?' Van Dieren guffawed loudly, in what seemed an unnecessary gale of mirth. 'That's a funny thing. You're going to have a hard time believing this, I know – but fact is, I can't tell you anything. We've *got* a Jones on our books, right enough. Who hasn't?' he asked, and went off into another fit of laughter. 'But nothing to do with the chap you want. I know because I rang him up and asked him.' He was silent for a moment, fingering his coat sleeve idly. He produced an enormous handkerchief from his pocket, blew loudly on it, and said abruptly, 'Glass of port?'

'No, thank you. Have you ever met Edward Hargreaves?'

There was another silence from Mr van Dieren's darkish corner – a silence with a quality of strain about it. Then Mr van Deiren said, 'Don't mind if I do?' and, with a hand that seemed not to be quite steady, poured out most of the port in the bottle into a dirty tumbler. He drank half the port at a gulp and said, 'Knew him in America a long time ago. Not seen him for years. Saw in the papers he lost his son. Sad thing.'

'That's what I've come about,' Bland said placidly. 'This man Jones who telephoned you bought the gun that killed Lionel Hargreaves.

There could be no doubt that Mr van Dieren's hand shook now, as he put down his glass of port on the dusty table. He fidgetted again with his coat sleeve, and finally settled on a button, which he tugged viciously. The deep roar of his voice was almost completely replaced by the querulous tone, as he said, 'They can't fix it on me. They're trying to fix it on me.'

'How could they fix anything on you?'

Mr. van Dieren seemed genuinely upset, and yet his dismay retained that curious theatrical flavour of which Bland had been conscious since the beginning of the interview. It was, as Carruthers had said, as if he were two men – as though he were pretending to be frightened, and yet had some real fright, which was still concealed. He began to talk now, very fast, and as though the words were dictated. 'Let me tell you a story.

'Thirty years ago I was a good-looking young man.' He stared at Bland as if he expected contradiction, but the detective had his head back and his eyes almost closed. 'And ambitious too. Had visions of myself as a big business man.' He laughed again, not loudly but a little pathetically. The edge of a curtain seemed to lift on a picture of frustrated ambition, to make clear some of the odd things about Mr van Dieren, his loud voice and ginger suit among them. 'Real estate. I was in real estate. In the Middle West in America. I've done most things in my time.' He poured the rest of the port into his glass. 'And though I say so, I was a damned good salesman.

'Well, there I was, eating my heart out in a little town named Abingdon, working for a couple of old boys who just about knew the motor-car had been invented. Then I met Eddy Hargreaves, and we cottoned to one another at once – at least that's the way I thought it was, though I realised later on I'd made a mistake. Anyway, I cottoned to him. He was smooth as paint was Eddy, a good talker, and a great mathematician too. I told him about my idea of starting up a real estate agency in Abingdon – it was a growing town – expanding fast – and I showed him my list of contacts. I knew I could take a lot of them along with me if I had my own agency. The difficulty was – money. I hadn't got any money. Eddy told me he could put up the money, and we agreed to split fifty-fifty on profits. We started in a small way, of course, but we both worked like niggers, and we showed a profit right from the start.

'After we'd been going three months Eddy made a suggestion. We were having difficulty because our capital wasn't enough to cover the outlay we had to make, and Eddy said he could arrange for us to become the local agents for the Nation-Wide Loan and Investment Corporation, a big firm in Philadelphia. What this meant in simple language was that they loaned us money for the purchase of real estate, and we passed the loan on to the chap who bought the real estate, taking a small percentage out of it. It meant that we made a bit less profit on each deal, but our turnover rocketed up, and we sent the two old boys out of business. Profits went up too, and we were both well in the money.

'Now, there was another side to this business we did for the Loan and Investment Corporation, and that was sale of the Corporation's stock to anyone who was interested. There were 100-dollar, 250-dollar and 500-dollar bonds, and they were easy enough to sell, because the Corporation was offering pretty good interest. I used to go around selling the bonds with my real estate, and Eddy did all the bookwork and handled our affairs with the Nation-Wide people. It was a very useful sideline, and I had more money than I'd ever had in my life. I used to sell the stock, and give them their stock certificate, and interest was paid every six months. We paid them their interest, and the Nation-Wide people paid us. Everyone was happy. That went on for a year.

'Then one day an old man named Schwartz called on me. We'd sold him a thousand dollars' worth of stock, and he hadn't received his half-yearly interest. Instead of speaking to me or to Eddy about it, he'd written off direct to the Nation-Wide people. He showed me their reply. Their letter said that they had no record of any shares held in his name, and that they had sold none of their stock through us, they had simply loaned us money for real estate deals.

'I had it out with Eddy that night – if you can call it that. First of all he denied the whole thing, said Schwartz must have made a mistake. Then he admitted it. I think that was my worst moment. I'd hoped against my good sense that it might have been some sort of mistake. And when he admitted it he changed his tactics entirely, and suddenly became furiously angry. I was taken aback for a bit by that, as he knew I would be. He was always smart, was Eddy Hargreaves.

'What did I think he'd been doing? he asked me. Where did I think the money had come from, the money I'd spent as well as him. Gradually I got the whole story out of him. He'd simply played me for a sucker all along the line. He'd had fake share certificates printed, and kept the money. I worked it out that the total sale of stock was something round about 30,000 dollars. All of it had been sold by me, all of it was worthless, and Eddy had had pretty well all the money. When I asked him where it was, he simply laughed. Finally, he promised to meet me in the morning. He said we could pay back most of the money out of profits.

'I was a fool, I see that now. I should have taken him to the police immediately. In the morning when I went round to the hotel he'd gone. I never saw him again.'

Bland had been scraping a small black scab off the back of his hand while he listened to the story. He said, without looking up, 'And you?'

Mr van Dieren gulped the rest of the port, and made a wry face. 'I'd sold all the stock, taken all the money. They gave me two years for embezzlement. It was a light sentence.'

Bland remained silent for a moment, thinking about this ghost from the past. 'Who would be trying to frame you?'

Mr van Dieren fingered his coat sleeve uncertainly and then blew his nose again nervously and loudly. 'How should I know?'

Bland said patiently, 'You've told me a story about Hargreaves and yourself thirty years ago. You said somebody is trying to fix his son's murder on you. If you're right, that could only be somebody who knew the story. Who would know it?'

The red-faced man glared at him and said querulously. 'Eddy Hargreaves would know it, wouldn't he?'

'So you think that he killed his son and tried to plant it on you. Why should he do that?' Bland held up his hand. 'You can't tell me? All right – I can't tell you, either. Who else might have known that story? It's not one Hargreaves would spread around is it?'

Mr van Dieren looked sly. He looked at the dirty window and at the port bottle on the table and at the worn carpet on the floor. 'How do I know who knew the story? When you find that one, you'll find the man you want.'

'Maybe,' Bland said. He opened his eyes wider and they began to water immediately. He dabbed at them, half-closed them again, and said, 'Do you know anyone else connected with Hargreaves?'

The art agent shook his head. He was looking straight ahead of him, and smirking slightly. Then he clicked his fingers. 'Carruthers.'

'Hargreaves' cousin. Could he be trying to fix you? Would he know the story?'

The smirk became more pronounced. The art agent fiddled with the watch key on the table, looked at it absently, and put it down. 'He's not the one who's trying to fix me – I doubt he'd know that story – but he might know something else. Might be interesting to have a chat with him.' Mr van Dieren had recovered his early jauntiness. 'Somebody's trying to frame me,' he said. 'But they'll have to get up early in the morning to frame Joseph van Dieren. And I think I know who it is.'

'Why do you want to see Carruthers?'

Van Dieren got up, grinning. 'Because he might be able to give me bit of information about – *somebody* – that I'd be very pleased to have. He doesn't know what this bit of information is, but he'd give it in spite of himself, if you see what I mean.' Bland didn't see, and said so, but this statement provoked one of van Dieren's loud, artificial guffaws, that followed him outside.

Slanting rain fell on Bland's shoulders as he looked up and down New Bridge Street. 'A chemist,' he said to himself, 'I must find a chemist.' He found one after three minutes' walk. A small brush dipped in oil and run across his eyelid removed the pain magically. Bland and the chemist looked at the brush afterwards, and the chemist pointed out what he said was a speck of dirt. Bland put a shilling in a collecting-box for Dr Barnado's Homes, and took a taxi to 27 Lexington Square.

Chapter Eight *3.15 to 4.00 p.m.*

William Weston, the Hargreaves lawyer, was a man in his late sixties, with a domed, bald forehead, jaws that drooped like a bloodhound's, and honest blue eyes. His voice was as decorous as his clothes, when he said, 'I don't know that I can do anything for you.' Bland raised his eyebrows in surprise. 'I mean,' the old man explained, 'I don't think I can tell you anything that will help you. You know that I am not permitted professionally to disclose any of my clients' legal secrets.' He smiled briefly, revealing a complete set of very white false teeth. Upper and lower set clicked emphatically as he finished speaking.

Bland said, 'I came to you chiefly because you've known Edward Hargreaves for a long time. I'm told that you're his oldest friend. I want you to tell me anything you can about his personal life that might give us a line on his son's murderer. From what I hear he must have made some enemies. Are there any of them who might have something to do with this case? Is there anyone who might want to strike at Edward Hargreaves through his son?'

The lawyer was silent for a moment, looking down at the papers on his glass-topped desk. Then, with a decisive click of his teeth, he got up and stood with his back to the fireplace, in which a large coal fire was burning. His hands were joined together behind his back. 'Your request, sir, is a curious one, and not the least curious thing about it is the form in which it is put. I should not describe myself as Edward Hargreaves' oldest friend – I should hardly describe myself as a friend at all. It simply happens that I have known him for several years. If you ask my opinion, I should say that Edward Hargreaves is a man who has no friends.'

Bland made a sound that might have indicated despair at the lawyer's loquacity, or surprise at his statement. Mr Weston, however, seemed to take it as an expression of discontent, for his immediate reaction was to offer Bland, with some apologetic clicking, a gold-tipped Turkish cigarette. Bland took it, settled back in his leather armchair, and half-closed his eyes. He seemed to be falling asleep. Mr Weston's measured voice went on:

'I am surprised also, sir, because such knowledge of human nature as I have gained during sixty-seven years does not lend me to suppose that the kind of business enmities I might know of would afford cause for murder. There was, for instance, a man named Morton. He came to Hargreaves from another advertising agency, and he brought with him an advertising account for the Monotone Electric Corporation – an account worth £100,000 a year. This account means a profit of £10,000 a year to Hargreaves, and because Morton was able to bring it with him he came to Hargreaves at a salary of £1,500 a year, on a three years contract. Within eighteen months Hargreaves had ingratiated himself personally with the Monotone people, broken Morton's contract on a technicality, and forced his resignation. You will hear many such stories. But they are not reason for murder. And if they were,' Mr Weston's tone was faintly ironic, 'they would be reasons for the murder of Edward Hargreaves, and not his son.'

Bland stirred in his chair, but if he had intended to speak, he was not permitted to do so. Mr Weston's teeth clicked again and he gave a bloodhound's sad but knowing smile. 'My professional experience leads me to suppose that there is a concealed motive behind your questions. Could it be, I wonder, that you are anxious to discover the relations that prevailed between Edward Hargreaves and his sons?'

'It could be,' Bland said. 'What were they?'

Mr Weston sucked air through his false teeth. 'They were not good. Edward was fond of Lionel, but his affection manifested itself oddly. He has an overweening family pride, coupled with a passionate family jealousy, and these warred with his personal avarice. He was alternately severe and indulgent to Lionel, who had a certain superficial dash and glamour. I should say that he had little but contempt for Richard.'

'What about the cousin, Carruthers?'

'Carruthers?' the lawyer said on a note of surprise. 'He was brought up with Richard and Lionel at Redfem Square, but he hasn't lived there since he was thirteen or fourteen. I shouldn't say Edward had any feeling either way about him.'

Bland looked with some distaste at his Turkish cigarette, and laid it down. 'Would the fact that Lionel Hargreaves had married a chorus girl have upset his father and caused a quarrel?'

The lawyer's bloodhound jaws drooped. His blue eyes fixed Bland with a hard, calculating stare. 'Do I understand that Lionel did in fact contract such a marriage?'

'Yes.'

'Then that would certainly have precipitated a quarrel. A very violent one. It might have caused Edward Hargreaves – ' Mr Weston stopped, and clicked his teeth loudly.

Bland leaned forward. 'To alter his will?'

Mr. Weston was cautious. 'Possibly.'

A kind of mist mingled with the electric light in the room, and made a halo round Bland's fair head. He said, 'What can you tell me about the death of Lily Hargreaves?' The lawyer was badly shaken. He took out a silk handkerchief, apparently from somewhere in his buttocks and patted his gleaming forehead as Bland went on, 'I know that she died on a cruise. I know that the sea was calm, and that she was in a part of the ship where she couldn't possibly have fallen overboard. I know that you were a guest on that cruise.'

Above the bloodhound jowl the blue eyes were grave. With less than his usual sententiousness, the lawyer said, 'There are some things about which one would rather not talk.'

Bland said sharply, 'There are things about which one has to talk. Did Lily Hargreaves commit suicide?'

'Her death can have nothing to do with this case.'

Bland tapped his teeth. 'It is an offence to withold information that may lead to the discovery of a murderer.'

With comic serenity Mr Weston said, 'I am well aware of that, sir.' He looked at the red and yellow flames of the coal fire and went on abruptly, 'Lily Hargreaves committed suicide.'

'Why?'

Still looking at the fire the lawyer said, 'She was disappointed in her husband. He was over sixty and she was twenty-two. She found out that he valued her simply as a possession. He loved her in his way, perhaps, as much as he could ever love anybody or anything – but it was a hard, inhuman way. She was delicate and easily hurt, and it was a mortal hurt to her when she found out the kind of vicious, bitter, ungenerous man she'd married.' He spoke with passion.

'Was that all the reason?'

Softly the lawyer said, 'She was frightened of her stepson.'

'Her stepson?' Bland frowned. 'I see – you mean Lionel and Richard.'

'They were her stepsons legally.' Mr Weston's voice was still soft. 'She was twenty-two and they were in their thirties. A curious situation.' Bland said nothing. 'It was Lionel who frightened her. Richard was never anything more than a cipher. You will have heard, perhaps, of Lionel's reputation with women.

'Lionel and Dick and I all joined the party at the same time. On the second night we were aboard Lionel had too much to drink. It didn't affect him in the way that drink affects most

100

people. He lost all his surface friendliness and became unpleasant, tried to pick a quarrel – I have seen him drunk once before, and I kept out of his way when he was drinking. That night Lily had gone to bed and we were playing a rubber of bridge, when Lionel practically accused Richard of cheating. We left the rubber unfinished, and about half-past ten we all went to bed. Edward Hargreaves had received a wire from Tracy, and had gone back to London – it was something that needed his urgent personal attention. At half-past eleven I heard a knock on my cabin door. I opened it, and there was Lily Hargreaves.

'She was panting with fear. There was a bruise on her arm and her neck was badly scratched. She told me that Lionel had entered her cabin, and that he had tried to make love to her. She was much distressed. I soothed her as best I could, told her that Lionel had been drinking, and promised to speak to him.'

Bland was tapping his teeth with a pencil. 'Why didn't she get off the yacht, go to her husband and tell him about it?'

Weston pulled at his bloodhound jowl. 'My dear sir – I don't think you fully realise the situation. Edward Hargreaves is not a man to brook such a thing. He might have done violence to his son.'

'Would that have worried her?'

'Besides, we – or rather, I – did not regard the matter with such seriousness. After all, Lionel had been drunk. It seemed that the reasonable and sensible course was to speak severely to Lionel, and to try to smooth the whole thing over. At least I thought so at the time. Perhaps I was wrong.' He sighed. 'I have been bitterly sorry since then that I did not take her off the yacht that night. But the fact remains that I took her back to her cabin, and advised her to lock the door. On the following morning I spoke to Lionel. He called me a meddling old fool, and said it was none of my business. He cooled down a little when I threatened to tell his father, and he promised to apologise to Lily. She stayed in her cabin all day, and would see nobody – she said that she had a bad headache. After tea Lionel, Richard and

I went ashore. I left them together – they said they were going to drink all the evening – and went off to look at the antique shops. Half an hour after I left them Lionel told Richard that he had left something important on the ship. He went back there alone. That night Lily committed suicide.'

There was a brief pause before Bland spoke, and his voice was much gentler than usual. 'You were fond of Lily Hargreaves?' The lawyer suddenly struck the desk in front of him, so that Bland thought the glass of it would break, in a gesture that fitted oddly with the placidity of his manner. 'I loved her. Nobody could help loving her. She was sweet and gentle, innocent and shy – it was a black day for her when she met Edward Hargreaves and his sons. I tell you, Inspector, she was killed by Lionel as surely as if he had thrown her overboard. I was sure of that at the inquest. I am sure of it now. And yet – what could I do, what could I say?'

'Did you say anything about her coming to your room at the inquest?'

'I didn't. It would have been simply my word against Lionel's. And what good would it have done her?'

'And you never told Edward Hargreaves?'

With a determined click of his teeth Mr Weston said again, 'What good would it have done her?'

'Are you sure that neither Edward or Richard Hargreaves knew anything? Did they accept the theory of accident?'

In the last few minutes, Bland noticed, the lawyer's face seemed to have sunk in, the hard lines become accentuated. He did not answer the question directly. 'They're a bad family. I'd not trust any of them.' Then his head jerked up, and he looked at Bland. 'I beg your pardon. Both of them guessed that it was suicide, but I'm sure that Edward, anyway, never guessed the cause. About Richard – I'm, not so sure. I've sometimes thought that he must have guessed his brother's secret – but if he did he never betrayed it to me.'

'And – supposing neither of them knew – what do you think would have happened if they'd have found out?'

Mr Weston's teeth clicked. 'Who knows,' he asked sententiously, 'the workings of the human heart? I have known murder committed by a girl of thirteen because of her infatuation with a man of fifty. I have known a criminal who had spent years in prison, and yet he fainted at the sight of blood.'

'I know a little about the actions and motives of criminals myself,' Bland said mildly. He made a mental note that the lawyer's pomposity made a good cover for evading awkward questions, and got up to go. 'Just as a matter of form, where were you between 7.30 and 8.30 last night?'

Mr Weston laughed and his heavy cheeks moved up and down. 'I am honoured to be on the list of suspects – but I fear I have an alibi. I dined at the Reform Club with a friend of mine who is a solicitor. His name is Geoffrey Matthews. We went into the dining-room at 7.15 and came out about a quarter to nine. Here is his address.' Still chuckling, he unscrewed a fountain pen and wrote a name and an address on a notepad in a firm, angular hand. Bland noted with faint surprise that, in spite of his decorous appearance, the lawyer was so dandyish as to use green ink. He asked abruptly: 'Do you know a man named Joseph van Dieren?'

The look that Mr Weston gave him out of his blue eyes was remarkably shrewd, and his reply remarkably brief. 'I don't. A suspect?'

Bland admired again the unobstrusive skill with which a question was turned aside. 'Hardly a suspect. A ghost.'

'Like Lily Hargreaves?'

'Like Lily Hargreaves. Except that, so far as I can see, they are two separate ghosts. It would be nice if one could find some connection between them.'

Chapter Nine *4.15 to 4.45 p.m.*

Bland sniffed appreciatively at the air as he came out of Weston's offices. The rain had stopped, and a damp, thick mist was hanging about Lexington Square. Fog, he thought, thick, delicious, soupy London fog, and he clicked his heels on the pavement. For some reason the dank mist made him feel more cheerful. Was it, he wondered, that it bore a relation in some way comforting to the fog that was settling down on this case? And was that fog really impalpable? Wasn't there rather a discernible pattern which narrowed down the suspects to two – or at most three people? He frowned, 'But what about Jones?' he said, and a taxi-driver who had moved noiselessly to the kerb in answer to Bland's raised hand looked alarmed. 'What's that, guv?'

'New Scotland Yard.' Bland said briskly, and stepped inside. Back in his office he called Filby, who said eagerly, 'What about old Jones' alibi?'

Bland tapped his teeth with a pencil. 'God knows. Jones only visited the place he was staying at half a dozen times, and never stopped the night. He left it just after four o'clock yesterday afternoon, after making a telephone call to an art agent named van Dieren. Then he vanished. He made himself a nice alibi for a time before the murder, and then abandoned it when it might have been useful. You can make what you like of that.'

'Maybe the murderer wasn't Jones, and it's all a red herring.'

'Then what was Jones doing with the gun?'

Filby shook his head, and his long, melancholy face grew longer. 'Beats me. But here's something for you. We gave Lionel Hargreaves' office a look over this morning, and what should we find but this, on his blotting-pad. I brought it away with me.' He showed Bland a yellow blotting-pad with the words 'Jones 7.30' written in pencil in one corner. Lower down, in ornamental lettering, as if the writer had been doodling while listening on the telephone, was the word 'Eve'. 'I've checked with Lionel Hargreaves' handwriting, and this is his all right. So he had an appointment with Jones.'

'It looks that way,' Bland agreed. 'And presumably it was made on the telephone. Did you check on that?'

'I tried to, but no luck. The girl on the switchboard couldn't remember any calls particularly.'

'All right, Filby – good work. I've got some more news for you.' Bland recounted the results of his interviews that day. 'Now – will you check this alibi of Weston's. He was very glib with it, but that's nothing against him. And find out all you can about van Dieren. Where he was last night particularly, but I also want to know where he lives, where he came from, how long he's been in business, how much money he's got – anything you can find out. Concentrate particularly on any details about his past linking him with the Hargreaves family or with anyone else at the house last night. Check whether he's a Dutchman – he's got a Dutch name – and try to find out whether he really was in America, as he claims to have been. You might get something out of that girl of his, Polly Lines. If you're looking for adventure, I think she may be interested.'

'Is that so?' Filby's eyes gleamed, and he went off at a tangent.

'This Lionel was a bit of a lad if what old Weston says is true I mean, hang it all, she was his – '

'Precisely.' Bland signed, and tipped back in his chair. He looked worries, and almost boyish. 'There's no means of checking Weston's story, but if it's true, and the old man found out about it, he'd have a good motive for murder. And there's quite certainly something fishy about van Dieren. And Carruthers was a nervous as a kitten when I talked to him this morning – quite genuinely nervous – I wonder why.' He tapped his teeth gloomily. 'Too many suspects.' He drew the anonymous letter from his pocket. 'And there's this, too. Get a check made on it, and see what comes out – make of typewriter, characteristics, and so on.'

'It could be,' Filby said, 'that this van Dieren rang himself up on the telephone to put you off the scent. After all, why shouldn't he ask for himself in the name of Jones? Who'd expect him to do that?'

Bland brought the legs of his chair gently to the ground. 'Who would? If he wanted to call attention to himself and get himself suspect of murder, he certainly couldn't find a better way of doing it. We shouldn't have heard of the name van Dieren unless Jones had telephoned him.' He walked over to the window, and stood looking out. 'It's going to be a foggy night. I'm going to the theatre – I'm anxious to see what Eve Marchant looks like in the chorus of the Splendid, and she's sent me a couple of tickets. I shan't be back till morning.' He picked up his fawn-coloured raincoat.

'I hate fog.' Filby said. 'It's dangerous. My aunt was knocked over one night in the fog. I wouldn't be surprised if there was another murder in this fog.'

'Dangerous,' Bland said. 'I wonder if you're right.'

Voicing Bland's own earlier thought, Filby said, 'Looks as if we're in a fog, too, eh?'

Bland stopped with his hand on the doorknob. 'Not altogether. Here's a couple of tips that may help you to see your way through it. The first is that marriage is a beautiful institution. And the second is that it's always nice to know you've got asbestos between you and the guests when you're shooting someone.'

Chapter Ten *7.15 to 7.45 p.m.*

'Just a snack,' Sinclair said cheerfully. 'Something to enable us to face the glories of the Splendid. I shall look forward to seeing this girl – Marchant, you said her name was? She must have something quite special to be able to hook *both* the Hargreaves lads – such different types too. I trust you're not going to put anything on those Whitstables? Pepper and salt – my God, what a barbarian.' They sat on high, uncomfortable stools, and looked at their reflections in a mirror. Bland thought that his companion seemed a little merrier than was justified by their three drinks. 'How did you get on with the mysterious art agent?'

'He told me a curious story about EH in his early days in America. It seems EH did van Dieren a very bad turn, and van Dieren landed in prison. Have you ever heard about that?'

'News to me, old boy, but I could believe anything bad about EH. Anyway, why would the man lie about it? I hope you didn't let Miss Lines seduce you – from your duty.'

'She's more interested in you.' And not surprisingly, he thought, as he regarded their images in the mirror: his own, well-brushed, blond, boyish, but a little insignificant; Sinclair's full of dash, and with a ready smile, like a film star. Which film star? Bland searched for a name and, while he rolled an oyster down his throat, settled on a fair-haired Robert Taylor. Taylor-Sinclair, and Van Heflin-Bland, he thought, with an inward chuckle – and doesn't Taylor-Sinclair know it! The Copy Chief had, indeed. looked rather smug at mention of Miss Lines' interest in him. The captain of the eleven, Bland thought a little nastily, still accustomed to conquests. He swallowed another oyster, and as he did so Sinclair gave him a Robert Taylor smile, and said, 'How about old man Weston and Lily?'

'He told me an extraordinary story too – one that reflects no credit on anybody. But I think I must regard it as confidential, even from my Watson.' He smiled amiably, and Sinclair looked almost embarrassed.

'Good Lord, yes. I'm interested, of course, but don't think I want to pry. Anyway, it's better that I shouldn't know secrets. I'm a tremendous gossip.' He looked at the clock. 'Just time for some lobster, and a glass of indifferent Graves on draught to wash it down. Suit you?' The tone was masterful, and one would hardly dare to say, Bland reflected, that it *didn't* suit. Was this perhaps still the captain of the cricket team regarding Bland as a boy trying, not very successfully, to bowl leg-breaks? Or was this the real and characteristic Sinclair? As these questions passed through Bland's mind Sinclair smiled again, and said, 'Think I've changed?' Without waiting for a reply he went on, 'I have you know. In one way, at least. I aspire to be an author. Detective stories. Tell me honestly, now, what do you think of them?'

Bland picked tentatively at half a lobster in its shell, and put a piece of firm white flesh into his mouth. 'Delicious,' he said, and then, 'Not very much like life.'

Sinclair pointed with a fork. His face was bright and enthusiastic. *'Exactly.* The essential thing about the detective story is that it's not very much like life. It doesn't set out to be like life – that isn't its function. The detective story is decidedly a romantic affair – something that brings a world they don't know, a world of romantic violence quite alien to their own lives to the sickly young men who spend their days in front of a ledger, the overworked and underpaid shop girls, the colonels in the clubs and the dowagers in their boudoirs. It isn't reality that these people want from detective stories – it's fantasy. The future of the detective story is in the field of fantasy.'

Bland drank some of the Graves. It was, as Sinclair had said, indifferent. 'You've written a fantasy?"

Sinclair swallowed a large piece of lobster quickly. 'A detective story to end all detective stories. It opens when the hero goes into the flat one day to find a dead man on the floor, and a girl, naked beneath a black mackintosh, standing over the body with a smoking pistol in her hand. An exciting opening?'

'Very exciting. Of course the girl didn't really kill the man?'

'Of course not. He'd been poisoned. The girl had been taking a bath in her hero's flat, and heard a prolonged ringing of the doorbell. Slipping on a black mackintosh, she went to open the door – '

'Why a black mackintosh?'

'She was a fetishist with a penchant for black mackintoshes,' said Sinclair imperturbably. 'She opened the door with a gun in her hand, and the body fell in. She was so startled that she fired the pistol.'

'What was she doing in the flat?'

'I'm not sure yet. I'm only in the third chapter, and I'm clearing up things as I go, along. But the germ of it is that there are ten characters, including the detective and the hero, and they're killed off one by one.'

'Including the naked girl?'

'Certainly. She is found, naked again, frozen to death inside a refrigerator. Finally, only the hero and the detective are left, and the hero realises with horror that the detective must be the murderer. At that time they're having a drink together. He sees the detective looking at him with peculiar fixity, and understands suddenly that the drink is poisoned.' Sinclair paused dramatically, with the last piece of lobster on his fork. 'And *then* – the detective drops dead. The drink was poisoned – but the hero has poisoned it. He's a schizophrene, and has murdered them all in his other personality. That's the end.' Dabbing his lips with his napkin, Sinclair looked at Bland. 'What do you think of it?'

'A little unsaleable.'

'Nonsense. You talk like a policeman. Of course it will be a terrific success. Let's go.' Before Bland had got down from his stool, Sinclair was half-way out, and looking at his wrist-watch. 'Just late enough. I'll get my car.' A swirl of fog met Bland at the door, and he groped in the thick white blanket in which Sinclair was hidden. He heard Sinclair's voice saying 'This way,' and then became conscious of two or three things at once: a violent jolt in his back that sent him reeling off the pavement into the road, the steady throb of a car engine, and a sudden feeling of danger and isolation. Then he heard a voice shouting, saw bright lights advancing terrifyingly towards him, and became conscious of the cold, hard road. When he picked himself up the car was not more than three yards from him. Sinclair jumped out of it, full of concern. 'Good Lord, old man, what happened? It's a good job my brakes are functioning.'

Bland picked himself up, brushed his hat carefully with his raincoat sleeve. 'It certainly is. Somebody pushed me.' He looked thoughtfully into the fog. 'Not much good going after him. Might have been a nasty accident.'

'Do you think it was an accident?'

Bland put his arm round Sinclair's shoulders. 'It's only in your detective stories that the criminal tries to kill the detective. Let's go to the Splendid.'

Chapter Eleven *8.00 to 8.45 p.m.*

'There she is.' Eve Marchant danced just where she had said she danced, three from the end at the left-hand side. Like the rest of the girls, she wore a black brassière, pink knickers and black stockings. She did not dance very well or very badly. She was in no way conspicuous in the chorus.

Sinclair seemed disappointed. 'She must have what it takes, but I can't see what it is, can you?' Bland did not reply, and they watched the show in silence, while the leading girl in the chorus sang:

> *'My disposition's for loving*
> *And though my intention is pure*
> *My disposition's for loving,*
> *And there isn't any cure...'*

Sinclair was using a ridiculous pair of opera-glasses which he had obtained by putting sixpence into a slot in front of him. 'My word, there's the old man.' Bland followed the direction of his gaze and saw EH sitting in a box, with another figure just behind him. 'When this figure leaned forward a little, it revealed the baldish head and snub nose of Carruthers. EH was sitting upright in his chair, staring down at the stage with an expression of complete disapproval. Bland whispered to Sinclair, 'See you at the interval.' As he tapped on the door of the box he heard the girl on the stage finishing her song:

111

> '*So, darling, although I may tell you*
> *I'll love you and always be true,*
> *Still my disposition's for loving*
> *And the lucky man won't always be you.*'

Carruthers came to the door. He looked startled, and almost apprehensive, when Bland beckoned him outside. EH did not turn round.

'The old man's in a pretty surly mood. He certainly doesn't like this girl. Do you want him?'

'Both of you. How do you happen to be with him?'

'I was in the office this afternoon, and as a mark of high favour was asked to share his box. Dick, as a mark of high disfavour, wasn't asked. What do you want to see me about?'

'I saw van Dieren today.'

Carruthers' look changed to one of positive alarm. 'He's been on the telephone to me at home, saying he wants to talk to me. He rang me up this evening. He seems very amused about something or other, as though there was a huge joke – and he asked me to go and see him tomorrow.' He paused and twiddled at a button. 'What did you think of him?'

Bland's fresh-coloured face was ingenuous. 'He seems a very odd character, and he's mixed up in all this affair somehow. There's something about him that's a fake – that's my feeling, I think.'

Carruthers nodded emphatically. 'I shall certainly take my work away from him.' He coloured suddenly, and for no apparent reason.

'Will you ask Mr Hargreaves if I can see him in the interval.' Carruthers turned, but before he could go back into the box the door opened, and EH appeared. He stopped short when he saw Bland and Carruthers, and said to Bland, 'You want to see me? We'll sit in the box. Do you mind, Arnold?' With an exaggerated deference that might have concealed annoyance, Carruthers said, 'Not at all. I'll go and have a drink.'

They went into the box. On the stage a man was throwing clubs in the air. Below them gleamed a hundred boiled shirtfronts. Still looking at the stage, EH said, 'You see, that postcard wasn't far wrong. She shows herself half-naked. A delightful daughter-in-law.'

'She's not your daughter-in-law now.'

'She has been once, and if my son Richard has his way she will be again. I find her fondness for my family distressing. I am not impressed by either her occupation or her talent.' EH fixed his cold blue eyes on Bland and said, 'Have your investigations led to any conclusions regarding that anonymous letter?'

'Not yet. I've seen van Dieren – he says he knew you in America. And I've seen Weston. He seems to think your second wife committed suicide.'

EH was still looking at the stage, where the juggler was now balancing three of the clubs on his chin. 'None of Weston's business. Anyway, it's all lies. Why should she commit suicide? She was happy enough with me.'

'You don't know of any other reason?'

'I don't know *any* reason.' EH rapped on the ledge in front of him with his knuckles. 'Don't try to be smart with me, young man. I've dealt with smart people all my life, and I've always been a little too smart for them.'

'Were you too smart in America, when you handled the affairs of the Nation-Wide Loan and Investment Corporation?'

Bland saw with some admiration that Hargreaves took this question without any sign of emotion other than a muscle twitching in his jaw. He said, almost to himself, 'Joe Riddell. I thought he was dead.' Then he looked at Bland. 'I suppose you got this story from the man you call van Dieren. What does he look like?'

'Seedy, thick grey hair, might be a wig, big moustache, about five feet eight inches, deep voice, ring-mark on third finger left hand but no ring. Theatrical manner. Looks in his late fifties.'

EH shook his head. 'That's not Joe Riddell.'

'This would be thirty years ago.'

'Joe Riddell was six feet tall. And he's dead. I thought he was dead. What story did he tell you?'

'He didn't mention the name Joe Riddell. He told it about himself – and you, of course.'

'What story?' EH had his voice under better control than his breath, which was coming in jerks.

'Something about embezzlement. He said you were responsible. He got two years. Did Joe Riddell get two years?'

'Yes. The rest of it is lies. I had no responsibility. That was made clear in court.'

Bland tapped a cigarette thoughtfully on his thumbnail and lighted it. 'Naturally not. Did your Joe Riddell have flaming red hair?'

'No. Why?'

'Just trying to fit Jones in the picture. But then Jones' red hair was probably a wig. How long since you last saw Riddell?'

'Nearly thirty years. I've never seen him since we parted. I had some threatening letters once – God knows how many years ago.'

'Was he a man who would bear malice that long – supposing he's still alive?'

'He was a fool. No, I don't believe he'd hate me for thirty years. Anyway, man,' EH's voice was impatient, 'if he hated me why should he kill Lionel?'

Bland leaned forward. Neither man was now watching the stage. 'Why, indeed? Let's not worry about Riddell. Who else knew this story about him?'

'No one outside the –' EH stopped and stared at Bland thoughtfully. He said, 'I don't recollect that I've ever told anybody.'

Bland pulled on his cigarette, and was silent for a moment. 'You didn't tell Weston? He's acted as your lawyer for a good many years.'

'Why should I tell Weston about something that happened before I knew him?'

Bland stood up. His face was a little pinker than usual. 'Well, if Joe Riddell's dead and if you've never told anybody about this thing, I suppose it must be Joe Riddell's ghost come back to put a spoke in the family wheel.'

EH stood up too. He was a little taller than Bland. 'I don't like – '

'*You* don't like,' Bland said furiously. 'You've tried to make a fool of me from the time the investigation started. You held out over that anonymous letter until you thought it might pay to show it to me. You're holding out over your wife's death. You're holding out over Joe Riddell. I can't make you talk, but I'm telling you now that you're being too smart for your own good. You may be a good businessman, but this isn't business. It's murder. It's not smart to play against murder – it's stupid, because the murderer's got no hesitations or compunction. Think it over, and if you want to come out from behind your barricade let me know. Until then, it's pointless for me to talk to you.'

Bland walked out of the box and went straight to the bar. Sinclair was sipping a pink gin and talking to Carruthers, who looked rather depressed. He brightened when he saw Bland.

'May one buy a policeman a drink? You look as if you need one.'

'Thanks. Whisky.'

'The old man a bit trying? It's something that comes naturally to him, doesn't it, Sinclair?' Carruthers seemed to be talking to hide his nervousness. 'Sinclair's had more recent experience of EH in his awkward moods, but my experience is of longer standing. I remember him as pretty trying ever since I was a kid. The old man paid for my schooling, and sent me to the same school with Dick and Lionel. He was really very decent about all that, although he wouldn't do anything for me afterwards. He wanted me to come into the firm and I wanted to stay on my own and do freelance work. I got my way in the end, but there were some awful scenes when he reminded me that he'd paid for my schooling, and so on.' Carruthers gave a mock shudder. 'He's never loved me much since.'

'Did you ever hear him talk of Joe Riddell? Years ago, I mean when you were a boy.'

'Joe Riddell?' Carruthers looked earnest. 'No, I don't seem to remember that name. I'm pretty sure I've never heard EH mention him. Who is he?'

'Just another mystery man,' Bland said gloomily. 'The case is full of them. What do you think of the show?'

Sinclair grinned. 'I should have thought our presence at the bar was sufficient comment. I can dispose of it in one word: wet. I'm looking forward to meeting the glamorous Eve at closer quarters, though. Is that on the programme?'

'She's sparing us ten minutes of her time after the show, at her flat. I think Richard will be there too, so you'll see him if you're coming along.'

Sinclair's fine eyes flashed, and Bland was reminded again of the Captain of the School. 'Good Lord, yes – I'd like it more than anything.'

'How about you Carruthers?'

Carruthers consulted his turnip-watch. 'I'd like to, although I've got some work to finish at home.' He hesitated. 'But I'm all agog to meet this charmer. I think I *will* come – if you're sure it's all right.'

Striving to catch some recollection, Bland said, 'Oh Lord, yes – she said bring anyone along. Sinclair and I must be getting back to our seats – Eve Marchant sent us complimentary tickets, and I'm willing to bet she'll be keeping an eye on our seats between kicks.'

Sinclair raised his glass. 'Back to the funeral.' The chorus was dancing again when they got back. This time they were wearing blue brassières, black knickers, and no stockings. 'Expanse of knickers in a waste of shame,' Sinclair murmured. They settled down in their seats.

Chapter Twelve *10.15 to 11.30 p.m.*

'How do you *do*?' Eve Marchant asked, raising her eyes to Sinclair's and then dropping them, with a revolting and yet somehow dreadfully attractive demureness. 'I've heard so much about you from Dick – and Lionel, too.' She shook hands with Carruthers with no particular interest, turned to Bland and spoke with a coyness that managed to be catty. "Did you enjoy the show? I noticed that you'd abandoned us once or twice.'

'Duty called,' Bland said solemnly. 'I was talking to Edward Hargreaves, who was in a box.'

She clasped her hands in an affectation of pleasure. 'What an honour. Did you know that the old man is my prospective father-in-law, Mr Sinclair?'

Sinclair moved uneasily. 'Congratulations.'

'Don't say that – he loathes me, although I'm sure I couldn't care less. But what will you think of me – I'm forgetting my manners. Will you have a whisky or gin? Really, though, I'm dying to hear what he said about the show.' While she was pouring a whisky Bland pondered again her curious sexual atractiveness, something distinct from her beauty. How could one define it? Something in the way she moved her shoulders, a contrast between the demureness of her manner and her brassy voice – what was it? He moved the base of his glass on the chair arm. 'You want me to tell you what he really said, Miss Marchant?'

Her colour heightened a little. 'More than anything.'

Bland sipped his drink. 'He said he was not impressed either by your talent or your occupation, that you showed yourself half-naked, and that he found your fondness for his family distressing.' He saw Sinclair and Carruthers looking at him in pained surprise, he saw the slightly increased rise and fall of Eve Marchant's breasts, and he saw that she was looking rather fixedly at a point beyond him. Richard Hargreaves was standing in the doorway, with a black homburg hat in his hand.

For a moment nobody said anything. Sinclair and Eve Marchant began to speak together, and stopped together. Richard came into the room, walked over to the cocktail cabinet and poured a drink. When he turned round his face was smooth and unworried. Bland turned the stem of his glass again, and wondered if this was the best time to ask his questions. Then he thought with faint impatience that it was no use being finicky, and dropped his words like stones into the troubled waters. He spoke to Richard. 'I'm sorry to seem officious, but I've come here to ask some questions.'

'Certainly. But that reminds me – I've got some information for you about this chap van Dieren. It seems that Bond, our Production Manager, had some dealings with him about a year ago. It was before Bond came to us, so that explains why no one else knew anything about him. Bond seemed to think he was a rather unsavoury figure, and I told him to get in touch with you.'

'Many thanks.' Bland asked Carruthers, 'Did you know that Bond knew van Dieren?'

'Well, I don't think I've ever met Bond. No, I didn't know.'

Richard Hargreaves stared at Carruthers with surprise. 'But do you know this van Dieren fellow, Arnold? I thought you didn't like to have anything to do with art agents.'

Carruthers wriggled. 'Well, I don't usually, but he was – ah – very persistent that he could do something with my work and I – ah – let him handle it. He hasn't been very successful.' There was a silence, while Richard still stared at Carruthers, who looked down at the floor. Then Bland said, 'Have you ever heard of Joe Riddell, Mr Hargreaves?'

'Joe Riddell? Good Lord, yes. Don't tell me that Joe Riddell comes into this?' Hargreaves looked at Bland with what seemed to be quite genuine amusement and astonishment.

'Just tell me what you know about him.'

'It dates rather a long way back, and really I don't know much, except that Lionel and I used to use the name of Joe Riddell as a kind of magic charm when we were kids together. He used to write threatening letters to my father – they came in the post regularly every week at one time, and I remember they were from all sorts of different countries. My father told us a bit about him when he was in a good humour. He often talked about the past to us then, and told us about adventures in America in which he'd been the hero – these last few years he's found it more convenient to forget all that. He told us about this Joe Riddell. It seemed they'd been partners in business together – some kind of real estate, I think it was – and in some way or another the old man was too smart for Riddell. Riddell went to jail for a term – I forget how long – and swore undying vengeance against the old man.

'That's the story, and that's really all there is to it. Nothing ever happened, and none of us ever saw Joe Riddell. These letters, and one or two postcards, came every week for some time, and then they became more infrequent. Finally they stopped coming. I should think, all told, they came for about a year. The reason it stuck so much in my mind that we were all of us kids at the time, and we built up Joe Riddell into a sort of bogey-man, a kind of O'Grady. You know: "Joe Riddell says you've got to do it" – that kind of thing.'

'Did any of you ever see Joe Riddell?'

'Oh no. That was the essence of the whole thing – that he was a sort of invisible man. When the letters stopped coming it all died down, and pretty soon we stopped talking about him.'

'Now, I want you to think before you answer this question. Do you know if your father ever met him – after the anonymous letters were sent, I mean?'

'I'm inclined to say "No," but I can't really be certain.' He looked up at the ceiling. 'I'm just trying to remember whether there was any ending to it all – whether I've forgotten something. All I can say is that to the best of my belief and knowledge the old man never saw Joe Riddell – but I don't absolutely *know*.'

'Was your father alarmed by these letters? Did he ever take precautions of any kind?'

'Good Lord, no. He treated the whole thing as a kind of joke. If he'd thought of it as anything serious, he'd never have told us about it.'

'Would it surprise you to learn that Mr Carruthers doesn't know the name of Joe Riddell?'

'Why, not particularly. Though I should have thought you'd remember the story, Arnold. You must certainly have heard it at one time.'

'I suppose I must, Richard, if you say so.' Carruthers was apologetic, but he did not sound altogether convinced. 'It's really rather odd that I shouldn't remember at all. My memory's not usually as bad as that. But still, I suppose it's passed out of my mind with the years.'

'It must have done,' Richard said, more emphatically than usual. He looked down at his long, elegant fingers. 'Perhaps the explanation is that even as a boy I was always rather exceptionally sensitive, and things like this always had a great deal of significance for me. Arnold probably wasn't influenced so much and so he doesn't remember the name.'

'H'm.' Bland looked at Eve Marchant. 'I'm sorry – I know I sound like the Grand Inquisitor. But doing this sort of ferreting is one of my penalties of being a policeman – and now I've got to go on doing it with you.' She fidgeted with a glass ornament on the occasional table by her side. 'Yesterday morning Edward Hargreaves received an anonymous letter. I won't repeat the terms of it to you, but it stated categorically that you were married to Lionel, which was news to him and everyone else at that time. Now, we don't know whether Lionel told anyone of your marriage, but it doesn't seem probable that he did, from what you've told us. Last night you said you'd not told anyone. Now, I want you to think – are you absolutely sure of that?'

There was a moment's pause – an almost imperceptible pause – before Eve Marchant replied. Then she spoke, with a bright emphatic air of sudden recollection. 'I'm too silly – Myrtle Montague.'

'Myrtle Montague?'

'My best friend. Well, she was my best friend. I mean – ' She seemed for a moment embarrassed. 'In show business you generally make friends with someone in the show, and when I met Lionel I was playing at the Follies in "Ladies, Let's Love". ' Myrtle Montague was a girl in the chorus and I saw a lot of her. Since I've been in this thing at the Splendid we've lost touch.' With a slightly artificial brightness, she said in her metallic voice, 'That's show business.'

'Yes, indeed,' said Bland. 'And you told Myrtle Montague?'

She talked fast and loud. 'We were friends at the time and it was really *before* Lionel had told me that I mustn't say anything to anybody. And I felt I absolutely *had* to tell somebody. But Myrtle said she wouldn't tell anyone, and I'm sure she didn't.' Richard was looking at her rather oddly. She continued breathlessly, 'If you say I shouldn't have done it, I simply couldn't agree more, but I do hope you won't hold it against me.' She looked at Richard and then at Sinclair, and her face puckered appealingly.

Bland said pleasantly, 'It's a good thing you remembered. Do you know Miss Montague's address?'

'No, I don't – yes, I do, though. She lives in a teeny-weeny little flat off Shepherds Market – I've got it down somewhere.' She fumbled in a suède bag with a claw clasp on it, and produced a small black and red diary. '86 Carteret Street, just off Curzon

Street,' she said triumphantly, rather as if she were handing Bland the murderer on a plate. She looked at him with an air of guilelessess that he found very attractive, and said, 'I do hope *you* won't hold it against me, Inspector.' Her legs were crossed, and Sinclair was gazing ardently at her knees.

Bland got up and looked at her quizzically. Under the lamplight the skin of his face showed fresh and pink. 'You're sure there's no one else you've forgotten to tell me about?'

She met his quizzical gaze with one of her own. 'Quite, quite sure, Inspector.'

'Then I think I should be getting along.' When he was at the door Richard Hargreaves said, 'Oh, by the way – just a minute.' He was tracing a pattern on the carpet with one pointed suède shoe, and he looked – it was odd, Bland thought, how often a theatrical smile seemed appropriate in this case – like an actor struck suddenly with stage-fright. When he began to speak, it was with a slight stammer. 'I don't know – I expect you all know Eve and I are engaged to be married, and EH has been pretty beastly about it all. Well, we don't feel that's the kind of thing that ought to be put up with and so we're – going to get married pretty soon. That's all.'

Nobody spoke for a moment. Then Carruthers wished them both joy with politeness, but a certain lack of enthusiasm. 'You know, this is going to make the old man awfully wild.'

'Damn the old man,' Richard said, in rather a high-pitched voice. Eve Marchant said nothing, but she smiled like a cat.

Sinclair came forward and said with his ready smile, 'Congratulations – and especially to you, Richard. I've only met Miss Marchant this evening, but I've seen enough of her to know that you're a lucky dog. Do you know, I have only one regret.'

'What's that?'

'That I didn't see her first.' As soon as he had spoken the words, Sinclair flushed a bright red. Carruthers said, with a malice that Bland had not seen revealed, 'No Lionel saw her first.' Richard looked up angrily, but Eve saved the situation by saying in her metallic voice, 'I think that announcement deserves a drink, Richard. And I'm intent that the great analytical mind should congratulate us. You haven't done that, Inspector.'

With a pleasant impersonality, Bland said, 'Of course I congratulate you. I hope you will be very happy.' He raised his glass and drank. They all drank.

'But what do you *really* think?' she asked coquettishly, and Richard moved unhappily, and said, 'For God's sake, darling.'

'You don't want to know what a policeman thinks. But the fact that you were Lionel's wife is bound to be known, and a good many people will say that you marry too often into the same family.' Richard made an angry, ineffectual movement. 'If it's any satisfaction to you, I think you're bringing things to a head – which, from my point of view, is a good thing.'

Richard Hargreaves looked puzzled. 'You mean you think our marriage is connected with all this?'

Bland picked up his hat. Sinclair and Carruthers moved towards him at the door. 'Directly – perhaps not. Indirectly – yes. I think you may be in some danger.' Richard looked at Bland with his mouth slightly open. 'Good night.'

FRIDAY, JANUARY 17

Chapter One *9.30 to 10.00 a.m.*

'Well, what do you know?' Filby said. 'She certainly is a cool one, that girl. One only ten minutes in the grave, and she's marrying another. And the same family, too.' He tapped his nose, and looked at Bland with a terrifying expression of low cunning. 'Let's hope she don't need to marry this one the same way as the other.'

'What do you mean?'

'She got him tight,' Filby said dramatically. 'Blotto. Stinking. One over the eight. Half seas over. The registrar was doubtful whether to marry 'em, he was so tight. But he could just about make the responses, and said he knew what he was doing. No difficulty in checking it, because of another thing. *She* got the licence – they remembered that. Enterprising girl, ain't she?'

Bland played with the paperweight shaped like a monkey which stood on his desk. 'Enterprising enough, yes. And far more intelligent than you'd think to watch her prancing about in the chorus. A good head, with her heart always at its service. You can get almost anything in this world, Filby, if you've got a sufficiently hard head and an equally hard heart.'

'She must be bloody Cleopatra and the Queen of Sheba rolled into one.' Filby's long, melancholy face looked indignant. 'By the way, I've found the taxi-driver who picked her up from her flat Wednesday night and took her to Redfern Square – so that's all okay.' He brooded again. 'Marrying two in the same family. What's she doing it for? She can't be in love with this one, too.'

127

'Money, partly. Don't forget the father's pretty well fixed.'

'But couldn't the old man cut her out of his will? He's mad at her, isn't he?'

'Perhaps she thinks he'll get used to her. He's very keen on his family. But I agree there must be something else driving her on to marriage – and I've got an idea what it is.'

Filby raised his eyebrows and whistled. 'A bit more mystery?'

'It might be very simple.' Bland leaned back in his chair with his trilby hat on the back of his head. Fog and damp hung about the room. Outside the window a thick creamy blanket had been placed over the world, dulling even the sound of traffic. He coughed, and the dry noise was odd in the quiet room. 'Any luck with that anonymous letter?'

'What you'd expect. No fingerprints, except Hargreaves' own. Typed by an amateur, or someone who was trying to look like an amateur, on an old Remington 12. Small letters 'e' and 'l' slightly out of alignment, small 'd' badly worn and 'n' a bit worn. Conclusive enough, if we could fix the typewriter. Shall we check on all the typewriters at that advertising agency?'

'Not yet. I don't want to alarm them at the moment. What about Weston's alibi?'

'Watertight. This chap Matthews was with him all the time between 7.15 and 8.30 except for ten minutes soon after 7.30 when Weston went outside to wash.'

'Yes, simple but sufficient. The first alibi we've come across.'

'Suspicious,' said Filby, pulled his lower lip, raised his eyebrows and looked like a horse. 'After all, he's the family lawyer. And he told you that tall story about Hargreaves' wife.'

'I wouldn't say it was a tall story – or if it is, Weston believes it himself. What did you get on van Dieren?'

'Mystery again.' Filby shook his head. 'He's been running this art agency for less than eighteen months. Dropped vague hints occasionally to various people that he used to know old man Hargreaves a long while ago, and that he's an old scoundrel.

Can't trace any connection between him and Hargreaves and can't trace him farther back than that period of eighteen months. Nobody knows where he came from, nobody seems friendly with him. Doesn't come into his office much, business is in decline – he bought it when it was a fairly good concern. Lives alone in a little place out Earl's Court way. Can't find out whether he stayed there last night or not. That's all.'

'Little enough. And yet there's a germ of something important in it. Consider, Filby: the study walls were lined with asbestos. Somebody sent an anonymous letter to Hargreaves about Eve Marchant. Edward Hargreaves' wife died two years ago, and he's shown no inclination to remarry. Joe Riddell is a figure out of the very distant past. Doesn't something about those things strike you?'

Filby's mouth was open. He closed it and said firmly, 'No.'

Bland's face looked white and a little strained. 'But I simply can't understand about Jones – I don't see where Jones comes in, and why. I sat up half the night thinking about it.'

'You think too much,' Filby said pityingly. 'What's the next move?'

'Eve Marchant's friend, Myrtle Montague. I hope she'll have something to tell us about the anonymous letter. I have a feeling it came from or through friend van Dieren.'

'You mean he did the murder?'

Bland paused at the door with his forehead puckered. 'If he did, he was acting for someone else. But don't ask me how that could be, for I don't know.' He put on his trilby hat, flipped the brim, and grinned. 'I'm off to see Myrtle.'

'Perhaps she'll give us a clue,' said Filby hopefully.

Bland looked at him seriously. 'Perhaps she'll be Mr Jones.'

Chapter Two *10.00 to 10.30 a.m.*

Sinclair was invariably punctual at the office. Or almost invariably: for this morning he was held up by the fog, and arrived half an hour late. His faint feeling of annoyance was not dispelled by Onslow, who came into his room and stood with his hands in his pockets. 'The old man's been asking for you. He's in a hell of a stew. Got in at 9.30 on the dot, and been asking where everybody's got to.'

Sinclair nodded, and vented a little of his annoyance. 'Right. Next time you come in here, knock on the door.' Onslow raised his eyebrows and went out without saying anything. His manner showed clearly that he classed Sinclair among the capitalist exploiters. Sinclair rang through to EH on the internal telephone. A voice at the other end said, 'Yes?'

'Sinclair, Mr Hargreaves. You wanted me?'

EH's voice was smooth but bitter. 'Oh, you've arrived.' He paused, but Sinclair saw no occasion for reply. 'I've been waiting to see you since 9.30, but I'm busy now. Come in at 10.30.' There was a click. Sinclair replaced his own receiver, just as the door opened and Bond came in. There was a gleam in the Production Manager's eye which Sinclair could see meant no good. He was not wrong.

'Spot of trouble, I'm afraid,' Bond said, with a hypocritically sympathetic look. 'Something seems to have gone wrong with the works somewhere.' Sinclair raised his eyebrows, rather like Onslow. With the same sympathetic look, Bond unfolded a copy

130

of that day's *Daily Express* and pointed to an advertisement for one of their clients, Quickshave Shaving Cream. 'See anything wrong with that?' he asked with intolerable smugness. Sinclair looked at the advertisement, which showed two men shaving, one with a look of disgust on his face, the other beaming happily. Above the first was written in a bold script, *'He* used "Shaving Cream",' above the second, *'He* changed to Quickshave.' There was nothing wrong with the blocks, or the headings or the copy. He put down the paper and said, 'Well?'

Even more smugly, Bond said, 'Price.' He pointed to the bottom of the advertisement – *In Tubes* 9*d*., *In Jars* 1*s*. 6*d*. 'Isn't it 7^1/2d and 1s. 3d. now? Remember the price reduction a couple of weeks ago? And we agreed it should be corrected on all proofs?'

Sinclair remembered it perfectly. He said sharply, 'Who passed the proofs?'

Bond produced from under his arm a proof, and said with what seemed to Sinclair obviously mock reluctance, 'It looks as if you did.' Sinclair bent over the proof and saw that it was perfectly true. He remembered also that the proof had come up when he was talking to Onslow about a new scheme for Flowspeed Airlines. He had been told that it was wanted urgently, and checked it for literals and initialled it. The mistake was certainly partly his responsibility: but it was also partly Bond's, for the Production Department had been informed of the change in prices, and had been told to alter copy accordingly. He said with no decrease in sharpness, 'I thought you were going to alter all proofs.'

Mock reluctance was replaced by mock sympathy. 'Sorry, old man. We altered all the rest, but the stereo for this had already been made.'

'Is that any reason why you shouldn't have altered it?'

Bond was imperturable. Well, old man, I suppose it isn't. But it is up to the Copy Department to check copy points, isn't it?'

With an effort, Sinclair controlled himself. Privately, he believed that Bond had noticed the price mistake, and let it through from pure malice. But he said pleasantly, 'OK, I'll deal with it. Thanks for pointing it out.'

'That's all right.' Bond hesitated in the doorway. 'What's happened to that friend of yours – the Inspector chappie? I believe he was asking questions about a lad named van Dieren.'

'Do you know something about him?'

Bond laughed. 'Do I not. I don't suppose it's important, but he'd probably like to know.'

'He's coming along here later this morning – I'll ask him to talk to you. Bond went out. Left to himself, Sinclair walked up and down on his green carpet. The mistake was annoying, but not serious. He pondered whether he should let it slide, or forestall criticism by telephoning Magee, the Advertising Manager, and tell him about it. He decided to telephone, picked up the external telephone and said, 'Get me Mr Magee of the Quickshave.' The internal telephone rang. Tracy's voice said, 'Sinclair? EH wants to see us both in his office. Will you come in.' Sinclair picked up the external again, and said 'Cancel that call.' He was feeling thoroughly sour when he walked down the passage and entered EH's office.

Chapter Three *10.30 to 11.10 a.m.*

'Well, the police,' Myrtle Montague said. 'This *is* a surprise. You don't look a bit like a policeman. *Do* come in.' She led him into a tiny sitting-room where a coal fire burned brightly, and photographs of male film stars lined the walls. 'Do let me have your hat,' she said. 'And your coat. You'll pardon my négligé, won't you? You see, I wasn't expecting you, I've never had a policeman come to see me before.' She said it as brightly as though Bland were a District Visitor. She was a small, blonde girl with china-blue eyes, and he wondered for a moment if she could possibly be as ignorant as she appeared. She was wearing a bright red dressing-gown, and it was clear that she had only just got out of bed. Bland offered her a cigarette. 'Well,' she said, 'State Express. *Super.* I don't think I can resist one, though I really shouldn't.'

Bland paused with a cigarette half-way to his mouth. 'You have a cough?'

'Oh no. I mean my voice – of course I'm resting now, but I have to look after it. Though with this *beastly* fog I don't think it matters about smoking, do you? Poor you,' she added suddenly, and Bland was amused.

'Why poor me?'

'Having to be out in the fog. It's quite true what the old proverb says, isn't it – a policeman's lot is not a happy one. Would you like a cup of coffee – my coffee really is something, though I say it myself.'

'I won't have anything, thanks,' Bland said a little desperately, and plunged in before she could say anything else. 'Miss Eve Marchant sent me here to see you.'

Myrtle Montague's china-blue eyes widened. 'Are *you* a friend of *Eve's?* And she asked you to drop in and have a chat when you were passing by? Well isn't that– '

'Super,' Bland said quickly. He had decided that her appearance told the truth. 'I'm here on business, Miss Montague. You were very friendly with Miss Marchant, weren't you?'

She bridled slightly. 'I *am* very friendly. We just haven't seen each other for a few weeks, that's all. She's in this new thing at the Splendid, and I'm resting. That's show business.'

'I'm sure. Now, did Miss Marchant tell you anything about a man named Lionel Hargreaves?'

'She certainly did.' Miss Montague tried to look crafty. 'But I don't know that I ought to tell *you.*'

'Then supposing I tell you. They were married, weren't they? You may as well say yes – Miss Marchant told me so herself.' She nodded. 'And you know what's happened to Lionel Hargreaves.' This time she shook her head, and he said a little impatiently, 'Don't you read the papers?' He was quite taken aback, when she said simply, 'No.'

'Oh,' he said weakly, and then pulled himself together. 'It doesn't matter. The important thing is that Miss Marchant says she told you about the marriage before anything was announced. Is that right?' She nodded again. 'And she say's she told nobody else. Is that right too – as far as you know?'

She seemed to have become suddenly impressed with the seriousness of the whole thing. 'I don't think she told anybody else.'

'Did you tell anybody?'

She shook her head happily. 'I wouldn't tell anybody about a thing like that, when it was told me as a secret.'

'You're sure you didn't tell anybody?'

'Certain sure.'

'Not even your father and mother?'

'Haven't got a father and mother.' She put a hand to her mouth. 'I'm a liar. I'm ever so sorry. Of course, I told my sister, Pauline. But that's the only person I did tell, cross my heart on it.'

'Pauline Montague,' Bland said thoughtfully. 'Or is your sister married?'

'Oh no, she's not married, but her name's not Montague, I mean my name's not Montague. It's just my stage name – I took it because it sounded distinguished.' She blushed. 'My name's really Ella Lines, but I wanted a super name for the stage, so I took Myrtle Montague.'

Bland realised why there had seemed to be something familiar about her face. 'So your sister's Pauline Lines – Polly Lines?'

'That's right.'

'And she works for a man named van Dieren.'

'Well, this is a surprise,' Miss Montague said. 'Fancy you knowing that. Do you know Polly?'

'We've met. Do you know anything about her boss? Does she talk about him?'

She pulled her dressing-gown about her, and frowned with an effort of concentration. 'That's a funny thing, too. And it's why I told Polly, though I shouldn't have done. Her boss is ever such a funny man. Of course Polly's a bit of a fast one.' She nodded sagely. 'She likes the men. Well, so we all do, but Polly's a bit naughty – if you know what I mean. But that's neither here nor there, except that I think her boss's business isn't quite straight, in some way or other. The real thing I was going to say was that I told Polly because her boss often talked about old man Hargreaves – that's Lionel's father – and how he'd cheated him over something or other. So naturally when Eve told me she'd got married to Lionel, I told Polly. I never breathed a word to anyone else.'

'And Polly might have told her boss. Is she friendly with him?'

'A bit too friendly, if you ask me.'

'I see.' Bland paused a moment and stubbed out his cigarette. 'What do you think of Eve Marchant? I'd better tell you why I'm asking all these questions. Lionel Hargreaves has been murdered, and now Eve Marchant's discovered that she wants to marry his brother, Richard.'

Her reaction to this was not quite what he had expected. 'Is she going to marry him?'

'She says so.'

'Good for her,' she said simply. 'She told me she'd met Richard too, and he was ever so nice. What a pity about Lionel, though.'

Bland blinked. 'But doesn't it seem to you a bit odd that she should marry again – and her husband's brother, too – so soon after her husband's death?'

Miss Montague looked at him, and giggled. 'Lionel wasn't very nice to her. And there's a very good reason, too, but wild horses wouldn't drag it out of *me*. You'll have to ask Eve about that. She's ever so nice, don't you think?'

'Very attractive indeed,' Bland said hollowly.

'Well, she's in show business. That's enough to explain anything. We're awfully funny people, you know, Inspector.' She looked at her watch. 'You'll pardon my saying it – it's been super meeting a real live policeman, but I've got to see my boy friend at the Savoy Grill at twelve, and I'm not dressed yet.' They moved towards the door, and she gave him a parting smile. 'I think you're ever so nice,' she said.

Bland walked slowly up Curzon Street inhaling great mouthfuls of fog. It was now so thick that he could hardly see the edge of the pavement. So van Dieren sent the anonymous note, he thought – or van Dieren had told somebody else, who sent it. All the trails led back to van Dieren – a man who had not the slightest reason for wishing Lionel Hargreaves dead, but who might have borne a grudge against his father. If van Dieren was acting merely as an agent, was not his employer taking a tremendous risk, in view of the fact that he must know all about the murder? Bland stood on the kerb and said aloud, 'It all depends on Jones.' A girl standing just by his side looked at him coldly, and moved a step or two away. 'I beg your pardon,' he said.

Chapter Four *10.45 to 11.10 a.m.*

EH looked at the three of them with an apparent urbanity that, Sinclair thought, presaged the worst. 'I should like to read you this letter, gentlemen,' he said. He read it. The letter was from Mr Ian Gordon, Managing Director of Furnishings Limited, and said that they regretted that they were unable to place their advertising with the Hargreaves Agency. The scheme submitted to them, the letter went on, was no doubt a sound one, but the Board of Directors felt that somehow it had not quite the tone they were looking for. In his, Mr Gordon's view, a view with which the other directors had concurred, it lacked, in a phrase, the spark of inspiration. He thanked them for the trouble taken in preparing the scheme and remained, with kind regards, theirs sincerely. EH read the letter in an impersonal voice, clasped his hands, looked at them, and said, 'Well, gentlemen?' Sinclair breathed in deeply and looked across the room, out of the big french window, at the people passing in the street. Richard Hargreaves stared at his suède shoes. Tracy looked straight at EH, his head thrown back a little self-consciously, the squint in his dark eyes very plain. Nobody said anything. Without any apparent loss of urbanity, EH tapped the letter and said, 'I want your observations.'

Richard's toe moved in a circle on the carpet, and he spoke in a low voice. 'Just one of those things. I don't see that there's anything much to be said about it. We've put up schemes before and had them turned down. So has everyone else. I can't see any point in holding an inquest.'

'I don't agree,' Tracy said, in his rich voice. He stared defiantly at EH 'This scheme was always an abortion. But maybe Richard's right, and there's no point in holding an inquest on an abortion.'

'Just what does that mean?' EH asked.

Tracy flung out his arm in the fine eloquent gesture that had so impressed so many advertising conventions. 'I mean that an advertising man is a creative artist. Or at least he should be. I am a creative artist. And no creative artist can do good work when he is hampered at every turn by pettifogging restrictions about spending a few pounds. We lost the Furnishings Account because I wasn't allowed to use the artists I wanted on it – they were too expensive. We lost it also because the original ideas I presented were altered and botched about by everybody who had anything to do with the account and especially by – ' Tracy stopped suddenly.

EH's lips were set in a thin line. 'I don't know why you should be affected in your speech by the fact that my son Lionel is dead. As I understand it, you put the blame for the loss of the account chiefly on my dead son, who interfered with your ideas – '

'Really, I protest.' But Tracy said it weakly, a little cowed by the unmistakable note of menace in EH's voice.

' – and my own refusal to allow you to spend an unlimited sum of money in indulging your desire to obtain the most expensive art work obtainable.'

Tracy got up. His squint was terrifying. 'I won't stay here to be insulted.' He lurched, rather than walked, out of the room, and slammed the door behind him.

During this altercation EH had not raised his voice, nor had Richard looked up from the floor. With almost an increase in urbanity, EH said, 'Have you anything to say, Sinclair? Do you attribute our loss of the account to interference with the work of the Copy Department? I hope that you will take a less purely departmental view than Tracy.'

'I don't think my view's departmental. Do you really want me to tell you, sir, why I think we lost the account?'

A shade of acerbity touched EH's voice. 'I hoped I had made it plain that that was my purpose.'

Sinclair said bluntly. 'We lost it because Mr Gordon doesn't want to be mixed up with a firm that's involved in a scandal. Stupid, no doubt, but that's the truth.'

EH stared at him, and then ran his hand through his white hair. 'But how could I have been so stupid? I should have realised that. You'll forgive me – I have been much upset by Lionel's death. I really am not myself.' It was typical, Sinclair thought, that the evident distress shown by EH, which in anyone else would have seemed pathetic, appeared in him simply a little unreal and disgusting. The telephone bell rang. EH picked up the receiver. 'Yes. Hargreaves here. Who is that? Who? Van Dieren oh yes, van Dieren. I should like to see you.' He looked at a diary on his desk. 'Two o'clock would suit me. I shall expect you then. Goodbye.' As he hung up the receiver, the clock above his head struck eleven times, with a silver tinkling note. EH rose and walked slowly over to a cupboard which stood in the wall opposite the window. He came back with a bottle and three glasses. When he spoke, his voice was as urbane and portentous as ever. 'You must drink a glass of wine with me, Richard, and you too, Sinclair. It is eleven o'clock.' It was EH's invariable habit to drink a glass of sherry at eleven o'clock in the morning and at five o'clock in the evening. The habit was known to all the senior members of his staff, but it was very rarely that they, or even his sons, were invited to drink with him. The glass of sherry was to be interpreted as a kind of discreet apology for the Furnishings episode, Sinclair thought, but also as a mark of high good humour. As though to confirm these thoughts, EH spoke again, with a touch of ponderous archness. 'I wonder if we should ask Tracy to come in here. I think not. He is so impetuous that I fear he might take the invitation in the wrong spirit.' He poured sherry into the three glasses. 'You will find this is a very decent Amontillado.' The liquid was pale amber against the electric light. As they sipped it EH said casually, 'A man named van Dieren is coming to see me this afternoon – he tells me that he has some information which may be relevant to Lionel's death.' Below the halo of white hair the small blue eyes looked at them both, keen and hard.

Chapter Five *11.20 to 11.40 a.m.*

Bland walked a few hesitant steps in the fog, wondering whether the information he had just received need affect his next move, which had been to speak to Bond about van Dieren. Was it perhaps more immediately important to check on what Ella Lines, or Myrtle Montague, had told him, and find out whether Polly had spoken to van Dieren about the marriage? He decided that it was, turned round and padded softly through the fog towards Piccadilly. The fog tickled his nose, and he sneezed. 'Damn,' he said, and stopped to light a cigarette.

He stood in front of the small hatchway that was now becoming familiar, and was about to ring the bell when the hatch popped open, and Polly Lines' round doll's head appeared. The physical resemblance between the two girls was a marked one, but there was a viciousness and intelligence in Polly's face quite absent from her sister's. She stared at Bland, and said immediately, 'He's out.'

'It's not Mr van Dieren I want to see. It's you.'

'Me?' Her blue eyes opened wide.

'Yes. May I come in?'

'I suppose so,' she said grudgingly, and opened the door to her room. 'I don't know what you want me for,' she said, and patted her hair. 'I've told you everything about that telephone call.'

'It's not about the telephone call. It's about your sister.'

'My *sister?*' She stared. 'What's she got to do with it?'

'Did you tell your employer anything about the marriage of a friend of your sister's named Eve Marchant to Lionel Hargreaves?'

Either she was a first-class actress, or her surprise was genuine. 'Why not? Yes, I did. He was always going on about old man Hargreaves, and saying he'd done him down and he'd get even one day, and I thought he'd be interested to know about this. It was just a bit of gossip, that's all. I haven't done anything wrong.' It was unpleasantly warm in the little office, and of necessity they were close together. One of Miss Lines' crossed legs was almost touching Bland's and he could not help seeing the sharp points of her breasts jutting out of her black jumper.

He leaned back in his chair. 'Cigarette?' She giggled. 'I don't mind if I do.' Her eyes, as he lighted the cigarette for her, were watchful. 'Damn,' she said. 'It's out.' She held his hand as he relighted it, with her small, rather pudgy hand, the nails tipped with scarlet, and she recrossed her legs, so that one of her knees was touching Bland's. 'Suppose you tell me what this is all about?'

'All right. Lionel Hargreaves has been murdered. His marriage to Eve Marchant was secret. Lionel didn't tell anybody, Eve says she only told your sister, and your sister says she only told you. Lionel's father received an anonymous letter before the murder, telling him that his son was married to Eve Marchant. That's the story in a nutshell.'

'And you think my old man here had something to do with it?'

'I know he had *something* to do with it, but I'm not sure what it was.'

'And you think I can tell you something else?' Bland shrugged his shoulders. Her voice was shrill as she said, 'I can't. It's nothing to do with me, and I don't know anything about it.' It seemed to Bland that the pressure of her knee against his increased slightly.

'And you didn't type that anonymous letter?'

'Typed!' she cried. 'You didn't say it was typed. I had nothing to do with it.'

He looked round the room. 'Where's your typewriter?'

'Mr van Dieren sent it away for overhaul.'

'What make is it? A Remington?' She nodded. 'A Remington 12?' She nodded again. 'Where was it sent for repair?'

'I don't know. Mr van Dieren sent it while I was out.'

'Did it need repair?'

She said reluctantly, 'Not much. Some of the letters were out of alignment.'

'Small "e" and "l"?' Her eyes were wild with alarm as she nodded a third time. 'All right. If you've nothing else to tell me – ' He stood up.

She came close to him, and took hold of his coat. Bland was not a tall man, but she was so small that she was a head below him. 'Listen,' she said. 'I had nothing to do with this, nothing at all, d'you hear? I don't want to get into any trouble.' She pressed herself against him, and he disengaged her, not gently. Her cheap scent was strong in his nostrils.

'What do you know about van Dieren?'

'I don't know anything,' she cried. 'Not anything.'

'Have you ever stayed at his place in Earl's Court?'

She stepped away from him, her face contorted with rage. 'Get out. Go on, get out. Before I throw something at you.'

Bland looked round critically. 'There's very little to throw. But I'll go. You're being very stupid, Miss Lines. If you change your mind, and decide you've got something to tell me, ring me up at once, or come to Scotland Yard.'

'Get out!' she screamed. 'Get out!'

He turned and went out. The last sight he had was of her china-blue eyes staring at him with hatred. Outside in the street he ran his fingers round his collar. 'Good Lord,' he said. 'The things I do for law and order.'

Chapter Six *11.45 a.m. to 12.15 p.m.*

'Darling, I thought we'd agreed that we shouldn't see each other alone in the office,' Jean Rogers said. 'It's really awfully tactless. You know how people talk.'

'I had to see you,' Tracy said, 'I simply had to see you. I just can't stand it.'

Her voice was not impatient, but rather elaborately patient, as she said, 'What's the matter now?'

'It's that bloody swine – the old man. He as good as told me I waste the firm's money. Well, by God, I only need to be told that once.' His face was very red. 'I shall hand in my resignation.'

She laid her hand on his shoulder. 'Don't do anything you'll regret.'

'I'll hand in my resignation,' Tracy said obstinately. 'I won't stand it. He's not the only pebble on the beach.'

'But he's a very good one. You'll not find anyone else who'll pay you what Hargreaves does.' As he started to protest she said hurriedly, 'Darling, I know you're worth every penny of it. But he *does* pay well.'

Tracy got up and walked about. 'So you think I should put up with it?'

She stood close to him. 'Just for a little while. You know I'll be seeing Alan again soon, and this time perhaps I'll really be able to make him agree to a divorce.'

'And then we'll get married?'

She said in a doubtful voice, 'Then we'll get married.'

His face broke into the fresh, attractive smile she knew so well, and he tossed back a lock of hair from his forehead. He took her into his arms and kissed her. 'Of course we will. Forgive me, darling. I suppose I shouldn't forget that Lionel was killed the night before last. I'm just a bad-tempered impatient devil, I know I am.' Since he was holding Jean Rogers in his arms he could not see the sudden change of expression on her face as he said these words: but he could not help seeing the door of the room open after a perfunctory knock and Bond put his head round it. Neither could he miss the long, malicious look Bond gave them before he said 'Sorry,' and closed the door.

Bond closed the door gently and stood in the corridor for a moment, his dark face happy with malice. He walked along the corridor to Sinclair's room, and looked in. He found Sinclair in the Copy Room next door, looking critically at a piece of Onslow's copy. Onslow was standing by his side, looking, if possibly, even more critical than Sinclair.

'These two are all right,' Sinclair said. 'But this third piece – I can't quite lay my finger on what's wrong, but somehow it doesn't ring the bell.' Onslow nodded. 'Have another shot, will you?' Sinclair said curtly to Bond, 'I've spoken to the Quickshave people, and settled that point.' But Bond was not so easily shaken off. 'Can I see you for a moment?' Sinclair paused with his hand on his door, and said, 'I'm very busy.'

'This won't take a minute,' Bond said, 'and it's most interesting.' As they went into Sinclair's room the door from the corridor opened and Miss Peachey, the receptionist, said, 'Inspector Bland'.

Bland was looking wonderfully fresh and unruffled, and he beamed at Bond. 'The very man I've been looking for. I understand you have something to tell me?'

'I certainly have. You were asking some questions about a man named van Dieren? Well, before I came here I was working with a firm of art agents myself, and believe me, I learned something about friend van Dieren.' He raised his eyebrows. 'Dirty work.'

'What kind of dirty work?'

'Dirty drawings – and photographs. It's not unknown and it's not unprofitable. Very few people, even inside the trade, know about it, but we had some dealings with him, and I called round once or twice. Devil of a queer cove he was, and his little bitch of a secretary too. Met her, Inspector?'

'Yes,' Bland said.

'*She* certainly knows what's what.' Bond said with a grin. 'And I'd lay a bet the old man's taught it to her, queer though he does look. One day when I was up there he asked me if I was interested in art studies – and then he showed me some of the filthiest photographs I've ever seen in my life.'

'And were you interested?' Sinclair asked. Bond laughed loudly. 'Another crack like that from you, my lad, and I'll tell the Inspector about your little slip-up on Quickshave.'

'You think van Dieren was making a good thing out of it?'

'If what I heard afterwards is true, he certainly was. He didn't do a lot of legitimate business, that I do know.'

'All right,' Bland said. 'Thank you, Mr Bond. That may be very useful.' Bond paused at the door and grinned again. 'I'm honoured if I've told the police something.' He said to Sinclair, 'I've got a titbit to tell you, but it'll keep.'

Bland breathed deeply when Bond had closed the door. 'As a policeman I try to feel no prejudices, but I must admit that I've taken a dislike to that man.'

'A dislike that's shared by almost everybody here.' Sinclair looked at Bland a little quizzically. 'Isn't your department falling down a bit – I mean, not knowing about these activities of van Dieren's?'

'No, I don't think so. He's never been in prison, and there's no special reason why the man I asked to make a check on him should have looked to see if he was running a separate pornographic business on the side.' He tapped his teeth with a pencil. 'You notice that every trail we have leads back to van Dieren. Jones telephones him, I've found out this morning that the anonymous letter came from his office, that curious story which should have been told by Joe Riddell came from him. And yet it's clear enough that he's merely acting for somebody else, or else he wouldn't move so openly. Bond's story would explain why Polly Lines was alarmed on that first day when we called, when she heard I was from the police, and why she was almost relieved when she found it was a case of murder.'

'You mean – she knows about these – other activities?' Sinclair flushed.

'I should think that almost certain.' Bland chuckled. 'She tried to seduce me this morning – at least I think that was her intention – but my purity remains untouched. I was going to say, though, that we have no proof whatever that Bond's story is true. I'm inclined to believe it because I can't see why he should invent it, but it's always possible that he's trying something on. In a murder story any character as obviously unpleasant as Bond would be clear of suspicion automatically, but in real life he's as likely as anyone else to have committed murder.' His unusually long speech was interrupted by a tentative knock on the door. It opened, and Carruthers' round face appeared. He spoke apologetically. 'I'm so sorry – I came straight in to see you about some work that Richard's given me to do – I didn't mean to disturb you.'

'Not at all,' Bland said casually. 'We were only chatting. I'm sorry to tell you, by the way, that your friend van Dieren seems to be in this up to the neck.'

Carruthers' Adam's apple moved up and down. His alarm would have been comic had there not also been something unpleasant and furtive about it. 'Are you going to arrest him?'

'Why, not at the moment, I think.'

'He's coming up here this afternoon,' Sinclair said, and Bland and Carruthers both looked startled. 'To see EH. I don't know what it's about, but he telephoned this morning and made an appointment. Richard and I were in the room at the time. It's something to do with Lionel's death, I think. So if you want to arrest him, he'll be here at two o'clock.'

'He'll be much more useful laying the trails somebody has carefully designed for him,' Bland said. 'If Mr van Dieren's given enough rope, I feel he'll hang – not himself, but somebody else. I think I'll pay another call on him this afternoon myself – some of the points in his story can be checked now. I feel the time has come to play what you, Sinclair, used to call a forcing game, when we were at school together.'

Chapter Seven *2.00 to 2.20 p.m.*

The hands of the clock above the reception desk pointed to two o'clock exactly when the disorderly figure of Joseph van Dieren pushed open the swing door and said to Miss Peachey, the platinum-haired girl who sat behind the reception desk, 'I want Mr Edward Hargreaves.' She noticed a general smell of drink that surrounded him. She could not help noticing also the frayed sleeves of his big raglan overcoat, and the great moustache and bushy eyebrows that gave a fierce expression to his face.

'I'll see if he's in.' She dialled a number on an internal telephone. 'Mr Hargreaves? Mr van Dieren here to see you. Certainly, sir.' She put down the telephone. 'Mr Hargreaves will be free in a moment, Mr van Dieren. Will you take a chair.'

'No I won't take a chair. I had an appointment at two o'clock and it's two o'clock now. Why doesn't he keep it, eh?'

Miss Peachey said nervously, 'Mr Hargreaves will see you in a moment, sir.'

'He'd better.' The man in the big coat began to walk up and down the reception-room with a ferocity which was somehow rather comic. 'I'm not hanging about for him. I've been waiting on this day for twenty years, and I'm not going to be done out of it now.' Two or three people came through the reception-room, and looked at van Dieren curiously. The internal telephone rang. Miss Peachey answered it, and said with relief, 'Mr Hargreaves will see you now.'

'And about time too.' He followed her along the corridor with a gait that was just perceptibly not straight. The last thing she saw before she closed the door was EH's face, grim and with no trace of customary benevolence, staring at his visitor.

Ten minutes later she heard a sudden crash, a sound of breaking glass, and EH's voice raised in anger. A series of large french windows with balconies outside them ran from the offices on this side of the corridor to the street. She opened one of these windows, and heard EH yell into the thick fog, 'There he goes. Catch the little devil. Catch him.' Following the direction of EH's finger, she saw a small boy running. EH's injunction to catch him was a vain one; visibility was not more than a few yards, and in a few moments the small boy had vanished.

'God damn and blast,' EH said. 'I'd like to wring that boy's neck.'

'What happened, sir?'

He held out for her inspection a large stone. 'Little devil threw this and broke my window, that's what happened.' By this time other french windows had opened, and Onslow, Mudge and Mrs Rogers had come out on their balconies. They stared at EH and the stone, and at the window, which had lost a good deal of glass. EH became suddenly conscious of their gaze, and stepped back off the balcony into his room. Miss Peachey carried back with her the smell of fog which, thanks to her incautious opening of the french window, had now pervaded the reception office. Miss Berry, her particular friend from Accounts, came in, and they agreed that the weather really was too vile, and that there was nothing worse than the English climate.

They were just speaking wistfully of the joys of Torquay in January when the door of EH's room opened, and van Dieren shot out of it, head down, scuttling along the corridor in his big overcoat. EH's voice followed him: 'And don't bring me any more cock-and-bull tales. When you've got something to say, I'll listen to you.' Van Dieren did not reply. With his head well down, without a glance at Miss Peachey or her friend, he charged out through the swing doors into the street. EH stood glaring down the corridor for a moment, and then slammed his door. Miss Peachey said to her friend, 'The old man certainly sent *him* off with a flea in his ear.'

Chapter Eight *2.20 to 5.00 p.m.*

Miss Peachey, the receptionist, liked her job. 'You see life,' she said, and she meant by the phrase that she preferred to sit at a reception desk, watching people pass by, swapping jokes with the boys from Production, and using her upper-class tone in the presence of upper-class visitors, to sitting in the unquestionably less lively but perhaps more discreet social atmosphere of one of the typists' offices. But although she talked to the boys from Production, although she kept her eye open for that Very Rich Young Man who would surely arrive one day and ask her out to lunch as a preliminary to marriage, Miss Peachey was an alert and conscientious, receptionist. It turned out that this fact was of some importance; or at least it was of some importance that she sat at the reception desk all the afternoon from the time Mr van Dieren left, until five o'clock, with the exception of a brief five minutes, when her place was taken by her friend from Accounts.

At ten minutes to three Mr Weston arrived. He had an appointment with EH at three o'clock, and although he hardly came into the category of Very Rich Young Men, and she did not expect him to ask her out to dinner, Miss Peachey was pleased to see him. There was something – she hardly knew how to put it even to herself something very trustworthy about Mr Weston. Whenever she saw his drooping jowls, his honest blue eyes and his respectable bowler hat and overcoat, she was reminded of a gentle St Bernard dog, and the portentousness of his manner somehow added to this impression. When she rang through to EH he told her to ask Mr Weston to come in at three o'clock. She put down the telephone, and gave Mr Weston what she classified as one of her genuine smiles, something quite distinct from the mechanical smile with which she greeted everyone, as part of her job.

'And how is our Miss Peachey in this vile weather?' Mr Weston's teeth clicked. 'Still breaking all the hearts?'

'*Some* people,' Miss Peachey said, 'have got no hearts to break.'

'If I were twenty years younger, I should know what answer to make to that.' Mr Weston twirled his rolled umbrella in a way that might have surprised Bland had he seen him. 'And how is our lord and master?'

'If you ask me, he's in a pretty bad temper, and has been for a day or two. But then he's had enough to make him. Wasn't it a terrible thing about Mr Lionel?'

'Terrible.' Mr Weston's teeth clicked again.

'And today some lad threw a stone and broke his window, and then ran away in the fog.'

'Tch, tch,' Mr Weston clucked.

'And then a man named van Dieren called – rather seedy looking, not quite a gentleman really, I think – and *he* seemed to rub up Mr Hargreaves the wrong way too.' Miss Peachey paused, conscious suddenly that she had said rather more than she should have done, even to so thorough a gentleman as Mr Weston. And indeed the lawyer, although he said nothing looked uncommonly thoughtful when he received this information. After a moment he looked at the clock. 'It is three o'clock,' he said. He rose and, carrying a fine leather despatch-case in his left hand and the rolled umbrella in his right, walked down the corridor with a step remarkably springy for his sixty-seven years. He stopped at the first door on the left, knocked, and went in. Miss Peachey returned to her invoices with a slight, nagging itch in her mind that she shouldn't have made that remark about another caller.

It was almost half an hour before Mr Weston came out, looking even more sober than usual. He settled his bowler hat on his head, and then thoughtfully lifted it to say good day to Miss Peachey. She noted it with pleasure as a mark of his absolute gentlemanliness, and she followed his tall, slightly stooping figure in its progress out of the swing doors with something like affection. She noted also the other visitors to EH's office during the afternoon, and was able to name them with perfect confidence later on, as Bond, Sinclair and Richard Hargreaves in that order.

At about four minutes past five o'clock when Miss Peachey was thinking that it was time to spend a few minutes in the washroom, she was startled by a sound which she took to be a strangled cry, coming from EH's room, followed by a heavy thud. She hesitated for a moment, but only for a moment, and then walked up to the door, and knocked on it lightly. There was no reply, but it seemed to her that she heard a scuffling noise, the kind of sound that might be made by a large rat. She pushed open the door. Fog was thick in the room, because of the broken window, and for a moment she thought that there was nobody there. She noticed a bottle and a glass standing on the desk, and then, while she stood with her hand upon the door, she heard a groan. Miss Peachey was a girl of common sense and courage, and though she jumped, she did not scream. She advanced cautiously towards the desk, and when she had taken two steps she saw a brown shoe and sock sticking out beyond the desk edge. The shoe and sock moved, and then suddenly were still. Then Miss Peachey screamed.

Chapter Nine *4.00 to 5.15 p.m.*

The fog was very thick, and it took Bland and Filby half an hour to get to New Bridge Street. As they turned the corner from Fleet Street, Bland gripped Filby's arm. 'What's that?' A moment later the sound became unmistakably the clang of a bell, and a fire engine moved slowly past them in the fog. The two men looked at one another. In Filby's eyes there was merely bewilderment, but in Bland's there was alarm. 'It's no use trying to hurry in this fog,' Filby said in a soothing voice, as Bland moved forward, and became entangled with a burly man's umbrella. For all that, they quickened their pace when they saw in front of them a patch of brightness glowing through the fog. The bright patch became an orange glare and Bland began to run. He pushed through a crowd of people, and came to a stop in front of van Dieren's office block. The building was on fire. Flames leaped from the ground-floor and first-floor windows, and the sharp smell of smoke mingled with the odour of fog in their nostrils. Two fire engines were at work, and Bland walked over to the officer in charge, and spoke to him urgently.

'Inspector Bland, CID. Did this fire start on the ground-floor?'

The man looked at him oddly. 'Certainly did. Someone pretty well soaked a couple of offices down there with petrol and set light to them – or that's the way it looks. Something else, too – we found a dead girl in there. Had a job getting her out. Our chaps thought the fire had made her unconscious, but I'm not sure. You'd better have a look at her.' He led the way over to a spot away from the fire engines, and pointed to a tarpaulin. 'Under there.' With Filby just behind him, Bland lifted the tarpaulin, and the face of Polly Lines looked up at him, hideously burned and distorted, but still recognisable. He pulled the tarpaulin right back, knelt by her side for a moment examining the body, and then got to his feet. 'There's a lump on her head,' the fire officer said. 'She could have been hit.'

'I saw it.' Bland's round face was grave and sad, and he spoke to Filby almost with a note of tenderness in his voice. 'Poor fool. If she'd talked to me this morning – if I'd known then what danger she was in – but I didn't.' He stood looking down at the tarpaulin for a moment and then said, 'You've seen no sign of van Dieren, I suppose? Theatrical-looking figure with grey hair and a big moustache? He's the man who rents those offices that are on fire.'

The officer shook his head. 'No one else. A girl on the first floor noticed the fire soon after it started – smoke coming under the door – or we might not have recovered her body at all. Had to break down the door, and no key inside. It's dirty work all right. Thanks to that girl who reported it, we've got the fire under pretty well.'

'Is there any chance of getting a look at the offices?'

'Not yet. Maybe in another half-hour. But everything will be pretty badly burnt – there won't be a lot left to look at.'

Bland turned to Filby. 'Will you take a look at the offices and salvage anything you can in the way of papers, files, metal objects – anything you can lay your hands on. If van Dieren comes, I want him at Scotland Yard for questioning. And let me know the result of the examination of that girl, and how she died.' Filby nodded without saying anything. Bland said, 'By God, I'll see somebody pays for this.'

When he got back to his office he found a note on his desk saying that Edward Hargreaves had been found dead in his office, and that poison was suspected as the cause of his death.

Chapter Ten *5.45 to 6.30 p.m.*

The little group of people gathered together round the reception desk met Bland with a cold hostility which he did not fail to notice. They are blaming me for this death, he thought. And in a way they are not wrong to blame me, because a policeman's job is primarily the prevention of crime, and not the discovery of criminals. A detective who is engaged on a case, holds the threads of it in his hands, and yet fails to prevent a crime, has failed. Yet that is a hard thought, for the detective starts at a great disadvantage against that very rare type of criminal who plans a crime, or a series of crimes, well in advance, and then carries them out methodically. In such cases the detective, even when he knows the name of the criminal, has no choice but to wait for a slip to be made.

These thoughts moved at the back of his mind while flash-light photographs of Hargreaves' room were being taken, while he was kneeling at the side of EH's body and looking at the dead face with its crown of white hair, and while he was listening to Dr McCullen telling him that Edward Hargreaves had been poisoned by hyoscine, and that the hyoscine had certainly been contained in the sherry. Such disturbing and unsatisfactory thoughts remained with him while he was told that the glass containing the sherry had no prints except those of EH, and that the bottle had apparently been recently wiped, and bore no prints other than those of EH. His face, when he went out into the reception hall again was stony.

'You probably know something of what has happened. I may as well tell you now that Mr Hargreaves has been killed by drinking sherry loaded with poison. Now, I want to know – '

'Just a minute.' It was Tracy, unexpectedly bellicose and unfriendly. 'We may not be detectives, but we can see what's in front of our noses. We could see that EH had been poisoned, and we've found out who did it. And God knows it's hard for a plain man to understand why this murderer's not under lock and key already. Of course it was this man van Dieren that you've been asking so many questions about. It's about time to stop asking questions. Let's get some action.'

Bland's voice was harsh. 'All right. Since you've constituted yourself the cheer leader, let's hear what happened.'

Tracy ticked off the points on his fingers. 'First, EH always has – had – a glass of sherry at eleven o'clock in the morning and five o'clock in the afternoon. It was a custom as regular as clockwork – something that several people in the office knew about, and that he never missed. Next, we can check that the sherry was all right at eleven o'clock this morning, because Dick and Sinclair here were in the room with EH, and drank with him.' Richard Hargreaves and Sinclair nodded. Tracy looked uncomfortable for a moment, but continued, serious and oratorical. 'So someone put poison in the sherry after eleven o'clock. It wasn't done during lunchtime, because he had sandwiches in his room, and no one came in to see him. His first visitor, at two o'clock, was this man van Dieren, who had telephoned this morning to make an appointment.' Tracy looked round, conscious that he was holding his audience. Sinclair was gazing rather anxiously at Bland, Richard Hargreaves looked almost as pale and shaken as Miss Peachey, Bond was staring sullenly in front of him, and Mrs Rogers was looking at Tracy. A little apart from the rest of them, Mr Weston listened intently, with one hand occasionally cupped to his ear. 'We don't know what happened between the two of them. Probably we shall never know. What we do know, thanks to the alertness of our receptionist here, is that EH turned van Dieren out after twenty minutes, saying that he wouldn't listen to his cock-and-bull stories.'

Miss Peachey interrupted. 'He didn't say exactly that, Mr Tracy. He said that if van Dieren had something to say, he'd listen to him.'

Tracy waved the remark away. 'But we know something more than that. An odd thing happened while this man was in the office. A little boy threw a stone, broke EH's window, and ran off in the fog. There was very little chance that he'd be caught on a day like this – and he wasn't caught. EH came out on to his balcony and stayed out there for a couple of minutes. During that time he had his back to the room. That two minutes gave ample time to the murderer. The bottle of sherry always stood in the same place, on the sideboard – the murderer simply had to distract EH's attention. And that was the only time during the afternoon when his attention *was* distracted. Miss Peachey was at the reception desk all the afternoon, and we had her word that EH didn't once leave his room. The conclusion is obvious. This man van Dieren put poison into the sherry. The case against him is cast-iron.'

Bland's face was not friendly. 'There's one flaw in that case – only one, but it's big enough to break it wide open. You make a great point of the fact that Hargreaves took a glass of sherry at eleven o'clock in the morning and five in the evening. It's obvious, therefore, that the crime was premeditated, and that the murderer brought poison with him, dropped it in the sherry and walked out.

'But that means that you can pretty well exclude van Dieren from the list of suspects. Yesterday, I described his appearance to Hargreaves, who said he'd never met him. He'd never been in the offices.' He turned to Miss Peachey. 'Had you ever seen him before?'

She shook her head decidedly. 'Oh no, sir. I shouldn't have forgotten him, I'm sure of that.'

'Quite so. His manner and dress would not be easily forgotten. Now – since van Dieren had never been here, since he had never met Hargreaves, how did he know about the bottle of sherry? Where did he get the information about Hargreaves' habits?'

There was silence. Tracy said lamely, 'He got it from somebody here. Somebody told him without knowing it was important. They must have done.'

'All the people here who would know Hargreaves' habits deny any knowledge of van Dieren, except Mr Bond here, and Carruthers, who's not here at the moment. Did you give van Dieren this information, Mr Bond?'

Bond laughed. 'Certainly not. Last time I saw van Dieren I'd never put foot inside this place, and never seen the old man.'

'We can also ask Carruthers. But if he didn't give this information,' Bland shrugged, 'where's your case against van Dieren?'

Tracy stuck out his jaw. '*Somebody* told him.'

'Not at all. Even if Carruthers did tell van Dieren, there's no cast-iron case against him – he's simply one of the suspects.' Bland spoke with a vicious pleasure, addressing himself particularly to Tracy. 'The trouble with amateurs is that they theorise from prejudice, not from facts. Let's work from the facts. There was only one door to Hargreaves' room. There was also the french window leading on to the balcony, but as it only fronts on the street, it's obvious that nobody entered that way to put poison in the sherry. Whoever came in must have had the chance of distracting Hargreaves' attention for sufficient time to poison the sherry. Either van Dieren did it – in which case he must have been told the exact geography of the room, position of the bottle of sherry and so on – or it was done by one of the other people who came in the room between eleven o'clock in the morning and five in the afternoon. You say you were at the reception desk during that whole time, Miss Peachey?'

'Except for the lunch hour, when Miss Bellamy was here, and she says nothing happened during that time.'

'She didn't know anything,' Tracy said. 'We sent her home.'

'So you sent her home. That was very kind of you. No doubt you thought you were assisting the investigation. If she didn't know anything, she could hardly have known less than somebody who sent home a witness who would obviously be needed. It's no use blustering, Mr Tracy, your interference and stupidity are both inexcusable.' The anger of men who are generally calm is always impressive. Bland's manner was normally so soft and placid that they were all to some extent cowed. Sinclair almost jumped when Bland said in the same tone, 'And you, Sinclair, you've seen enough of this case to know Miss Bellamy would be needed for questioning.'

'Really, I – she said no one went in during the lunch hour.'

'And did you make absolutely sure that she hadn't left the desk for ten minutes of that time? Of course you didn't. And you, Miss Peachey – are you sure that you really remained at your desk the whole time?'

'Quite sure,' Miss Peachey said with composure. 'Except when the stone was thrown – then I looked out of the french windows, but I didn't leave the reception hall. I should have seen anyone walking along the corridor.'

'All right. Who else did you see go in there during the afternoon?'

Miss Peachey was conscious of the importance of her answer. Her voice had a hollow sound. 'Mr Weston, Mr Bond, Mr Sinclair and Mr Hargreaves.'

'In that order?' She nodded. 'Can you remember the times? Don't say you're sure of them if you're not.'

'I am sure – within a minute or two, anyway. Mr Weston went in at three, and came out just before half-past. Mr Bond went in just after half-past three, and stayed about five minutes. Mr Sinclair was in for about a quarter of an hour, and I should think he came out about four o'clock. Mr Richard was in there from about ten past to half-past four. And then, of course, I went in just after five o'clock, and saw – '

'All right,' Bland said. 'Now, would you swear to those times?'

She nodded. 'Within a minute or two, yes. I always notice people going in and out of Mr Hargreaves' room, because he hates to be disturbed when he's engaged, and I used to tell people if anyone else was in there.'

'Thank you very much. You've done extremely well, and that's very helpful. Now, Mr Bond, do you agree that you went in for five minutes?'

'That or less. I went in to give him the price of a printing job. He queried one or two details about it – asked if it wouldn't be better done in colour lithography, rather than half-tone. I told him it wouldn't be so suitable.'

'Did you notice the bottle of sherry?'

'Can't say I did. Wouldn't say it wasn't there, though.'

'Did Hargreaves seem just as usual?'

Bond pursed his lips. 'He was pretty short with me. But then he was a man who'd often be pretty short.' He looked at Richard, and added, 'If you don't mind my saying so.'

'Mr Sinclair why did you go in to see Mr Hargreaves?'

Sinclair's handsome features were set in a sulky expression. It was clear that he resented his reprimand. 'He'd asked me in the morning to come in sometime to show him the copy and layouts on a new scheme for Flowspeed Airlines. He asked me to come in between three and four o'clock. It was a custom of his to look at absolutely everything that was going through, so that he kept his fingers on every account. I didn't notice the bottle of sherry, but then I don't suppose I should have done, if it were on the sideboard.'

'He didn't offer you a drink?'

'No, he didn't drink with his staff – unless it was a special occasion of some sort. We had a drink this morning, I know, but that was unusual.'

'*We* is Mr Richard Hargreaves and yourself, I gather. What was the special occasion?'

Sinclair moved uneasily. 'Nothing much. EH got upset – he was very worried about Lionel, I think – and blew off the handle about our losing an account.'

'Who did he blow off the handle, as you put it, against. You?'

Sinclair moved again. 'Really, it's – it was all over in five minutes – '

'It was me,' Tracy said in a deep voice. 'Make what you can of it, Inspector. I walked out of the room before the olive-branch was extended and the sherry bottle produced.'

'It was all over in five minutes.' Sinclair repeated. 'And we had a drink because it was eleven o'clock. That's all I meant by a special occasion.'

'Mr Hargreaves.' Richard Hargreaves was scuffing the carpet with his pointed shoe. 'Why did you go in to see your father?'

'A private matter.' He did not look up.

'We'll talk about it later. Did your father offer you a drink?' Richard shook his head. 'Did you notice the bottle of sherry?'

'I've been trying to remember.' Richard wearily passed his hand over his eyes. 'I *think* – I'm almost sure – it was standing in its usual place on the sideboard.'

'You couldn't swear to it?'

'No-o, I don't suppose I could.'

'All right. Mr Weston, I'd like to talk with you privately, and you too, Mr Hargreaves. Mr Tracy, if you'll leave Miss Bellamy's address, I'll be grateful. Then the rest of you can go.'

Bland sat at Lionel Hargreaves' old desk, and looked over it at the lawyer. 'I didn't question you out there, because I think I know part of what you've got to tell me. But I'll ask you the routine question. Did you notice the bottle of sherry?'

'Yes.' Weston nodded, and his jowls moved. 'It was on the sideboard when I left just before 3.30. I'll swear to that.'

'Why did you notice it?'

The lawyer's jowls shook a little as he laughed. 'Because I always look at it expectantly, in the hope that he'll offer me a drink, and he never has yet.' He stopped laughing, and added solemnly, 'And never will now, poor fellow. But let me tell you what I have to say, Inspector. I came along to see Hargreaves by appointment at three o'clock today, about a case the firm has against a man named Fairbrother, who has refused to pay for some display work done for him. And that time he seemed rather gloomy, but fairly calm and reasonable. Just after 4.30 he telephoned my office and said he wanted to see me as soon after five o'clock this afternoon as possible, for a specific purpose.'

'Let me guess,' Bland said. 'He wanted to make a new will.'

Weston's teeth clicked. 'Now, how did you know that?'

'Not very difficult. One, Richard told me last night that he was going to marry Eve Marchant very soon – you remember, I mentioned her to you yesterday. Two, his father strongly disapproved of the marriage. Three, EH telephoned you just after he saw his son. It might have been something else, but a new will seemed a good bet. Did he say anything to you about this will, its provisions, and so on? And what was his old will?'

'The existing will,' Mr Weston said portentously, 'shares the estate equally between Lionel and Richard. There are a few minor bequests of a hundred pounds here and there – I am myself beneficiary to the extent of a thousand pounds, which is more than I deserve, as I said to him at the time.' He coughed.

'What about Carruthers? Does he come in the will?'

Mr Weston's eyes were raised in surprise. 'He is one of the small beneficiaries. He is left a thousand pounds. I do not imagine he expects more, because he was down and out two years ago and EH gave him two thousand pounds, and told him then that he should not expect to be remembered in his will.'

'And the will means that when Lionel was murdered the estate went wholly to Richard, with the exception of those few items?'

'There was a clause to, cover the death of either brother, in which case the other brother inherited. On the death of Lionel, Richard became the sole legatee.'

'All right. What about the new will?'

The lawyer spread out his hands. 'I wish I could tell you. All he said on the telephone was that he wanted me to come along to his office – he wanted to make a new will. I was surprised not particularly by the request but by the urgency of it – and I asked him if it was really essential for me to come along this afternoon. He said, in a tone that indicated annoyance, that it *was* essential. No word passed between us about the provisions of the new will.'

'He didn't say anything to indicate what changes he had in mind?'

'Nothing at all. He merely said he wanted to make a new will, and said nothing at all as to it's nature.'

'So that, for all you know, he may merely have wished to change a few minor bequests?'

Mr Weston pursed his lips. The effect was to make him look remarkably judicial. 'It is not likely that he would have asked me to come along here at such very short notice to change a few minor bequests.'

Bland stayed for a few moments staring into space, and then gave Weston a mechanical smile. 'One more thing. What is the size of the estate?' As the lawyer pursed his lips again, Bland said, 'I don't want anything more than a general idea.'

'In general terms,' the lawyer said solemnly, 'between ninety and one hundred thousand pounds.'

Bland whistled. 'As much as that? All right, Mr Weston. Thank you.' When the lawyer had gone, Bland sat still for a few moments, and then walked out of the room and across the corridor. Richard was standing in EH's room, looking at the men who scurried about the room like ants. On his face was an expression of sullen despair. 'Come now,' Bland said, and his voice was kind. 'Things are not as bad as they seem. This routine activity must be endured. And after all – you were not so very fond of him.'

The young man looked up. An expression of surprise was on his face, and his voice was high-pitched and hysterical, as Bland had heard it once before. 'I hated his guts. But don't you understand what's happened?'

Bland steered him gently into Sinclair's room, and said, 'You tell me. Or would you prefer that I told you, and you can correct me when I go wrong. First of all – this afternoon you told your father that you were going to be married. He threatened to cut you out of his will, and you told him, I imagine, that he could do what he liked, but that you intended to marry Miss Marchant.'

Richard struck the desk with his fist. 'Why should I put up with everything all the time? I've been bullied all my life by him and Lionel.' His voice was shrill.

'Precisely. Now – can you tell me in detail what happened when you went in this afternoon? And what are – and were – your plans for the marriage?'

'I told him that I'd arranged to get married to Eve next week, by special licence. Now – I just don't know – I haven't seen Eve.' He flapped with his hands in the air. 'He asked me to forget it, and then at least to wait, and I wouldn't. That was what really upset him, I think – the fact that I insisted on holding out against his will, for once. He said all sorts of awful things about Eve – hateful things about her character, and about her being at the Splendid. He said she was nothing better than a prostitute, and that he'd send for Weston to alter his will. He said he'd wished I'd died instead of Lionel. In the end I walked out of the room.' Richard gave a curiously ladylike nod of the head.

'Did he say anything about the change in the will?'

'Yes – he was leaving his money to charity. He said, "I'm leaving my money out of the family now, Richard, so you can

cease to worry about it. It won't be of interest to you any more."
Then he said something about selecting a charity.'

'He didn't have time to make a will. He telephoned Weston,
but he died before seeing him.'

'Yes, I know.' Richard stared at Bland. 'You mean – you can't
mean – oh, this is too much.' Suddenly he put his head in his
hands and began to sob. There was no doubt that the sobs were
genuine. Bland stood looking at him thoughtfully until they had
subsided, and Richard looked up, revealing a tear-stained face.
'I'm sorry. It's not that I was fond of my father, or of Lionel for
that matter. But all this happening in a couple of days – I'm
afraid it's upset me.' He wiped his eyes with a fine linen
handkerchief. 'I swear to you that I had nothing to do with all
this.'

Bland was a little impatient. 'I didn't say you had. Are you
sure you've nothing else at all to tell me? Either about your
conversation this afternoon with your father, or about anything
else?'

Richard shrugged his shoulders with a girlish and appealing
gesture, and spoke with what seemed to be complete sincerity.
'Before God, Inspector, I swear to you that I've nothing else to
tell.'

Chapter Eleven *6.30 to 7.00 p.m.*

Filby's face was rather red. 'It seems a bit hard to blame me for not finding out about the dirty pictures, I must say, sir. After all, you never said anything about – '

'I didn't say I blamed you, Filby. Don't be so sensitive. Let's have a look at these drawings you've found. I'm a bit puzzled about them. Tell me again, and carefully, how you came to find them.'

'Well – it's a bit of a funny thing at that. These drawings were out in the passage. Fire had burned pretty well all the papers in the rooms – wooden filing cabinets make beautiful firewood.'

'No indication of how they had got into the passage?'

'None at all. Fire was in the rooms, so they're only a bit singed.'

Bland went over to a side table and carefully unwrapped the tissue paper in which Filby had put the drawings. He studied them for some time without expression, while Filby stood by his side with his hands on his hips. 'Filthy, aren't they?' Filby said with relish.

'They're competent, too – that's the thing that interests me. And another thing that interests me is the signature.' Bland pointed to the bottom of two of the drawings, where the letters ARTES were printed neatly. 'All the same, aren't they?'

'Yes, all signed like that. What d'you make of that?'

'It gives us a lead. Put someone on to watch van Dieren's place at Earl's Court and bring him in if he turns up there. And pack up these drawings and bring them with you – I want you to come with me on these calls tonight.'

"What me? I'm tired. Haven't had any sleep since this thing started. What d'you want *me* for?"

'Witness to things said and done,' Bland said curtly. 'Now tell me about Polly Lines.'

'She was murdered. Hit on the head first, and then suffocated. If the girl had given the alarm a bit later, we might never have known about it. But now that we do know, what have we got?'

'No word of van Dieren or anyone else having been on the scene this afternoon?'

'Not a word or a sign. How did you get on over the old man being popped off? Any clues?'

'There are a few things, but nothing important or decisive. Tracy made a lot of fuss about van Dieren – he was there this afternoon and behaved suspiciously – but I don't know. I'm being led to a conclusion I don't like at all, Filby. I don't believe it's true, either, but I can't get away from it,' He stared at Filby. 'I wish I could understand about Jones.'

'If you ask *me,* Jones was an absolute and complete red herring,' Filby said. He fumbled for a handkerchief in his coat sleeve, failed to find it, and wiped his nose with the back of his hand. 'I can't see he links up with anything. He's been put in simply to exercise your brains.'

Bland was still staring at Filby, with his eyes wide. 'My God I wonder if that's it.'

'What's what?' Filby asked, bewildered by the fact that his remarks were taken so seriously.

'Shut up, Filby. I must think.' Bland sat down at his desk, and put his head on his hands. Filby looked at him with complete incomprehension. When the Inspector looked up two or three minutes later, his eyes were shining. 'I believe it is,' he said softly. 'I believe that's the way it's being worked. Talking to you does me good, Filby.'

Filby beamed. 'Talking to you does me good, too,' he said handsomely, and Bland was momentarily disconcerted.

'I don't know that it's necessary to pay those calls now – but perhaps we'd better. After all, I may be wrong.' He walked over to the window. 'The fog is lifting.'

'Who are you going to call on?'

'As many people as we have time for – Bond, Sinclair, Carruthers, Tracy, Mrs Rogers, pretty well everyone connected with the case. And we must certainly pay a visit to van Dieren's house. That may be useful.'

'We shall never get round London tonight.'

'We certainly shan't if we don't start soon.' Bland said cheerfully. 'I'll pay a call on my friend Sinclair first, and you wait downstairs – I shan't want you with me for that interview.'

Chapter Twelve *7.00 to 7.20 p.m.*

'I must say,' Sinclair said, 'I think you were awfully rude.'

'That was partly tactical, and partly that I felt sour,' Bland said. 'It did seem to me that one of you should have put a spoke in Tracy's wheel, and that you could have done it. But it also seemed to me that it would ease a difficult situation if I got a little tough.' He sipped reflectively, and looked at the amber liquid in his glass, then at his surroundings. His eyes moved from the early Picasso and Rouault reproductions, to the Finnish wood tables and chairs, the plain maroon carpet, and finally came to rest on the flickering glow of the fire. 'This is a pleasant flat. Do you look after yourself?'

Sinclair laughed. 'I'm not so industrious, or so domesticated, as all that. These are service flats – a woman comes in and does for me. This is her evening off. And my brother lives here with me, and lends a hand. My elder brother,' he said, as Bland raised eye brows in surprise. 'Ten years older than I am – before your time at school. He's a stock jobber.' With no change of tone, and with his usual bright smile, Sinclair said, 'I'm in the top class of suspects now, I suppose?'

'Why?'

Sinclair's grin was engaging. 'It seems to me that in what may be called the Case of the Poisoned Sherry there are only five starters – the people who went in the room and had a chance to poison the sherry. Van Dieren, Weston, Bond, Sinclair, Richard – you pays your money, gentlemen, and you takes your choice.

And since you seem to think it's not van Dieren, can you wonder that my collar feels uncomfortably tight, especially when you snap at me because I didn't stop one of our directors from sending home a member of the staff?'

'I didn't say it wasn't van Dieren – in fact, I'm prepared to agree that he seems to have had the best chance of dropping the poison in the sherry. I simply pointed out that there's no cast-iron case against him.'

'Have you seen van Dieren – has he offered any explanation?'

'If he explains, it will be at Scotland Yard,' Bland said grimly. 'His so-called art agency was a cover for selling dirty drawings – but, somehow, I don't feel we shall see friend van Dieren again until we look for him.' He told Sinclair what they had found at Old Bridge Street. 'Now, he may or may not have killed this girl, but he almost certainly knows the game is up at Old Bridge Street, and he won't go back there. There are only two explanations of his conduct – either he's the murderer, in which case we've got to find a genuine motive and link between him and the Hargreaves family – or he's acting for the murderer, without knowing what he's doing. If we adopt that second idea, then the window might have been smashed deliberately, and the fire started deliberately, to throw suspicion on van Dieren. But if that's so, I wouldn't be much inclined to take out an insurance policy on van Dieren's life – from the murderer's point of view, he'll have served his purpose, and can now be eliminated.'

'What about these drawings – is there any clue in them?'

'They're signed ARTES. Does that suggest anything to you?'

Sinclair pondered. 'Not unless the artist's initials are RTS. Is it an anagram or something?'

'Something like that, I think. But I don't know that it has anything to do with the murder.'

'So we're left with the problem of the five suspects,' Sinclair said. He poured more sherry in Bland's glass. 'It's narrowed down now, isn't it, to one of the five people who, if Miss Peachey is telling the truth, went in the room and had the opportunity of poisoning the sherry. Or do you think there was an unseen person? – like someone in a John Dickson Carr locked-room mystery?'

'There was no unseen person.'

'Then it was one of those five people?'

'It was one of those five people.' Bland drank his sherry at a gulp, under Sinclair's disapproving eye, and stood up. 'Look for the question of motive – and remember that the obvious is very often the truth.' As Bland put his hand on the door, the handle turned from the outside, and a man came in. He was an older edition of Sinclair, with the same tall, graceful figure, the same fair hair and bright blue eyes, but with a gravity that contrasted sharply with Sinclair's air of slight irresponsibility. 'I beg your pardon, Charles,' he said. 'I had no idea you were engaged.'

'This is my brother Edgar – genius of the Stock Exchange. Edgar, this is Inspector Bland, who was at school with me, but is none the less just about to arrest me for poisoning my employer's sherry.' With a friendly grin, Sinclair said, 'Have a drink?'

Bland's last impression was of Edgar Sinclair saying, in a voice that sounded as if he had a plum in his mouth, 'I do trust you are joking, Charles. Thank you, I do not think I will have a drink.' When he got outside, Bland saw with some pleasure that visibility had improved. After lending its assistance to the murderer during the afternoon the fog, he reflected, was now obligingly giving the police a hand. He got into his car, and sat for a moment at the wheel. 'Carruthers,' he said. 'Yes, next, I think, Carruthers. But I must pick up Filby.'

Chapter Thirteen *8.00 to 8.30 p.m.*

Mansfield Court was a small block of flats in dirty red brick, just off Balham High Street. It had an air of genteel dinginess, the hall was badly lighted, there was no porter and no lift. Rows of numbered doors ran along either side of an uncarpeted corridor. Number 73 was on the first floor. When Bland knocked there was silence for a moment, and then he heard a key turn in a lock. It might have been half a minute afterwards that the door opened and the figure of Carruthers, collarless and a little flustered, stood in the doorway. He took a step back when he saw Bland and Filby behind him, and an expression of dismay showed on his face. He said, with an attempt at composure, 'I was just having supper. Come in.' He waved apologetically to, a table where bread and cheese and half a beetroot lay like a still-life. 'I should like to ask you to share it, but you see my meal is simple. If you'd care for some bread and cheese – or some coffee – He began to flutter towards the door. 'This is my little kitchenette– '

'No thank you.' Bland's tone was not pleasant. He took from under his arm the drawings Filby had found in van Dieren's office, and put them on the table. 'I believe these are your work.'

'Mine?' Carruthers gasped. He almost danced round the table in his excitement and alarm. After a first horrified glance he made no attempt to touch or look at the drawings. 'Not *mine* – you must be mistaken – these have nothing to do with me.'

'Come now, do not be ashamed of your handiwork. I am no art expert, but these seem to be competently done.' Bland's voice was menacing. He pointed to the signature, and said softly, 'ARTES. Doesn't that mean anything to you?'

'Certainly not.' Carruthers' eyes were wild.

'Next time, use another pseudonym. It doesn't need a cryptographer to discover that the letters A-R-T-E-S in that order are alternate letters of your surname, beginning with the second and ending with the tenth. If further evidence is needed, I imagine our art experts can provide it.'

'Further evidence.' Carruthers sat down suddenly, and his face white. 'You don't mean you're going to prosecute me?'

'You acknowledge that these are your work? I'm asking you in front of a witness.

'I – I don't know – you must realise my position, Inspector – '

'Do you admit it?'

'Yes,' Carruthers said, and looked away.

'All right. You understand that the dissemination of this kind of stuff is punishable by law? If you want to avoid that, you'd better answer some questions. Truthfully, this time.'

Carruthers' voice was muffled. 'Anything. I've been a fool, I know, but – '

'When did you start doing these things? Who put you in touch with van Dieren?'

'It all began eighteen months ago – '

'Just about the time van Dieren set up in business, in fact?'

Carruthers seemed disconcerted. 'I don't know. Was it? It may not have been so long.'

'Did you know him before he took over this business?'

'No, no.' He shook his head emphatically. 'I think it was soon after he'd started up. I was very hard up at the time – you see the style in which I live.' He waved a hand round the tiny flat with its worn blue carpet and hideous furniture. 'It's not easy to make a living and stay free and independent. It's an important

176

thing to be independent,' he said, and looking at his wistful, weak blue eyes, Bland recognised him as a type of the defeated artist, the sensitive man who has not the capacity or the strength of will to produce a work of art.

'Did you ask Hargreaves to help you?'

'I'd rather starve,' Carruthers said, and the detective was surprised by the violence of his tone. 'You know what they say about him – he throws his money about like a man throwing fly-paper. My God, no. I asked him for money once, and he gave it me, but the way he did it – I'd never ask him for money again.'

'It was while I was on my beam ends that someone told me about this man van Dieren, and that he'd pay good money for stuff like this.'

'Who told you?'

Carruthers said readily enough. 'Somebody named McGillivray, in an advertising agency. But he died last year, so you can't ask him about it. Well, I started working for van Dieren, and he paid me – not very much, but a good deal more than I'd been getting. He always paid me by cash – said it was better that way. I used to take the things up, wrapped in brown paper, and give them to that girl Polly Lines – she knows all about it, of course,' he said spitefully. 'Van Dieren tried to browbeat me, and I wouldn't stand for that. You've got to preserve your independence – it's what I've been trying to do all my life.' His mouth set in a weak but obstinate line.

'You choose a queer way of doing it,' Bland said coolly. 'Did van Dieren ever ask you anything about the Hargreaves offices?'

'The Hargreaves offices?' Carruthers echoed, on a note of surprise. 'Why, no; he said something about how badly EH had treated him – I told you about that.'

'He didn't ask about a bottle of sherry, and where it stood in Edward Hargreaves' room? You didn't tell him anything about that?'

'Good Lord, no.' Carruthers was staring in astonishment. 'What on earth made you think so?'

Bland did not answer. 'When I saw van Dieren he chuckled, and said he was going to see you. Last night you told me he'd telephoned you, and you were seeing him today. What did he talk to you about?'

'I never saw him. He sent a telegram, telling me not to come. Here it is.' Carruthers took down a telegram, still in its orange envelope, from the mantelpiece, and handed it to Bland. The detective read: CANCEL ARRANGEMENT THIS AFTER-NOON SOMETHING CROPPED UP UNEXPECTEDLY GOING OUT LONDON FOR A FEW DAYS VAN DIEREN. The telegram had been handed in at 9.30 that morning. 'I had an appointment for half-past three this afternoon. But what's the matter – what's all the trouble about?'

'This afternoon Edward Hargreaves died in his office from drinking sherry that had been doctored by hyoscine. There is a strong possibility that your friend – ' Carruthers made a movement of protest ' – your *employer* van Dieren was responsible for the insertion of the hyoscine. This afternoon also van Dieren's offices were burnt down, and this girl, Miss Lines, found dead, under conditions which makes us suspect that she had been murdered. Your works of art were salvaged from the fire.'

Filby stuck his neck forward and spoke for the first time. 'Where were you this afternoon?'

'I was at home here, doing some work. But I can't prove it. I haven't an alibi, I'm afraid.' He smiled weakly. 'My best alibi is that I only benefit to the tune of a thousand pounds. EH told me that a long time ago. Not much reward is it? But, my God, what a terrible thing it is. Poor EH – what an end, after a life like his, to die from drinking doctored sherry.'

'When did you last go up to van Dieren's office?'

'Three or four weeks ago, I should think. I haven't been there since you said he was mixed up in Lionel's affair. I didn't want

178

to have anything to do with all that.' An earnest, pleading look was in Carruthers' eyes, and he made a motion towards the drawings on the table. 'What are you going to do about those things? For God's sake give me a chance. I swear I'll never touch this kind of thing again.'

Bland stood staring at the floor. Then he picked up the drawings, walked over to the small coal fire, and put them on the red coals. He held them there with the poker until they were ash. When he turned round there was tears in Carruthers' eyes. He started to speak, but Bland stopped him. 'There's no need to say anything. I've burnt those drawings because I'm looking for a murderer, not a petty crook, and some of the things you've told us may be useful. But if I find you playing about with this kind of thing again I'll crack down so smartly you'll be in prison inside twenty-four hours.'

When they were outside Filby said, 'It's something to have got those things cleared up, but you were too easy. He's a slimy little devil – why did you let him go?'

'He'll do us more good outside prison than in it. I think, with what we know now, we can really forget our other calls, but perhaps a visit to Bond may be useful.'

Chapter Fourteen *9.10 to 9.30 p.m.*

Bond's house in Highgate was a semi-detached two-storey house in a row of semi-detached two-storey houses. A step up, Bland thought, on Mansfield Court in social solidity, but still nothing very impressive – hardly a house that justified the air of a successful man that Bond maintained. The small iron gate creaked a little, and a light came on in the front room downstairs. A tall woman, running to fat, appeared in the doorway in answer to Bland's ring.

'Is Mr Bond in?'

'Who wants him?' Her voice was shrill. 'Anyway, he's not in. You'll find him at the Crown if you want him.'

'I'm a policeman,' Bland said, and he took a step backwards. 'There's nothing at all to be worried about, Mrs Bond. May we come in for a moment?'

'All right,' she said grudgingly, and Bland walked into a suburban sitting-room, filled with knick-knacks and photographs. Two armchairs were placed symmetrically in relation to an electric imitation coal fire. Lace curtains were at the window, and two pink basket chairs stood on a maroon carpet patterned in yellow. Bland sat down in one of the chairs, and Filby sat opposite him on the edge of another. Bland said enthusiastically, 'What a charming room. Have you lived here long?'

'Ten years.' In the light Mrs Bond was revealed as a big sulky -looking woman in her late thirties. She might have been handsome in a hard way ten years ago, but now she had a pronounced middle-aged spread. She wore no make-up. 'What do you want him for? Is anything wrong?'

'I simply want to ask him a question. Is he usually out at this time in the evening?'

She drew herself up. 'He certainly is *not*. Tonight's his night for going to play in the darts team, otherwise he's home as regular as clockwork every night. My old man may have his faults, but he's always regular coming home, though I won't say he's always in a good temper when he comes. But what's the question you want to ask?'

'After all, which of us hasn't got his faults?' Bland laughed pleasantly. 'Your husband was a bit late home tonight, though, wasn't he?'

She nodded. 'And his dinner in the oven for an hour and a half. But what did you want – ' She paused as the front door slammed. 'There he is now. They must have got the darts over quicker than usual.' They heard the clatter of a stick in the hall.

Bond was neither pleased nor surprised to see them. 'What's the trouble now? It's bad enough to be mixed up in a lot of bloody murders at the office without having them brought into your home. What do you want?'

His wife interpreted his mood correctly. 'Did you lose at darts?'

'Yes, I did. And who wouldn't lose at darts when they've been put on edge by a lot of people being shot and poisoned? And everyone asking questions about it down at the Crown. I wish I'd never gone down tonight.' He sat down and began to unlace his shoes.

'There are just two questions, and the first one is personal. Why do you use a stick for walking?'

Bond looked up with a startled and furious face, and then decided to laugh. 'Well, I don't know. Don't tell me you've got around to suspecting *me*. That's a bit too much of a good thing.'

'Why don't you tell them – show them you've got nothing to hide,' his wife said anxiously. She turned to Bland. 'He's always had – '

Bond turned on his wife. 'Shut up. I'll tell them all right and in my own way. I've had one leg shorter than the other since birth.'

'That's true.' His wife nodded solemnly. 'That's absolutely true. He should wear a surgical boot, but he won't.'

'You look a little doubtful, Inspector,' Bond said sardonically. 'Perhaps this will convince you.' He took off his sock and stood up. His left leg was smooth and white, and it was immediately apparent that it was a little shorter than the right.

'Thank you. Just one more question. When you went in to see Hargreaves at half-past three, was he smoking a cigarette?'

'I don't have to think much about that one,' Bond said. 'He wasn't. He was a non-smoker.'

'Thank you.' Bland got up and put on his hat. Filby got up, and put on his hat too, looking absolutely, bewildered. 'I'm sorry if I've been a trouble to you.'

Bond stared at him. 'Do you mean to say you came out here to ask those two questions? You must be crazy. I always thought the police force wasted a lot of public money, but this beats everything.'

'There *was* another reason, but I hardly like to mention it,' Bland said. 'We came here because I never can resist your sweet smile. Good night.'

Chapter Fifteen *9.30 to 10.30 p.m.*

'I can't make head or tail of all this,' Filby said. 'I understand why you wanted to know about his leg – to make sure he wasn't Jones – but what the devil was all that about a cigarette? What does it matter whether Hargreaves was smoking or not?'

'It doesn't matter – I just said that to give him something to take his mind off the other question. But it might matter that Bond is a good family man, who comes home punctually in the evening. I didn't care much for his wife, but I don't think she was lying about that. What are the other names on our list?'

'Tracy, Mrs Rogers, Richard Hargreaves, Eve Marchant, van Dieren, Weston. Shall we go and see Eve Marchant?'

'I think not. Telephone the Yard, and see if there's any news of van Dieren.'

'Okay.' Filby returned in five minutes. 'Not a trace,' he said cheerfully. 'They're keeping a watch on his flat in Earl's Court, but he's not turned up. Smelt a rat all right.'

'Let's have a look at his flat, and then call it a night.' He put the car into gear, and then swung away from the kerb.

'Why don't we call on Tracy?'

'If you tell me how he could have poisoned the sherry, we'll go along and see him.'

'Then the murderer did go into the room?'

'Of course he did.'

'I don't see why you can't simply tell me who it is, if you think you know.'

'I don't tell you, because this is still all purely theoretical. I'm still in need of proof. If my ideas are right, this story is so astonishing that nobody will believe it without proof. It's possible that I shall find some of the things I'm looking for at van Dieren's flat. Or I may find that I'm making a big mistake – but I don't think I am.' Filby lapsed into a sulky silence which he preserved until they reached Earl's Court. There, in a narrow street of small shabby houses, Bland stopped the car, and they got out. 'Where's – oh, there you are, Hemming.' A man who had been concealed in the shadow said, 'Evening, Inspector. Good thing the fog's cleared. Couldn't see much before that.'

'But you're sure no one's been in the house?' Bland's voice was sharp.

'No doubt about that. It's the second on the right, dirty little place it looks. No back entrance and no garden.'

'Did you make enquiries about van Dieren in the neighbour-hood?'

'Ridley did that, sir. Seems nobody knows much about him – bit of a mystery man, and they didn't see much of him. Used to come home late, and go out early. One thing that may be interesting – a girl used to come home with him sometimes – somebody saw her leave about two o'clock one morning.'

'What did she look like?'

'Only a vague report, but they saw she was short and fair.'

'Polly Lines,' Bland said thoughtfully. 'Good work, Hemming. Filby and I are going in now, and we shall probably be half an hour. Who's on with you?'

'Peplow, sir. He's down the road.'

'If anybody approaches while we're in there follow them and stop them from coming in. Then let me know.' They moved silently along the pavement, and turned in at the second house on the right. Even in the dim light of a street lamp they could see that the windows were dirty, and that paint was flaking off the door. Bland produced a bunch of keys and fiddled with the lock. Behind him Filby was breathing heavily. 'Shall I do it?'

'If you'll stand to the left so that I have a little light,' Bland said rather irritably, 'I may be able to – ' He stopped, for one of the keys had unlocked the door, and it had swung open with a slight creak. 'Now, first of all let's make sure there's no one here.'

'Dead, you mean?'

'Dead, drugged, or alive and kicking.' They searched the house. There were two small rooms and a scullery on the ground floor, and two rooms on the first floor, and it did not take them long to discover that there was certainly no one in the house. When they had finished, Filby pushed his hat to the back of his head and looked at Bland, with an expression of astonishment. 'This is a damned rum go if you like. What the devil does it mean?'

'Let's have another look at these rooms downstairs.' The sitting-room was decorated with a dark-blue paper covered with magenta flowers. A piece of dirty hair carpet was on the floor, and the furniture consisted of a small dark wooden table, an old padded easy-chair, and a bookcase containing some dozen books in brown-paper wrappers. The bedroom contained a divan bed, with the bedclothes made, an inset cupboard, and a chest of drawers. Both cupboard and chest of drawers were empty. In the scullery they found crockery on a small dresser, stale bread in a bin, and some liver sausage in a small blue safe. The upstairs rooms were covered in dust, contained no furniture at all, and were plainly unused. The small table in the sitting-room and the chest of drawers in the bedroom looked remarkably clean among the surrounding dirt. Curtains that were almost black with dirt covered the windows in sitting-room and bedroom, screening them from the road.

'What a bloody awful place to live,' Filby said, and shivered. 'And what an empty one too. No secrets here.'

'No bodies, you mean.' Bland's eyes were gleaming. 'The place is full of secrets. One, the mystery of the missing clothes. Two, the mystery of the polished furniture. Three, the mystery of the paper-covered books. Why did he put those books in paper covers?'

'Perhaps he was fussy about them.'

'If you can judge by the dirt, that's the last thing he was. But let's have a look at them.' Bland opened one, and his eyebrows went up. *Justine* – the Marquis de Sade.' He opened another. *'The One Hundred and Twenty Days of Sodom* – more de Sade. *Miss Smith's Torture Chamber*. There's one mystery cleared up – anyone would want to keep these in brown-paper wrappers. But it's curious that van Dieren's own tastes should be pornographic, like the things he sold, don't you think?'

'I can't see anything curious about it. If he wasn't interested in the damned stuff he wouldn't have started selling it, or asked that little pip Carruthers to do it for him in the first place.'

'You're perfectly right, of course.' Bland tapped his teeth. 'And yet I feel it's suggestive. Doesn't it suggest anything to you, Filby?'

'No.'

Bland sighed. 'Then take the most mysterious thing. Where are van Dieren's clothes? It's clear that since he lived here he must have kept them here. Did he take them away himself this morning, with the intention of skipping – or did someone else remove them, and why? For that matter, why did van Dieren do it? What could his clothes tell us about him that we don't know already? And then the polished table and chest of drawers, and the neatly-stacked washing-up, compared with the surrounding dinginess. Don't those points add up to something?'

Filby pushed his hat to the back of his head. 'They add up to a headache. The whole case adds up to a headache.'

Bland opened the front door. 'I want men kept on here in case van Dieren should turn up, though I don't think he will.

And get the place fingerprinted in the morning. We may get something out of that.'

'Did you find out what you wanted?'

'I found what I expected, but I don't know that it does any good. We need our small piece of luck now to clinch the case.'

SATURDAY, JANUARY 18 to
SATURDAY, FEBRUARY 1

Bland's attitude and activities during the next fortnight bewildered Filby, who became doubtful at times whether the Inspector was not losing his grip on the case. At first he was keen, and nervously anxious for news; as days went by without any dramatic development, it seemed to Filby that he became gloomy about the case though he seemed less to show gloom than an apathetic lack of interest in what was happening. Nor did some of his enquiries seem to Filby to make very good sense.

The first of these activities, which Bland put in hand with a good deal of enthusiasm, was to issue a warrant for van Dieren's arrest on a charge of murder. 'Murder?' Filby said. 'So it was van Dieren – I said so all the time.' Bland was non-committal. 'We've certainly got enough evidence to call him in, and if he's innocent this may make him show up. I want a special watch kept on ports – it's most important that he shouldn't get out of the country. And the papers can splash it as much as they like – but perhaps I'd better see to that myself.' And he did see to it, so that headlines like HUE-AND-CRY FOR VANISHED ART AGENT and ADVERTISING MURDERS: POLICE WATCH PORTS appeared in the *Howl* and *Shout*. 'He'll not get out of the country,' Filby said confidently. But he was not so confident when some days had passed without anything being seen of van Dieren. Dozens of reports of people seen 'answering the description of the wanted man' (a description provided by Bond and Carruthers, and checked by Bland from his recollection of the art agent) were followed up without success.

Nor was there any success with the fingerprinting of van Dieren's little house. There were very few fingerprints, and it became obvious that the table and chest of drawers found in the cottage, and some of the kitchen utensils, had been carefully cleaned and polished so that there were no prints at all on them. A few prints were found elsewhere, some of them on the books in the brown-paper covers: but these proved to be the prints of Polly Lines. No other prints were found in the cottage. This worried Bland more than Filby. As the tall man very reasonably said, why worry about prints when they hadn't got van Dieren? And when they got van Dieren they would hardly need the prints. But this argument did not make Bland less depressed.

It was on the first day of this dreary fortnight that Bland, to Filby's surprise, put a man on to trailing Richard Hargreaves. 'I told him a couple of days ago that he's in a dangerous situation,' Bland said, and when Filby asked why, the Inspector merely smiled and said facetiously, 'Isn't marriage always a dangerous project?' The reports of the men who trailed Richard, however, made dull reading. His days were fully occupied at the office, where, they learned from Sinclair, he was working surprisingly hard, and with surprising enthusiasm, to fit himself for the post which he now occupied as head, and in fact owner, of the Agency. 'Where he had been lackadaisical he was now energetic; where he had once confessed ignorance with a shrug of the shoulders, he now showed himself keen to learn. His evenings were spent with Eve Marchant, in a round of dinners, cinemas and theatres. He did no entertaining, and drank very little.

Most of the other instructions Bland gave him seemed to Filby very curious. The telegrams to New York, Paris and Amsterdam, asking whether anyone answering the name or description of Joseph van Dieren was known to them, were, of course, more or less routine matters – and Bland seemed even slightly cheered when they were answered in the negative. Further enquiries to New York produced information regarding the mysterious Joe Riddell whose story van Dieren had told to Bland as his own. The Inspector did not seem particularly pleased or surprised when he learned that Joe Riddell, who had indeed served a sentence of two years' imprisonment for embezzlement in an affair in which a young man named Edward Hargreaves had been mixed up, died in 1933. He had been in prison several times on charges of embezzlement and fraudulent company promotion.

A mysterious line of enquiry which produced surprising but hardly useful results was an attempt to obtain some traces of van Dieren's past activities. About these it seemed to Filby that Bland was unnecessarily and uncharacteristically fussy and irritable. He insisted, for example, on an elaborate investigation being made among all van Dieren's neighbours in Earl's Court to discover whether any of them recalled his personal habits, or remembered details of the visits of Polly Lines. Had anyone noticed van Dieren smoking a pipe or a cigarette when he came out in the morning? Did he carry an umbrella? How many times had Polly Lines been seen entering and leaving the house, and was there any indication whether or not she had stayed the night? How much milk did the milkman leave? Where did van Dieren get his groceries, and how often were they delivered? These were some of the extraordinary questions to which Filby found answers. The answers were all of them what might have been expected, and they did nothing to lift Bland's gloom. Very few people remembered van Dieren leaving his house – they had other things to think about – and nobody recalled him smoking a pipe or a cigarette, or using an umbrella. Polly Lines (or somebody answering her description) had been seen to enter the house some half-dozen times, and twice had been seen to leave in the early hours of the morning. Nobody remembered other visitors, and van Dieren was known as a man who kept himself to himself, and never talked about his business. The milkman left half a pint of milk every other day, and was paid at the end of the week. The groceries, delivered weekly, were such as it might have been expected a single man would order.

One curious thing was discovered when Bland ordered an investigation into the length of time that van Dieren had lived in the house, and occupied his office, and asked Filby to obtain the agreements. There was no agreement for the office, which had been rented monthly, but the house had been taken on a year's tenancy, and the house agent had a copy of the agreement. It was not, however, made out in the name of van Dieren, but in that of Polly Lines! Filby saw the house agent, who was able to remember quite clearly the letting of the house. Van Dieren had called on him, had inspected the house, and agreed to take it. He had paid a year's rent down, so that the agent, very pleased to let the place that was in a poor state of repair without doing any work on it, had made no enquiries about his financial status. And when the time came to sign the agreement, he had telephoned and said that for private reasons the agreement was to be made out in the name of Miss Lines. This had been done, and although the agent thought this a curious thing, he had thought it wise to ask no questions.

Bland received the news with more annoyance than he had yet shown over the hold-up in the case. 'He's a cunning devil.' He walked up and down his small office with furious impatience. 'If something doesn't break soon, Filby, I shall have to do something to make it break, and I don't want to do that.'

'I've got an idea about this agreement,' Filby said, and although Bland's raised eyebrows were not encouraging, he proceeded to unfold it. 'What's to have stopped them getting married?'

'Who?' Bland asked. He sounded quite startled.

'Van Dieren and Polly Lines. *There's* a reason why the agreement was made out in her name. She had some sort of hold over him, made him marry her, insisted on the agreement being in her name, so that she kept hold on his affairs. In the end he had to kill her to break the hold – some form of blackmail maybe, mixed up with the Hargreaves family. How's that?'

'Out,' Bland said, and laughed when Filby looked annoyed. On the same day the Inspector, who had spent a good part of the past two days sitting at his desk in what appeared to be a trance of inaction, got up and went out. When he came back he looked a little happier. 'I've been to see Myrtle Montague,' he said, 'to ask some more questions about her sister.'

'Did you ask whether she'd ever said anything about getting married?'

'I did, and she hadn't. Myrtle says she wasn't the marrying kind.' Filby looked disappointed. 'What she did say was that her sister told her once or twice that she was frightened of van Dieren, and that he did ever such funny things. When Myrtle asked what kind of things she giggled, and wouldn't say. Once she said she thought he was mad. Polly didn't tell her sister anything about staying at Earl's Court, although Myrtle knows she went there, from remarks she dropped at odd times. But Myrtle's quite certain that Polly never married van Dieren – she was too much afraid of him for that.'

Filby was not dismayed. 'It was an idea, anyway,' he said rather nastily, and it was certainly true that Bland had contributed nothing in the way of ideas lately. 'And here's another one, that's been going round in my brain for a day or two. Suppose van Dieren's dead.'

Bland was playing with his monkey paperweight. He did not say anything.

'If those early ideas of yours were right – and he's *not* the murderer after all, but some sort of – ' Filby reached for a word, and discovered it with some pride, ' – *scapegoat*, then he might have been bumped off. It's funny he's not turned up by now.' This was a week after the news had been splashed in the papers.

'Not so funny,' Bland said rather absently. 'Don't forget that there are indications that he planned a getaway, eliminated traces by which he thought we might follow him, and so on. It's one thing to go into hiding when you've made no preparation for it, and another to proceed according to an elaborate and well-laid plan.'

Filby was irritated. 'You don't seem to have any constructive suggestions.' Before Bland could reply the telephone bell rang, and he picked up his receiver. 'Sinclair? Show him in.' He turned to Filby a more cheerful face than he had shown for a couple of days. 'Prelude to action, I hope,' he said. 'I'll see him alone.'

Sinclair's bright handsomeness illuminated the drab room. 'So this is your cubby-hole,' he said, as he sat down. Bland laughed.

'Not quite so impressive as an advertising executive's office, I'm afraid.'

'But socially much more useful. I came in, like a faithful Watson, to see if there was any news on the case, and to give you one or two snippets, if you're interested. We've not seen you around the office lately.'

'I've been busy,' Bland said vaguely. 'Thinking and worrying. And I find this is the best place to do that. As for news, if you mean news of van Dieren, there just isn't any. He's vanished into thin air for the moment, but it's only a matter of time before we get him.'

Sinclair looked at him curiously. 'I suppose you're quite sure he's the murderer? But you're bound to say yes to that – after all, there's a warrant out for his arrest. But there are some pretty queer rumours floating round the office. I don't know if you're interested – '

'I'm always interested in rumours.'

'I don't know where to begin,' Sinclair pondered, frowning. 'And I hardly know where the rumours started. But it's about Dick Hargreaves. Should I be right in thinking that there's a hell of a strong circumstantial case against Dick?'

'You might be. Let's hear it.'

'Point one – as Bond said to me a couple of days ago – *cui bono*? And Richard certainly profits, whereas it's hard to see that van Dieren or anyone else does, or did. From being a humble younger son, rather out of the limelight, he's become sole owner of a big advertising agency, and worth a hell of a lot of money.

'Next this is a bit intangible, but it's been noticed by most of the people who come in contact with him – there's been a change in Dick since EH died. He's much more pleasant, works harder, even seems a bit less of a pansy. I dare say that's partly the influence of Eve Marchant, and it's certainly all to the good. But somehow – so soon after EH's death – although nobody loved EH, people don't like it.'

'I see.' Bland was looking at the paperweight on his desk. 'There's nothing else – nothing more tangible?'

'Only the fact that Dick is going to marry this girl very soon. Nobody likes that – it leaves a bad taste in the mouth. But he seems to have been completely under her thumb.'

Bland was looking depressed. 'Any other developments?'

'Only a bit more marriage news. Tracy and Mrs Rogers. Her husband's agreed to divorce her at last. I'm very pleased – they're both nice people.' Sinclair's forehead crinkled as he leaned forward. 'Look here, it *is* van Dieren, isn't it? I've been puzzling my brain trying to work out what you told me a few days ago. You as good as said you knew the name of EH's murderer.'

'I do.' Bland's voice was impersonal.

'And he was one of the people who went into EH's room that afternoon?' Bland nodded. 'Then it *must* have been van Dieren. I can't see that anyone else had a chance to do it.'

'I haven't said it wasn't van Dieren. There's a warrant out for his arrest, you know.' Bland got up from his desk, and took his hat and coat. 'Thank you for the news. I've got to pay a call now.'

'Something to do with the case?'

'A call on Eve Marchant.'

In the sitting-room of the flat in Catherine Street two tall french windows reached almost to the ground. The thin January light came through them and showed the furniture that was too new, the china dogs standing on the mantelpiece, and the gay chintz curtains. Eve Marchant stood by the french windows and said, 'When are you going to catch this wretched man, Inspector? Not, personally, that I could care less.'

'You aren't interested in the arrest of your husband's murderer?'

She waved her hands. 'I don't think of him as my husband any more. Dick and I are going to be married soon, probably next week.' In her shrill voice she said, 'I don't see why we should put it off. Let people talk – I don't care what they say.'

'Don't you think you should tell him?'

'Tell him what?'

Bland looked at her unlined, smooth white neck, where a muscle was throbbing. 'About the little stranger. I know he's a nice chap, and you think you've got him taped, but he won't be very pleased if he finds out afterwards.'

She stared at him without saying anything. An ormolu clock on the mantelpiece ticked through the silence. He said, 'If you're wondering how I know, let's be frank and say that I don't. But anyone can make a guess. You wouldn't have got Lionel tight and made him marry you unless you had some very good reason. Your friend Myrtle Montague used those exact words – a very good reason – and giggled over them. She didn't give you away – she told me she couldn't say what the reason was, because it was a secret, but one doesn't have to think very long or hard to discover it. You knew Lionel wasn't the sort of man who would give you what you wanted, you knew he'd never live with you or give you a home, but you thought you might be able to use the fact that you were married to him and that you were going to bear his child as a lever to work on his father. When you saw the way in which Lionel behaved you saw it was no use hoping for anything from him, and you turned to Richard. After Lionel was murdered and you saw what EH was like, you saw that you could never convince him of the truth of your story. It became imperative then that you should marry Richard as soon as possible.'

He thought that he had never seen her look more beautiful. She stood facing him, with her dark eyes staring, her hand gripping and twisting a paper spill, and the pulse throbbing in her neck. When she spoke she made no attempt to deny his assertion, but said simply, 'What business is it of yours?'

Bland's voice was quiet and friendly. 'It's not my business, and I'm sorry to hurt you by talking about it. But it's a piece of the puzzle, and I want you to tell me that it's true.'

'You're a good guesser. But not quite good enough, Mr Police Inspector.' I've lost another friend, Bland thought. She doesn't love me any more. 'I've told Dick already. He knows about it, and it doesn't make any difference. I told him, if you want to know, on the day he announced that we were going to be married.'

'I'm glad, Bland said. 'Will you believe me when I say I'm sorry – '

She put her hand on her hip and struck a pose reminiscent of any bad actress playing the part of outraged but contemptuous virtue. 'No, I won't. It's no use trying any of your smarmy civility on me, do you understand that? I don't like insignificant little police sneaks. There's the door, and you can get outside it now. I don't want to see you again.'

'I couldn't care less,' Bland said. At least, he thought, when he was out in the street, she had given him an exit line. Unfortunately, it was one that was not quite true.

Bland told Filby about this visit to Eve Marchant, and the tall man was incredulous. 'But what's he marrying her for? Do you think she's telling the truth, and she has told him about it? Are you going to ask him and find out?'

'I don't think she'd try to bluff by saying she had told him when she hadn't. Too dangerous. And as the reason for why he's marrying her, don't forget that she's a very beautiful woman. This guess helps to get a bit of the puzzle out of the way, that's all.'

Filby was disappointed. 'You don't think it's got anything to do with van Dieren or the murders, then?'

'Not directly. Is there any news on van Dieren, by the way?'

'Nothing, and if you ask me there won't be. Somebody's knocked him off.' Half an hour late Filby was dumbfounded when news came through that a man answering van Dieren's description, and giving that name, had been arrested in Liverpool, while boarding a ship for New York. Bland took the news coolly, but he left for Liverpool on the next train. While he was away, Filby read with some disgust more reports by the detectives put on to trail Richard Hargreaves, who was still living a blameless and uninteresting life, read the answers to *The Times* crossword puzzle on the previous day, compared them with the clues and still failed to understand them, disposed of several false reports of people who claimed to have seen van Dieren, and received another negative report from the men who were trying, so far unsuccessfully, to trace the purchase of the hyoscine. His spirits were maintained, however, by the thought that van Dieren had been taken and they were even raised during the afternoon by a visit from Myrtle Montague. He received her in Bland's office, and she seemed disappointed not to see the Inspector.

'He's away today,' Filby said easily. 'But anything you can tell him you can tell me. I'm his right-hand man.'

She looked a little doubtful, but she said, 'It's simply that I've remembered something. I mean I forgot to tell Mr Bland something, and as I thought it might he important, I thought I'd drop in. I've never been at Scotland Yard before, you see.'

Filby beamed. 'What do you think of it?'

'*Super.*' She looked round. 'But this is a poky office. Yours, I suppose?'

'Certainly not.' Filby was more indignant than if it had really been his own office. 'This is the Inspector's room. What was it you wanted to tell him?'

'He came round to see me the other day – I must say he's ever so nice – and he was asking me what poor Polly said about that beast who killed her.' Filby took in suddenly the significance of her demure black dress, with its edge of white at the throat. 'And I told him that she said van Dieren sometimes did funny things and had funny habits, and then he asked me if she ever said what things and *what* habits, and I said she'd never mentioned any.' She paused to take a breath. 'That wasn't right. She *did* mention one thing.'

'Is that so?' Filby affected a little indifference, and pushed the Inspector's chair on to its back legs, as Bland did.

'She said he was so much afraid of soiling his hands that he always wore gloves at home.'

'Gloves.' Filby let down the chair with a hump that certainly was not typical of Bland. 'He wore gloves.'

'That's what Polly said. Is it so important?'

Filby's eyes were bulging, and he rubbed a slightly bristling cheek quickly with his hand. 'I should think it is.' He said craftily, 'She didn't say anything about the colour of the gloves.'

'I don't – think – so. She was always hinting that she could tell me terrible things about him, but she never said what they were. I'm sorry.'

'Not at all. You've been most helpful.' Filby showed her out with a vast and uncharacteristic beam spread over his features, and she stared at him as if he were a lunatic. Then he sank back into Bland's chair and began to tap his teeth with the Inspector's pencil. This, he thought, will certainly be something to ask van Dieren when the Inspector brings him back.

But he was wrong, for when Bland came in next day, as neatly dressed and as gloomy as ever, it was to say that the arrested man was not van Dieren, or not the right van Dieren. He was a perfectly respectable Dutch commercial traveller, who bore a slight resemblance to the wanted van Dieren in height, age and build, and who had booked a passage in the name of van Dieren for the very good reason that it was his own name. He was furiously angry that he had been detained and had missed his ship, and complicated explanations and elaborate apologies had been necessary. The Dutch Embassy had been called into the matter, and further explanations had been made to them. All this had not made Bland lose his temper, but it had not made him happy.

He listened to Filby's excited description of Myrtle Montague's recollections without visible pleasure. At the end of them he said only. 'It's a pity she couldn't remember that before.'

'But don't you see what it means,' Filby cried. 'It means van Dieren and Jones are the same person after all.'

'It doesn't necessarily mean that, I'm afraid. It only shows that van Dieren had something to hide, and that was plain as soon as we found that there were no prints in his house. It's obvious that he must have taken good care that they should be eliminated. But we can't deduce from this that there's any *proof* of his identity with Jones. Remember, if van Dieren *isn't* guilty, then someone's been framing him as the murderer from the word go. If he is guilty, and if he masqueraded as Jones, you still have to explain his apparent foolishness in drawing attention to himself by making that telephone call.'

Before Filby could reply, a policeman brought in two letters and put them on Bland's desk. The Inspector looked at one of them, after he had opened it, with such an expression of concentrated attention that Filby asked, 'What is it?' Bland passed it over without saying anything. It was an invitation to the wedding reception of Richard Boynton Hargreaves and Eve Marchant, to be held at Johnson's Hotel at one o'clock on the following Wednesday, the fifth of February. Filby was surprised to see that the Inspector's eyes were sparkling with an eagerness that had been missing from them for a few days. 'I think this is what we've been waiting for, Filby.'

'You mean that there's something special about this wedding that will bring van Dieren out of hiding?'

Bland laughed and then nodded. He was looking out of the window, and from between his lips came a singularly tuneless and dreary whistle. 'He must alter the place of the wedding reception. It must be at the house in Redfern Square.'

'Where his brother was killed?' Filby's eyebrows went up. 'He'll never do that.'

'He must do it. The solution of the case may depend on it.' Bland brought his fist down with a crack on the table. 'I must go and see him. We're on the last lap now, Filby.' He put on his trilby hat and his raincoat. When he went out he was still whistling.

WEDNESDAY, FEBRUARY 5

Chapter One *9.30 to 12.00 a.m.*

Early on Wednesday morning Miss Berry left the sham-Tudor house in Pinner where she lived with her mother and father, and went round to the almost identical sham-Tudor house where her friend Miss Peachey, the receptionist lived with *her* mother and father. The Peachey family stood on a rather higher social level than the Berry family, because Miss Peachey's father was a bank manager whereas Miss Berry's father was an electrical engineer, who worked with his hands; but Miss Peachey and Miss Berry did not allow these social differences to influence their friendship. They had already gone over pretty thoroughly the ground of Richard Hargreaves' marriage, canvassing it from almost every possible aspect, but it was the kind of subject that can never really be exhausted, and when Miss Berry had admired the rather startling fur-trimmed coral coat and matching dress that Miss Peachey was wearing (though privately she thought that her own sober black coat and neat pale-blue crêpe dress with the lace collar were far more appropriate to the occasion) they settled down happily to a half-hour's gossip before catching the train up to town.

'It's easy enough,' Miss Berry said, 'to see that *she's* just after his money, but what I can't understand is how *he* can be so taken in.'

Miss Peachey, it has already been indicated, was a girl of shrewd common sense, and she now made a common sense remark, which she had made several times before. 'There's more

203

in this than meets the eye. I don't mind telling you, Rhoda, that if we hadn't been given the day off and practically ordered to attend the reception, I shouldn't be going.'

'What *do* you mean, darling?' Miss Berry asked, although she knew very well what her friend meant.

'Why do they want to get married when his father and brother are only just in the grave? And she married to the brother, too. And then to hold the reception in the very house where his brother was killed. It's a regular scandal, Rhoda, and you know it.' Miss Berry shrugged her shoulders to, imply that, after all, it was the way of the world, but she made no attempt to contradict her friend. Miss Peachey turned round from the mirror in which she was putting the finishing touches to her complexion, and waggled a powder-puff at her friend. 'I shouldn't wonder if they *have* to be married.'

'Do you really think so?' Miss Berry breathed. It was a fascinating speculation.

'Indeed I do.' Miss Peachey drew a delicate cupid's bow over her upper lip. 'She was married to Lionel, we all know that – but suppose she was carrying on with Richard all the time.'

Even the gravity of the speculation could not prevent Miss Berry from giggling. 'I've never thought Richard was that kind of a man.'

Miss Peachey scraped a fleck of lipstick off a tooth. 'Every man is that kind of man.' She pointed dramatically at the window. 'Look, it's beginning to rain.' The day was indeed exceptionally dark, and a few heavy drops of rain were falling out of the lowering sky. 'That's a bad sign,' Miss Peachey said with relish.

Mrs Bond regarded the whole affair as a nuisance, and her husband's insistence on pressing his dark-blue suit when she wanted to use the electric iron provoked her to say so. When she complained that he was making a lot of fuss about nothing, Bond hummed to himself, and went on pressing his trousers. At length he laid down the iron and spoke with what was, for him, extreme good humour. 'Look here, old girl, just keep your nose out of this, will you? I know what I'm doing.'

'I wish I did. I don't believe you're up to any good.'

'I'm not up to anything except trying to look smart so that the new Managing Director will notice me, and give me a rise.' Bond put on the trousers, still humming. 'Not but what it might be useful to find out how this marriage is linked up to the murders – it must be linked up somehow.'

'You mean so that you can tell the police?

'*That* for the police.' Bond spat accurately into the fire. 'You get nothing out of telling the police, and there's no taste in nothing. Besides, why should I tell that little rat anything, coming here and asking questions about my leg, and whether old man Hargreaves smoked cigarettes? No, my dear, anything I find out will be used for the exclusive benefit of yours truly. And I *have* found out one or two things already – or at least I've got my suspicions. I told you about Tracy and Mrs Rogers, didn't I?'

'But they're going to get married.'

'Ah, but they weren't going to when I spotted them – and old man Hargreaves wasn't dead then, either. I don't say there's anything in it, but you never know. And if I could find out anything about the reasons for this marriage – well, it might be useful.'

'Take care you don't burn your fingers.'

Have I ever burnt 'em yet?' Bond asked jauntily, as he pulled on his pointed patent-leather shoes.

Sinclair spent the morning at the office. Richard had announced that his wedding-day was to be a holiday, but Sinclair had a good deal of work to do, and took this chance of making up arrears. As he was one of the few people invited to the registry-office ceremony, he had dressed with a good deal of care, in a sober suit of clergyman grey, a white shirt and dark tie. The effect of these clothes was to make him look more like a film star than usual.

Soon after eleven o'clock he was surprised to hear footsteps moving down the corridor of the deserted offices. They stopped outside his door, and Bland came in, looking dapper and conventionally respectable. A keen eye might have noticed that his hair was brushed with particular care, that his nails had been recently manicured, and that his eyes were exceptionally bright and sharp. Sinclair greeted him with a smile, and slipped the papers he had in front of him into his desk. 'How did you know I was here?'

'Your brother told me when I telephoned this morning.' Bland sat down and looked at the flower in Sinclair's buttonhole. 'I've been invited to the reception, but not to the wedding. I see you've been more greatly honoured.' Sinclair nodded. 'And what do you think about it all?'

'I think they're damned fools not to wait a bit. I must have heard pretty well everyone in our office express shocked surprise about the way the marriage is being hurried through or the fact that she's marrying again into the same family, or the holding of the reception at Redfern Square. The three put together – well, I must say it does seem a bit steep, even to me.'

'Are there any rumours about the fact that the reception's not being given at a hotel?'

'The general view is that she's keen to hold it at Redfern Square, and that Richard's putty in her hands. Though I heard Carruthers the other day saying it was the family home, and perhaps that was why Richard wanted to hold it there. He's best man, you know – nearest relative and all that. By rights, of course, it should be *her* family that arranges the reception, but I gather there's no question of that – she prefers to forget her father and mother.' Sinclair leaned back in his chair. 'But what was it you wanted to see me about?'

'Partly to discover what you're telling me now – the way that people are thinking and feeling about it. Partly to tell you that I hope to break the case today. There may be some surprises at the reception.'

'Really.' Sinclair's face showed his pleasure. 'Do you mean that some fresh evidence has turned up? I was beginning to think you'd come to a dead end. Have you got van Dieren yet?'

'Not yet. But I'm hoping that this marriage may bring him into the open.'

'Out of the place where he's hiding, you mean?'

'You might put it that way.'

Eager and enthusiastic. Sinclair leaned across the desk. 'Tell me one thing – I can see you've come to a conclusion, in some way I can't fathom. Do you believe that van Dieren was responsible for EH's death?'

'Yes,' said Bland.

Carruthers got up late, and moved about his Balham flatlet humming the 'Wedding March'. He ate some toast and marmalade, drank three cups of coffee and read the morning paper until, looking at his watch, he discovered that it was a quarter past ten. He dressed in a hurry, telephoned Richard and apologised for being late, and set out for Redfern Square at a quarter to eleven.

Jean Rogers and Tracy had also been invited to attend the registry-office wedding. 'What I can't understand,' she said, as they set out from Hampstead in the car, 'is what Richard sees in her. I grant that she's attractive and all that, but then she really is *such* a tarty piece. I shouldn't have thought Richard would have cared for a tarty piece. But there – I suppose he's just bowled over.'

Tracy grunted from behind the wheel, and then said, 'She's very beautiful.'

'And has such a delightful voice,' said Jean Rogers, who was not without malice. 'And no doubt equally delightful parents – except that nobody has ever seen them.'

'You know what she says – her mother divorced her father, and then married again. Mother's in India, father's in South Africa. No particular reason to doubt it.'

'It's wonderfully convenient. Father and mother in East End, daughter in West End, is more likely, I should think.'

He pulled at his stiff collar. 'Really, you're uncommonly catty this morning. Don't forget what people might say about us. He that is without sin, you know.'

She put her hand on his arm. 'I know. I'm sorry. But I do dislike that woman.'

Mr Weston tapped the top of his egg and looked seriously at the elderly housekeeper who was pouring out his tea. 'Young Richard Hargreaves is getting married today.'

'I know, sir.' She pursed her lips. 'Saw it in the papers. Scandalous, I call it.'

'Rarely, I am bound to agree, can nuptials have been celebrated under less auspicious circumstances.' Mr Weston fished behind him, produced a large coloured handkerchief, and blew his nose with a honking noise. 'And you see also, Mrs Harrison, that Jupiter, or whoever rules upon Olympus, is concerned, like yourself, to express disapproval. In other words, it is raining. But let us hope, none the less, that this youngest member of an ill-fated house will contract a happier marriage than his brother.' He neatly sliced off the top of the egg and ate it. 'Perfectly done. I shall be attending the wedding reception, Mrs Harrison, and perhaps I shall bring back a piece of cake.'

'I don't believe I could eat it, sir – it'd choke me. It's my belief the two of them did in his poor father and brother. A scheming hussy that girl is, if half what they say is true. I believe she's been behind all these murders.'

Mr Weston dived further into his egg, and looked profoundly shocked. 'Such sentiments, my dear Mrs Harrison, should hardly be voiced within the privacy of these four walls.' He waggled his spoon at her. 'If I were to repeat them, now, to Mr

Hargreaves or Miss Marchant, who knows but that they might bring a suit against you for slander in which I should be regretfully compelled to testify against you.'

This elephantine playfulness was lost on his housekeeper. 'I don't care about any of that. And what's more, I shall always believe that that Richard – nasty effeminate young man he is – had something to do with the death of that poor Lily Hargreaves.'

There was a clatter. Mr Weston dropped his spoon on the floor. Mrs Harrison stooped and picked it up for him.

'Thank you,' he said. 'That will do, Mrs Harrison.'

And the actions and emotions of the bride and bridegroom on this momentous morning? They shall he left in obscurity with the hope that both Richard and Eve entertained all the feelings appropriate to a wedding-day.

Chapter Two *12.00 to 12.30 p.m.*

Richard Hargreaves slipped the ring on Eve Marchant's elegant third finger, and took her into his arms. Both of them were smiling happily. Carruthers tapped Richard on the shoulder and said, 'Best man's privilege – after you, old boy.' Richard still smiling, relinquished his wife, and Carruthers kissed her – not on the cheek, but on the mouth. Tracy, Mrs Rogers, and Sinclair gathered round to offer congratulations, which Eve accepted with a demure smile. The registrar beamed. They went outside in an atmosphere of rather forced heartiness and good fellowship, Eve, Richard and Carruthers walking ahead together, arm in arm, and the others following a few steps behind.

The day was still dark, with a thin, penetrating rain falling. They ran to get into the cars, Richard waved a hand, shouted 'See you later,' and they drove off in turn, Richard and Eve first in the new Lagonda that he had given her as a wedding present, Carruthers and Sinclair in a hired Buick, and Tracy and Mrs Rogers in Tracy's Morris. None of them saw a man sitting in a Ford V.8 on the other side of the road, reading a newspaper, who put in his clutch when the Lagonda had gone a few yards, and moved after it.

Neither Richard nor Eve spoke for five minutes, and then he said, 'Thank God that's over. It will be wonderful when we can leave all this, and get away by ourselves.' She simply looked at him, and placed her hand on his knee. 'Arnold seemed to kiss you rather enthusiastically.'

She laughed. 'Do you blame him, darling?'

'It's in the family tradition that you should marry a jealous husband,' he said, and then quickly put his hand on her as he saw her flinch. 'I'm sorry. I'd really forgotten for the moment about Lionel, and everything else. But don't worry – it will be over soon, and we shall be by ourselves.'

'I know. You're very sweet to me.' A genuine, incongruous tenderness sounded in her brassy voice, and she hesitated before she said, 'Darling – you know, I couldn't care less what people say – but do you think we shall have to stay long at this reception? I know it's going to be fiendishly difficult, and that all the women will he awfully catty. I really am dreading it.'

'I know.' Richard sounded a little hesitant. 'But I suppose I shouldn't dash off too quickly, now that I'm in sole charge at the office. You can disappear after half an hour, if it's too great a strain. Our plane for Paris doesn't go until six, you know.'

'There's no doubt she's a beautiful woman, but I wish Richard joy of her all the same. She's too beautiful to be true.' Carruthers laughed at his own joke. Sinclair was silent, and Carruthers said reflectively, 'It's certainly remarkable, the whole affair, and most imprudent. I advised against it, but I think she hurried Dick into it. It's certainly odd that she didn't bring any relative along to the wedding, isn't it? Of course, we all knew she wasn't out of the top drawer, but it rather looks as if she were out of the bottom.'

Sinclair was looking out of the window. He said without turning his head, 'Malicious,' and Carruthers coloured slightly, and stopped talking.

In the third car Jean Rogers was talking to Tracy. She had changed her mind about Eve Marchant. 'Do you know, I believe she'll make him a good wife.' She said this as if surprised by her own daring. 'I saw her looking at him in that certain way, and I think she's fond of him.' Tracy grunted. 'She's too beautiful for any other woman to look at her without feeling jealous – and I suppose a woman can't help being jealous in a sort of way of the fact that she's carried off this rich young man and is dashing away with him to a honeymoon in Paris – and she *has* got the most awful voice – but I believe she's fond of him, and I'll be prepared to throw my old shoe with a good heart when they drive away.'

'I suppose she's leaving the stage?'

'I doubt if Dick wants her to go doing that act in the chorus at the Splendid. In fact, I doubt if she wants to go on doing it herself.'

Tracy dexterously steered his way through half of a traffic jam. 'I wonder why the devil they're holding this reception at Redfern Square? There's something queer about that. Sends a bit of a shiver up my spine, I must say, when you remember what happened there last time.'

'I dare say that it was just the most convenient place.'

Tracy spoke emphatically. 'Whatever the reason, it's in damned had taste, and I don't like it.'

Chapter Three *1.00 to 1.45 p.m.*

From the first, the reception did not go well. Perhaps it was partly the day, heavy, cold, dark, with the thin rain persistently falling and a faint threat of snow in the whipping east wind; partly the fact that, by what seemed to be, as Tracy said to Jean Rogers, the very peak of bad taste, the reception took place in the very drawing-room in which the party had been held on the night of Lionel's death, with the folding-doors into the dining-room thrown open; perhaps the guests were disturbed by the fact that the newly-married pair seemed very obviously to find the occasion a severe strain on their nerves. Not all the people present, of course, had been there on that earlier occasion, but the uneasiness felt by the people from the Hargreaves Agency who had attended the other party communicated itself to the whole company. It seemed to spread even to the additional servants who were helping Jackson and Williams on this occasion, causing one of them to drop a tray of drinks, and another to spill a glass of sherry over Tracy's suit. Conversation was uncertain and uneven with silences punctuated by bursts of laughter like the clatter of gunfire before a battle.

Among those people, almost all of whom seemed to be waiting for something to happen, Richard and his wife moved with a discomfort that grew steadily with the uneasiness of their guests. Richard was not, indeed, an inattentive host, but he seemed to be conscious that he moved in an atmosphere of disapproval and coldness which in one or two cases was hardly concealed. This hostility was even more apparent towards Eve, who had only one or two acquaintances in the room. The men were altogether too friendly to her, while some of the women, who had known Lionel Hargreaves and his father, were barely civil. Sinclair, who had seen nothing of what was going on, said to her. 'Can I get you a drink? I'm afraid all this must be rather a strain.'

'Nothing to drink, thank you.' She clasped her hands. 'Strain isn't the word. I never knew women could be so catty. It's these friends of the family who're the worst. Some awful old spinster sister of an advertising man who just had to be asked said to me that it must be interesting to be married so often. I told her it was more exciting, no doubt, than not being married at all.' Her large eyes looked pathetically at Sinclair, and her voice was almost a wail. 'But it's not very nice, is it, to have things like that said to you on your wedding-day? Oh, here's Dick.' She went up to him and took his hands. 'Dick, darling, I'm having such an awful time I could cry. This really is the end, darling, the dreaded end. Can't we go away now, and leave these people to themselves?'

Richard looked pale, but determined. 'I don't think we ought to go away quite yet. We've only been here half an hour.'

'Then for God's sake let's start on our cold buffet, and stop talking. It's driving me crazy.' The long refectory table in the dining-room was laid for a meal. Richard looked miserable. 'I don't think everything's quite ready yet.'

'It *must* be ready.' There was a touch of hysteria in Eve's voice.

'And people keep coming in and out. I said they could have a look over the house, and a lot of people are doing just that.'

'Dick, I can't stand much more of this.' The hysteria could be heard plainly now. 'I wish I'd never let you alter the arrangements, and hold the reception here. I wish – '

'Here's Bland,' Sinclair said, and she swung round and stared at her husband.

'You didn't say he was coming.'

'Why, darling – ' Richard protested when Bland, in the doorway, saw her hand swing up and slap Richard's cheek, as it had been raised to strike his father in the next room three weeks ago. Her hand left a shaped red mark on Richard's white face. Everybody in the room heard the sharp report, and looked at Richard. He stood motionless, while his wife walked away with a firm, quick step which became almost a run as she neared the door. She went past Bland without a word or look and ran upstairs, quite plainly sobbing.

Something had happened at last, and the hum of excited voices testified that it was for an incident like this that the guests had been, perhaps half unconsciously, waiting. 'Isn't she *awful*,' Miss Peachey said to Miss Berry. Onslow and Mudge, both of them wearing their sports jackets, corduroy trousers and knitted ties, exchanged significant glances. Jean Rogers, standing next to Tracy, suddenly gripped his arm tightly, and he looked down at her in surprise. Richard Hargreaves walked away from Sinclair and across to Bland, straight through the crowd of people who looked at him, some of them with sympathy, and others with satisfaction. He said to the Inspector with some bitterness, 'You saw that?'

'I'm sorry,' Bland said, with a warmth that seemed hardly warranted. His eyes were watchful. 'I know this is an inappropriate moment, but I offer you my congratulations.' Richard seemed hardly to have heard. He was looking up the beautiful curve of the stairway after his wife. She disappeared at the head of the stairs, without looking back. Bland placed his hand on Richard's shoulder, and spoke gently. 'Do not expect too much of marriage, my friend, do not imagine that the rose is without its thorns. And don't forget that your wife has had a great deal to endure in these last few days.'

'I don't forget anything.' Richard made an impatient gesture, and suddenly swung round to show Bland a face distorted by

215

fear and passion. 'If Eve's come to any harm because of this crazy notion of yours, I'll – '

Bland was not listening. 'There are some people I do not see here. Where are – '

They were standing in the doorway, and there was suddenly a good deal of noise and commotion in the hall. Out of this noise Filby emerged, with his lean long-nosed face excited, and his hat on the back of his head. Two of the assistant men-servants were following him. 'Downstairs,' Filby said, and Bland jumped into action. 'Come on,' he said to the two assistant servants, and went after Filby, down the staircase to the servant's quarters. Richard Hargreaves looked again up the staircase, and then followed them like somebody in a dream. Sinclair followed Richard.

They went down the narrow winding staircase, and were in a long corridor with doors leading out of it on either side. 'Servants' quarters,' Filby said. 'But they're upstairs now, of course.' He led them along the corridor, to a door at the end of it, outside which another man was standing. This man said, 'In the cellar, sir,' and Sinclair gaped. He whispered to Bland, 'These are your men?'

'Of course,' Bland said impatiently. Then to Richard, 'Is the door of the cellars left open generally?'

'No, locked. The key hangs in the pantry just along the passage.'

'How far do the cellars extend?'

'Right underneath the house and almost into the road. There are six of them – wine cellar, a couple of empty rooms and then three lumber rooms with all sort of odds and ends. Can't think what anyone would want down there.'

Bland said to the man on guard, 'Do you know which cellar, Burke?'

'Somewhere up the other end, sir. Not in those first two any-way.'

'Is there any way out the other end?' Bland asked Richard, who shook his head. 'Good. All right, let's go. No torches if you can help it. Ready for anything, but I don't think there'll be much trouble.' He raised his eyebrows at Richard and Sinclair. 'What about you two?'

Sinclair's eyes were shining. 'Yes, of course I'll come. Who is it – van Dieren?'

'Yes, van Dieren.'

'You've lured him out at last.'

Bland did not answer this, but said impatiently. 'You, Hargreaves?'

Richard swallowed, and said simply, 'Yes.'

'Right.' Bland spoke with a note of command in his voice that Sinclair had not heard before. 'Take off your shoes and let's go down.'

While Sinclair was unlacing his shoes, Richard whispered, 'It's awfully dark down there, but there's a light switch in every cellar, and I can show you where they are.'

'No lights unless I give the order,' Bland said sharply. 'We need surprise. Open the door, Burke, and then stay at the top of these stairs. The rest of us will go down.'

Chapter Four *1.50 to 2.05 p.m.*

When Burke opened the door they saw at first nothing but darkness. Then Sinclair's eyes became a little accustomed to the gloom, and he made out the dim outline of two or three stone stairs, and a rail at their side. Filby went down first, followed by Bland, Richard and Sinclair himself, the two detectives following behind. As they went down the steps Sinclair lost the sense of identity of other people, as one does easily in darkness. He knew that Richard was before him on the stone staircase, and that one of the detectives walked behind, but so silently did they move that until he put out his hand and touched Richard's jacket he could have believed himself to be descending the stairs alone. When they had gone down six steps the staircase curved sharply to the right. He heard in front of him a hoarse whisper, 'How many more?' and Richard whispered back, 'Seven or eight.' It seemed minutes later, but was no doubt only a few seconds, that Sinclair reached the bottom of the stairs, and was conscious of bodies near him. Bland said to Richard, 'What's the geography?'

'We go straight through to a door at the other end. This is the wine cellar and there are racks about everywhere. I think you'll need a torch.'

'Torch, Filby,' Bland said. 'But no longer than you need.' The yellow torchlight cut slices of darkness, and revealed in flashes the steel racks in which bottles presented themselves like guns. There were paths between racks and Bland said, 'The one to the

218

left.' Filby put out the torch and they moved again, so quietly that Sinclair was painfully aware of somebody, he supposed one of the detectives, breathing heavily by his side. He could just make out the shapes of the racks on either side. When he put out his hand he felt the cold touch of the neck of a wine bottle. Ahead he heard a voice which he recognised as Richard's say, 'The entrance to the next one is just ahead on the right. The next two cellars are empty. The others contain old boxes, trunks, and so on.'

'Doors to the cellars?'

'Yes, but they're usually left open.'

'Flash your torch at the entrance of each cellar, Filby, and see that there's no one in it.'

'Okay,' said Filby hoarsely, and flashed the torch. An open door stood in front of them. Beyond it the second cellar stretched, square, clean and empty, just a little more than Sinclair's six feet in height, so that he had to bend a little in passing through the door. The torch played round, and made it plain that there was no place in this cellar for anyone to hide.

While they were passing cautiously through the second and third cellars Sinclair lost the sense of time so that he could not have said within minutes how long they had taken to walk through them. There was no sound in the cellars except the occasional drawing-in and sharp expulsion of breath, and Sinclair found himself moving like a careful automaton, while he wondered what they would find in the fourth, fifth or sixth cellars. Van Dieren, Bland had said, but how had van Dieren got there? And why was he there? What possible reason could the art agent have for coming out of hiding on Richard's wedding-day, and entering the cellars? Had he simply walked in as van Dieren, or in some disguise? Disguised, perhaps, by the red wig of that Mr Jones, who had never appeared in the case since his first dramatic entry. Suddenly Sinclair touched Richard Hargreaves, who moved in front of him. Richard was trembling.

Richard's whisper, however, was clear enough when he replied to Bland's question: 'Old boxes in this cellar, but I can't remember where they are.' Bland spoke to Filby and the torch played again, on books and files, cases filled with papers, a bicycle with broken spokes standing against the wall. At the same time they all saw a gleam of electric light in the next cellar. Richard drew his breath sharply, and Sinclair felt a coldness in his stomach. Bland said to the last man, 'Stay here and cover this door. The rest of us across – and quietly.' They moved towards the gleam of light slowly and noiselessly, in an atmosphere of growing tension. Once there was a rustle of paper, and Sinclair could have cried aloud with hysteria, and then with relief as something scurried over the floor and away. At last they were near the half-open door and could see the interior of the fifth cellar.

One dirty electric lamp threw a dim light in the cellar, and by this light they saw that the middle of the room was piled high with cases, trunks, boxes and all sorts of household odds and ends. Behind this pile somebody was bending down, apparently turning out the things in one of the boxes. The face and body of this person were invisible, but as a hand came up and took from the top of the pile of cases what looked, in the dim light, like an article of clothing, Sinclair saw something – and saw it with a shock of surprise that made him feel slightly sick.

Whoever was behind the pile of cases was wearing lemon-yellow gloves.

They stood behind the door, while the yellow gloves appeared again, and took something else – again it seemed to be an article of clothing, but Sinclair could not be quite sure – from the top of the pile. Then Bland stepped forward, flung the door into the cellar wide open, and called in a voice which contained a tone of mockery, 'You can come out, Mr van Dieren.'

The rustling behind the pile of boxes stopped at once, and the image came suddenly to Sinclair's mind of an enormous frightened mouse running back into its hole. But there was no hole here for the mouse – the trap had fastened on it. Or was that thought too dramatic? Bland called again: 'It's no use. I know what you're doing down here. You may as well come out.' There was a scuffling noise, and the figure darted into the last cellar, and slammed the door. They heard a key turn. Bland said sharply to Richard, 'You're sure there's no way out?'

Richard shook his head. There was sweat on his brow, and he seemed unable to speak. They advanced into the cellar, to the spot where the figure had been, and saw that a number of trunks and cases had apparently been moved to reach an old box at the bottom of the pile. This box had been opened, and its contents scattered around. Old shirts and pillowcases, a pair of dirty green curtains, a hairbrush, a camera, bits of lace, some broken picture frames – these had been placed at haphazard on the floor. But they noticed these things afterwards, for they looked first at what lay at the bottom of the trunk. This was a rather worn and frayed ginger coloured suit. Bland bent down and lifted it. 'Van Dieren's suit,' he said. 'Quite unmistakable, to anyone who'd seen him wear it.' He ran his hand through the pockets. 'Nothing here. I should have thought – ' He bent down to look at the box again and picked up from the bottom of it a piece of paper with typewriting on it. He read this, and said to Richard with a grim smile, 'This seems to be addressed to you. I'll read it. It has van Dieren's address at Earl's Court on the top, and it reads:

'Dear Richard, I cannot go on with this. You have made me act as your dupe through this whole affair, because of what you know about me, and I have always suspected your motives. But now your father is dead, they say he has been poisoned, and I hear that the police suspect me. You have forced me to do a lot of things for you, but I can't be an accomplice to murder. I shall go to the police and tell them I have acted as your tool, because of your hold over me. I know what the consequences will be for me, but I am prepared to face them. I write to you so that you shall have a chance to get away – '

Bland stopped and said, 'The letter is torn off there, at the end of a line, and there is no signature. An incriminating document.' He put it in his pocket.

Richard's face was white with terror. His voice was high, and the words tumbled out. 'I didn't do it – I swear I didn't. I don't know anything about that letter. I've never met van Dieren.'

Bland said sharply to Filby, 'Break that door down.'

Filby and Hemming put their shoulders to the oak door. It shivered, but did not move. 'All of us,' Bland said, and attacked the door with Sinclair. Richard Hargreaves stood with his hands hanging at his sides, and his eyes staring into space. The third time they attacked the door there was a sound of tearing wood, the lock gave way and the door opened. One of the policemen was taken off balance and slipped over on his side. There was no sound from inside the room, and Bland snapped. 'The torch, Filby.' Before the tall detective had time to take the torch out of his pocket a figure in a dark coat and yellow gloves rushed head-down out of the darkness, and butted him in the stomach. Filby said 'Ouch' and went sprawling, with his torch clattering on the stone floor. Richard Hargreaves made no move to stop the advancing figure, but in order to reach the door it had to dodge round the boxes, so that Sinclair and Bland had time to make an intercepting move. Sinclair caught hold of the dark coat from behind, but with an astonishingly quick movement the figure wriggled out and away so that Sinclair was left with the coat in his hands. But Bland was coming fast and straight from the other side of the room. The other swerved to avoid him, a little too late. Bland's rush carried them both to the ground. There was a flurry of arms and legs, and then Filby and Sinclair joined them, and the struggle was over. Bland got up from the floor and dusted his suit carefully, his face impassive. It was then that Sinclair saw the face for the first time.

SATURDAY, FEBRUARY 8

Chapter One *3.00 to 4.00 p.m.*

In a room on the first floor of the Richard the Third Restaurant, that last resort of the witty and beautiful, where all the men speak in epigrams, and all the women smile as if they understood them, Detective-Inspector Bland was giving a luncheon party.

There was a particular reason why this luncheon party, which was a celebration of the end of a difficult case, should be held at the Richard the Third Restaurant – for this restaurant had seen the successful end of another case in which Bland had been engaged.* Now, as the six of them sat sipping liqueurs at the end of a luncheon in which everything from pâté Richard the Third to cheese soufflé had been chosen with some care, Bland's smooth, round face was beaming with a pleasure not quite unmixed with smug satisfaction at a job of work completed. They had talked during luncheon of English, French and American police methods, of ways of cooking turbot, and the possibility of another war ('There won't be a war this year, or next year either,' Filby, who was a reader of the *Daily Express*, had announced confidently): but now Sinclair, his face bright and handsome, looked across from the other side of the round table at which they were sitting.

'What I can't understand, and what we'd like you to explain more than anything, is how you solved this case.'

Bland moved the stem of his glass between his fingers, and said with an affectation of coyness that Filby found altogether

*See The Immaterial Murder Case.

intolerable, 'It won't sound very impressive, but if you're interested, I'll be pleased to run through the way in which things worked out.' Filby covered his mouth with his hand to hide a yawn. It was pleasant to have been asked to lunch, and an honour, of course, and the food – and especially the drink – had been grand, but it was really a little too much to expect him to listen again to something that he had heard two or three times already. He rested his head on his hand, for Bland was already speaking in his pleasant, monotonous voice.

'Let me give you first of all the facts about the murder of Lionel Hargreaves, as I formulated them on that Wednesday evening. He had been shot through the back from close range, by somebody who had presumably worn a pair of yellow gloves, which were left behind as a present. Nobody heard the shot fired because the library, where he was killed, was soundproof. The murderer could have come from outside, through a door in the garden wall, or he could have entered the room by walking out of the drawing-room, where a party was going on, down the corridor and into the library. We were able to prove, thanks to the presence of servants in the hall, that there were only six people who walked out of the drawing-room during the relevant times Bond, Sinclair, Richard Hargreaves, Tracy, Onslow and Mudge. The last two went out together, and vouched for each other, and although it was theoretically possible that they might have committed the murder together, in practice we were soon able to clear them from suspicion, since they had absolutely no motive for committing the joint crime. This left, therefore, these four people – or someone from outside. Anyone else at the party was automatically excluded from suspicion, although the possibility of some sort of complicity between two people couldn't be ignored. Suppose, for example, Mrs Rogers had made an appointment with Lionel to meet him in the library – and it had been kept by Tracy. That kind of possibility had to be kept in mind.

'But as soon as the possibility of two people being concerned is mentioned, we come across another question which was generally ignored – why did Lionel go into the library? Since the library was a soundproof room, it was essential that the murder should be committed there, if the shot was not to be heard. The fact that the murder took place in the library indicated strongly that it was premeditated, and the presence of the gloves and gun made this almost certain. But if the murder was premeditated, the murderer must somehow have arranged that Lionel should be in the library. How? The obvious answer was that he met him there by appointment.

'Accepting this answer, I was brought up against the inherent improbability of anyone actually at the party being able to make such an arrangement without making Lionel suspicious. It *might* be that Bond, Sinclair, or Tracy would be able to say, "I've got something awfully important to tell you, old man – can I have a chat about it in the library?" – but that didn't seem at all likely. It was more likely that Richard, as Lionel's brother, could say such a thing – but more likely still that the appointment had no connection with the party at all. This was confirmed the next day when we found on Lionel's blotting-pad the note "Jones 7.30" and the word "Eve". The obvious conclusion to be drawn was that "Jones", who soon appeared in the case, had telephoned and made an appointment which referred to Eve Marchant.

'A further point was immediately apparent. If the murder was premeditated, and if the murderer had chosen the library deliberately, as a soundproof room, that could be done *only by someone familiar with the house*. By questioning I discovered that neither Sinclair nor Bond had been inside the house before. For the time being, therefore unless something new turned up – they were eliminated from suspicion.

'The dramatic entry of Miss Marchant on that evening, her statement that she was secretly married to Lionel, the fact that Richard was obviously in love with her, the mysterious telephone call made to her to ask her to come along at half-past nine – all this added further complications and possibilities. Her statement provided Richard with a motive. He said that he knew nothing of her marriage to Lionel – but supposing he had found out about it suddenly? If Miss Marchant's story was true, however, who had telephoned her?

'Later on various suggestions about the murderer were made. Bond made one out of pure malice. Mrs Rogers made another to try to lead suspicion away from Tracy, because she feared he might have committed the murder. Sinclair suggested that I should investigate the death of Lily Hargreaves two years before, and this idea proved useful. That ended the investigation on Wednesday evening.'

Mrs Rogers looked meltingly across the table at Tracy. Delicious, she thought, a delicious lunch, and delicious the candlelight and the drawn curtains, the candles now guttering, so that one could see faces dimly and softly. It was good for the Inspector to have given them this wonderful lunch, and of course his account of what had happened was fascinating. If only his voice were a little less monotonous! If only she had drunk a little less wine! She blinked quickly, to overcome the feeling of drowsiness that had almost made her close her eyes, and lit a cigarette. Bland was talking again.

'On the following morning the case unfolded, and presented its central problem – a man called Jones.

'You all know now that Jones bought the gun with which the murder was committed, that he made himself as conspicuous as possible with his red hair and yellow gloves, that he vanished at four o'clock on the day of the murder, and was never seen again. One could easily enough understand that the murderer would wear a disguise when buying the gun, but why should he wear such a conspicuous disguise and go to the lengths of hiring a room and living in it though the landlady said he never stayed the night? Why, why? I thought at first that Jones was used to create an alibi for the murderer in some way – but since he disappeared *before* the murder, what kind of alibi could possibly be created? Or perhaps he was simply an accomplice, a red-haired herring designed to lead us off the trail? I couldn't dismiss this altogether, but it seemed unlikely, because the accomplice would know too much of what went on. I considered the possibilities that Jones might be part of the pair Richard Hargreaves-Eve Marchant, or part of the pair Tracy-Mrs Rogers, working in collusion, but I couldn't see what they gained by such an elaborate fandango. Throughout the case, when incomplete and partial solutions were suggested, I went on asking myself the question "Why Jones?" – and when I answered it the case was solved.

'The other action of Jones we knew about, apart from his purchase of the gun, was his telephone call to Joseph van Dieren. When I called on van Dieren I found that he was an eccentric figure who denied all knowledge of Jones, but told me an extraordinary tale about EH having got him into prison in America many years before. I noticed, without paying any special attention to it, that van Dieren had a curious habit of plucking at his left coat-sleeve. When, later on I asked EH about van Dieren's story he did not deny its truth, but denied that it had anything at all to do with anyone who looked like van Dieren.

'With the help of Mr Weston I was able to clear up the mystery of Lily Hargreaves' death. But although her death was an indirect cause of the murders that followed two years later – I think, indeed, that her death put the whole idea into the murderer's head – it had nothing directly to do with the case, and I don't propose to talk about it.

'I began to build up a case – or rather it built itself up – against van Dieren. The telephone call had been made to him, he had known of an episode in EH's early life that was known to very few people, and I discovered that an anonymous letter received by EH about Eve Marchant had been typed on van Dieren's machine. It was clear that there was something wrong, and even criminally wrong, about him – his secretary shivered when she knew I was a detective, and Carruthers, the sole link I could find between van Dieren and the Hargreaves family, shook with terror whenever I mentioned his name. At the same time I had nothing like sufficient evidence to arrest him – a fact which I mentioned to Sinclair and Carruthers on the day that van Dieren was to call on EH. As it turned out, if I *had* arrested him then – even though I had only an inkling of the truth – I should have saved two lives...'

Below that domed brow Mr Weston's small, intelligent eyes were heavy. A good chap, Bland, he thought, a *very* good chap. Look at this lunch he had provided for them. And then such an excellent cigar! He took the giant Upmaish from his mouth, and looked at it appreciatively. Delicious fragrance! Through the blue smoke he looked at Mrs Rogers – a fine figure of a woman, and how pleasant it was that everything had worked out well for her and Tracy. What a good world it was altogether, Mr Weston thought; but when he closed his eyes he saw behind the lids an image of Lily Hargreaves. He opened them again, and it seemed that Bland's voice was coming from far away.

'We have reached the time of EH's murder. I don't need to recapitulate the circumstances of it to you, except to point out that it shortened our list of suspects, which in the first murder was Richard Hargreaves, Tracy here, or an outsider. In the second murder we could reduce the suspects quite definitely to van Dieren, Richard Hargreaves, Sinclair, Bond and Mr Weston. You won't fail to notice that one name appears on both lists – Richard Hargreaves. Two other names, those of Weston and van Dieren could be added, because both might have filled the role of "outsider" in the first murder, but Weston had an alibi for that murder which we were unable to break, and van Dieren could presumably have no knowledge of the asbestos-lined library.

'The case against both Richard and against van Dieren were strengthened by this second murder. Against van Dieren, because he had been sent away by EH "with a flea in his ear", having apparently told "a cock-and-bull story", and because he was the person who most obviously had an opportunity of adding poison to the sherry, because in the thick fog a small boy broke a window in EH's room, while van Dieren was there and EH's attention to what was going on inside the room was relaxed for some minutes. Against Richard, because it appeared that EH had been in touch with Weston that afternoon with the object of changing his will, cutting Richard out of it and leaving his money to charity.

'On the same afternoon van Dieren's offices were burned down, and his secretary found murdered. At the same time, although everything in the office was burnt, some pornographic drawings were found just outside the office, signed ARTES. I soon saw that this was a code name for Carruthers, consisting of alternate letters of his name. I had already been told by Bond that van Dieren carried on this kind of business, and the drawings provided an explanation for Carruthers' cold sweat of fear whenever van Dieren's name was mentioned. But why were the offices burned down? to conceal the fact that a murder had been committed? Hardly – why bother to do that when two unmistakable murders had been committed already? To conceal, then, something in the offices? It looked like it. And if this had been done by van Dieren, or by his order, then it was likely van Dieren would disappear. But one could argue, then, that anything left lying about on the premises, as those drawings of Carruthers were, was left for us to find, as a red herring.

'All this added to the conclusion that was slowly and inescapably being built up. That there were two murderers, one the executant, and the other the guiding hand. The executant – the person who appeared always in a suspicious light – was van Dieren, who seemed almost to go out of his way to court suspicion. The guiding hand was obviously the younger son, the person who stood to gain overwhelmingly by the death of a brother of whom he was jealous, and a father who had always behaved to him ungenerously, who was to be cut out of his father's will because he threatened to make an unsuitable marriage – Richard Hargreaves.

'That,' said Bland, drawing breath, 'is what we were meant to believe. I might have believed it, but for a trivial incident in which Filby was the central character. It was a gesture of Filby's that led me straight to the truth.' A sigh went round the table, passing from Filby to Mrs Rogers, from Mrs Rogers to Sinclair, on to Weston and Tracy, and back to Bland. A sigh of suspense – of anticipation – or merely of boredom? In the gathering dusk faces were almost invisible, and it would have been hard to say. But Bland, at least, was interested in the story he was telling, and was obviously determined to pursue it remorselessly to the end.

'When Filby was talking to me about the case he made a gesture as if to take a handkerchief out of his sleeve. But he had mislaid his handkerchief, as men sometimes do who carry them in their sleeves, and he quickly – and rather inelegantly – wiped his hand across his nose instead. Now, the point is this – I had seen van Dieren make an identical gesture towards his sleeve, not once, but two or three times during our short interview. But he had restrained himself, and drawn back his hand quickly or fiddled with a button on his coatsleeve, so that I had not realised that he was looking for a handkerchief. Was it that van Dieren, like Filby, had no handkerchief? No – for he produced a handkerchief from his jacket, and blew his nose on it loudly. Had he changed over from keeping his handkerchief in his sleeve to keeping it in his pocket? Possibly – but that could not account for my impression that he did not want me to know the meaning of his gesture, that he had drawn back suddenly and avoided putting his hand into his sleeve. Was it possible, then, I asked myself, that van Dieren when he saw me, was playing some kind of part? And when I had asked myself that question I asked myself another: *was not one impersonation involved, but two?*'

'When I had answered that question I had solved the case. I understood what really happened, and – most important – what the murderer was trying to do. And I saw that the clues did not lead to two persons but direct to one. I knew then that the murderer could be nobody but Arnold Carruthers.

'If one looks at the whole thing through those distorted eyes,' the detective continued, his own blue eyes looking dreamily into an unfathomed distance, 'one can recognise that the idea probably came into his mind when Lily Hargreaves died. He had been brought up with Lionel and Richard, on terms of comparative equality, had gone to the same school with them – and then he had been suddenly transformed from an equal to a poor relation. He reacted to this treatment as many young men might have done – he determined to be independent, and to be an artist. He was lonely, poor, sexually frustrated (as I learnt from Sinclair), and it must have become plain for him after a time that he wasn't, and never would be, a serious artist. Like all frustrated people he found compensation in a daydream in which he was free and rich, with unlimited opportunities for enjoyment. For he was not moved by one frustration only, but by two. He was shy and uneasy and unsuccessful with women – and he compensated himself for this by making pornographic drawings.

'But the further a compensation is removed from reality, the less satisfactory is it as a substitute for reality. And there is a time when the substitute altogether ceases to satisfy, when the heart cries out for reality, whatever the cost of obtaining it. Carruthers reached the point when, to obtain what he conceived as reality, he was prepared to commit murder. He became what we can call, for convenience, mad – but not certifiably mad. The scheme which entered his head was highly complex and hardly sane. Its purpose was nothing less than to inherit the Hargreaves fortune by eliminating everybody who stood between the fortune and himself. I suggest that Lily Hargreaves' marriage

233

put the idea of inheriting the Hargreaves money out of his mind. Her death, in curious circumstances, with a strong hint of suicide, brought it back with a rush.

'His first step was taken six months after her death, when van Dieren first appears on the scene. An existing, moderately successful art agent's business was bought, with the aid of a loan from EH, who did not know, of course, what he was lending the money for – a neat ironical touch that must have touched Carruthers' sense of humour. The character of Joseph van Dieren was created. Van Dieren had, of course, no background and no history. Instead of trying to provide him with a false background, Carruthers very sensibly set to work to create a real one. One suspects an impersonation when a man suddenly appears and disappears, but hardly when he had been in physical existence, with a business of his own, for eighteen months.

'It was not very difficult to create and maintain the separate character. Carruthers lived alone in Balham. Van Dieren lived alone in Earl's Court. Their acquaintances were different, their appearances different. Physically, van Dieren was composed of a large false moustache, a fairly obvious wig – so obvious that nobody guessed it was meant to conceal anything – a suit of clothes that was too big, a deep bass voice and a bit of make-up. About half of Carruthers' time was spent in the character of van Dieren, and through the art agency he was able to find an easy market for his pornographic drawings. For eighteen months he bided his time and perfected his scheme. He might have been prepared to wait even longer, but for the coincidence – the only one in the case – that Eve Marchant's friend in the chorus was the sister of van Dieren's secretary. Eve told her friend that she'd been secretly married to Lionel, and, of course, the news came through to Carruthers in his role as van Dieren. It must have decided him to act – because if there were a child of the marriage it would inherit legally when Lionel died. So Mr Jones appeared on the scene.'

Bland paused and looked round in the dim light at the assembled company. Filby was looking at his pipe with a disgusted air. He had, of course, heard all this before. Sinclair's customary bright look was somehow blurred, as if there were a film over his eyes, but he was staring at the detective with what might be thought flattering attentiveness. Tracy's head was in his hands, Mrs Rogers seemed to be looking at the ceiling, and Weston was frankly nodding. Not an altogether satisfactory audience, Bland reflected, and thought rather wistfully of Eve and Richard, who had sent a cable from Paris where they were honeymooning, 'CONGRATULATIONS TO SLEUTHERY.' Perhaps they would have improved the standard of listening. Perhaps the lunch had been too good. He plunged on, like a swimmer in difficult water.

'Jones was a bold and successful conception, who again helped to conceal the truth by appearing to reveal it. He flaunted his red hair and yellow gloves – he was concerned to give an address to which the revolver he bought could be sent – he positively advertised himself as the murderer, and also as somebody wearing a disguise. He made a quite unnecessary telephone call to van Dieren's office, which he made sure that his landlady would overhear – what landlady wouldn't listen to the telephone conversations of a red-headed man who always wore yellow gloves, and who never stayed overnight in his lodgings? The gloves were really necessary, of course, so that no fingerprints should be left in "Mr Jones'" room. If fingerprints were left, and found later to check with Carruthers', the fat would really be in the fire. This question of fingerprints worried Carruthers all along, and he went to extravagant lengths to eliminate them, as we shall see. The purpose of Mr Jones was to create the character of van Dieren even more firmly – since nobody expects, nor was there any obvious reason for, a *double* impersonation. But his subsidiary purposes were to cast suspicion on van Dieren, for reasons that I'll explain in a moment, and to make it quite clear that Jones, whoever he might be, was *not* van Dieren. Filby once suggested that the two of them might be identical, and I remember that I answered caustically that if van Dieren really wanted to draw suspicion on himself he couldn't have done it better. But van Dieren (it's easier to keep the names separate than to call them all Carruthers) did want to draw suspicion to himself. Why?

'There lies the key to the whole plot. If Carruthers had gone about eliminating everybody who stood between him and the Hargreaves fortune in a straightforward and simple manner he would (as he realised) very soon have been caught. By arranging this elaborate build-up he thought he stood no chance of being even suspected. For in his plan he did not mean to kill Richard Hargreaves – he meant to arrange things so that Richard should be hanged as the murderer of his father and brother, so that he should inherit as the next in line. In Carruthers' plan van Dieren was to be used to cast suspicion gradually on Richard. Gradually – for it would never do if Richard were arrested for murder of his brother alone. Carruthers' role as van Dieren was to draw suspicion on himself, and to show at the same time that van Dieren could be only a pawn in somebody's hands. Since Richard was the person who profited by the crimes the conclusion was that he must be a pawn of Richard. Incidentally, he was used to make it absolutely clear that Carruthers himself had nothing to do with the crime, by various remarks and innuendoes and by the picturing of Carruthers as a tool of van Dieren. Jones was probably intended to have a final unveiling as Richard by the discovery of his red wig in Richard's possession, or something like that; but if he remained forever unexplained, that would do almost as well. Jones served the purpose of drawing attention to van Dieren, but here and elsewhere Carruthers overplayed his part a little – Jones was rather too palpably a figure in disguise, so that one asked awkward questions about him. 'When he vanished from the scene at four o'clock on Wednesday, the stage was set for Lionel's murder.

'The mechanics of that were simple. Lionel was telephoned by somebody calling himself Jones, who said he knew about Lionel's marriage to Eve Marchant, and wanted to see him about it. Lionel was, we know, anxious to keep the marriage secret, and agreed to meet Jones that night at 7.30. Jones must have threatened to tell EH if Lionel would not agree to see him, and then no doubt said something like, "You won't need to leave the house – I'll come up through the back entrance and see you in your library." When Lionel entered the library he may have found "Jones", but I should think it more likely that he found Carruthers, from the fact that he was shot in the back. He would hardly have turned his back on a stranger, especially so odd a stranger as Jones.

'On the same day, to thicken up the plot a bit, Carruthers telephoned to Eve Marchant, to say that Lionel wanted to see her, and he typed on van Dieren's machine an anonymous letter about the marriage, which he sent to EH.'

'Then came one of the most difficult things he had to do – to face me as van Dieren. He couldn't have looked forward to that, especially when he was unlucky enough to meet me by chance for the first time as Carruthers, a couple of hours before he was due to meet me as van Dieren. He seemed, and no doubt was, frantically nervous. But he got away with it all right as van Dieren, partly because of a piece of good acting but chiefly because by bad luck I got a piece of grit in my eye, which was watering so badly that I had to keep it half-closed. He very wisely sat half in the shade, so that I could see him only dimly. He spun me this tale about EH in America, which was meant to link van Dieren up with Richard who knew the story, but linked him up with Carruthers just as effectively. He was guilty of another piece of over-subtlety here, because when I asked him as Carruthers if he remembered the story he said he didn't whereas Richard remembered it at once. If Richard had been guilty one would have expected that he would deny the story.

'He was over-subtle about his drawings, too. When he burned down the offices – '

'Why did he do that?' Sinclair asked. The words fell startlingly in the thick and hazy twilight.

'Fingerprints again. He was terrified of a fingerprint verification. And because of another of his mistakes – Polly Lines.'

'How much did she know about it all? And why did he kill her? And, by the way, who pushed you in the road that night when I nearly knocked you over? Or was that really an accident?'

Bland laughed. 'Of course it was. I told you at the time that it's only in books that the murderer tries to kill the detective. Polly Lines knew about the pornographic racket, but of course she wasn't an accomplice in the murders. He was madly foolish to let himself get mixed up with her, but he was a sexually frustrated man, and Polly Lines was no doubt one of the few women he could get. But she must have learnt he made up. I doubt if we shall ever know what story he told her to explain that, but the fact that he was in such a shady business made it possible for him to tell one of half a dozen plausible tales. When she heard talk about murder she became suspicious and frightened, and he killed her because of that, and burned down the offices to avoid any chance of fingerprint recognition. He also destroyed all the letters and correspondence of the firm, including samples of van Dieren's handwriting. He was extremely careful about handwriting – she signed all the letters, and he even got her to sign the agreement for his cottage. After the offices were burnt we couldn't find a scrap of paper signed by van Dieren, so that we could compare his handwriting with Carruthers'. He made a big mistake, though, in leaving those Carruthers drawings outside the office for us to find. His idea was to confirm once again that van Dieren had Carruthers on his books, and that they weren't intimate friends and the drawings were left to give a plausible reason for their tie-up. Carruthers' reasoning probably went something like this. It might be dangerous to conceal the fact that van Dieren and Carruthers were linked in some way. All right then, let's admit it. Let Carruthers appear frightened when he hears van Dieren's name. And then, at the right moment, give evidence to show *why* Carruthers was worried – because he was afraid that the business about the pornographic drawings would come out. It's an old trick, to admit responsibility for a minor offence to avert suspicion about a major one, but it's still an effective one.

'In this case, however, the trick was spoilt by the signature. What pornographic artist in his senses would sign his work – and with a signature consisting of alternate letters of his own name, at that? And it was only a step from wondering about the signature to wondering how and why these particular drawings happened to escape the fire, and if they'd been left deliberately.

'Before I realised the significance of the handkerchief, I was just working by guess and by God, trying to separate what was genuinely important from the trails that, I could see, had been laid by the murderer. I even played around for some time with the idea that Jones had been invented to conceal a non-existent physical defect – if Bond's limp wasn't real, for instance, he might create Jones just to give himself an alibi. I tried to make something, too, of the fact that Jones never stayed overnight – if he were a married man, of course he probably wouldn't be able to do so. And all the while I saw this case building up against Richard, through van Dieren – a case which puzzled me because it was too obvious. If Richard was the murderer, then he'd behaved with astonishing stupidity.

'EH's murder of course, was done in the obvious way, by van Dieren dropping poison in the sherry while EH's attention was drawn away by the small boy who'd been engaged to throw the stone. The beauty of this was that it was made absolutely clear that Carruthers couldn't have committed this murder, because (as Carruthers) he'd never entered the room. After that van Dieren vanished, and Carruthers hoped I would arrest Richard, because of his obvious motive. But by that time I knew exactly what was happening, and I was determined to force Carruthers to make a further attempt to incriminate Richard, which might allow us to catch him in the act. I put a man on to watch Richard, simply to make sure that no attack was made upon him, because that couldn't absolutely be ruled out. In the meantime I tried to find some link that would identify van Dieren and Carruthers as the same person. I failed in that – he'd covered the two main tracks of fingerprints and handwriting too carefully. Since his arrest, however, we've found, by advertising for them, some receipts signed incautiously by "van Dieren" in the early days of his agency, which present the same characteristics as Carruthers' hand.

'Carruthers must have been disappointed by my failure to arrest Richard, but he was prepared for it. He couldn't produce van Dieren's body, so his last and most ingenious idea was to show unmistakably that Richard had killed van Dieren, and by extension, therefore, must have committed the two other murders. I was prepared for this, and while Carruthers was playing cat-and-mouse with Richard, I was playing cat-and-mouse with him, I asked Richard to alter the place in which his wedding reception was held to his house in Redfern Square, because I thought it certain that Carruthers would think that too good a chance to miss planting incriminating evidence. I had men watching Carruthers from the moment he left home that morning, and when he went down into the cellars they knew what he was going to do. That was the only way we could catch him – as we had to catch him – redhanded.'

The room was almost dark as Bland stopped speaking, and there was no sound in it but the gentle rhythmical breathing of five people. They were all asleep. With a sigh Bland got slowly to his feet, raised one of the wine bottles and poured the few drops of it down Filby's neck. With a horrified look on his face Filby opened his eyes and shook himself. 'All over?' he said.

'All over. They can't take drink, I'm afraid.' Bland stood up. 'We must go.'

'The Jones case is closed?'

'From the point of view of investigation it's certainly closed. Finished. I don't want to hear about it or him any more.'

'Neither do I,' said Filby handsomely. 'But aren't we going to say goodbye to those people?'

'We'll just get our coats, and then say it.' They met a waiter at the door, who peered at them both. 'Inspector Bland? There's somebody to see you downstairs. Something to do with some criminal case, he said it was.'

'Oh yes. Who is he?'

The waiter said, 'A man called Jones.'

JULIAN SYMONS

THE BROKEN PENNY

An Eastern-bloc country, shaped like a broken penny, was being torn apart by warring resistance movements. Only one man could unite the hostile factions – Professor Jacob Arbitzer. Arbitzer, smuggled into the country by Charles Garden during the Second World War, has risen to become president, only to have to be smuggled out again when the communists gained control. Under pressure from the British Government who want him reinstated, Arbitzer agreed to return on one condition – that Charles Garden again escort him. *The Broken Penny* is a thrilling spy adventure brilliantly recreating the chilling conditions of the Cold War.

'Thrills, horrors, tears and irony' – *The Times Literary Supplement*

'The most exciting, astonishing and believable spy thriller to appear in years' – *The New York Times*

Julian Symons

The Colour of Murder

John Wilkins was a gentle, mild-mannered man who lived a simple, predictable life. So when he met a beautiful, irresistible girl his world was turned upside down. Looking at his wife, and thinking of the girl, everything turned red before his eyes – the colour of murder. Later, his mind a blank, his only defence was that he loved his wife far too much to hurt her...

'A book to delight every puzzle-suspense enthusiast'
– *The New York Times*

The End of Solomon Grundy

When a girl turns up dead in a Mayfair Mews, the police want to write it off as just another murdered prostitute, but Superintendent Manners isn't quite so sure. He is convinced that the key to the crime lies in The Dell – an affluent suburban housing estate. And in The Dell lives Solomon Grundy. Could he have killed the girl: so Superintendent Manners thinks.

JULIAN SYMONS

THE PLAYERS AND THE GAME

'Count Dracula meets Bonnie Parker. What will they do together? The vampire you'd hate to love, sinister and debonair, sinks those eye teeth into Bonnie's succulent throat.'

Is this the beginning of a sadistic relationship or simply an extract from a psychopath's diary? Either way it marks the beginning of a dangerous game that is destined to end in chilling terror and bloody murder.

'Unusual, ingenious and fascinating as a poisonous snake'
– *Sunday Telegraph*

THE PLOT AGAINST ROGER RIDER

Roger Rider and Geoffrey Paradine had known each other since childhood. Roger was the intelligent, good-looking, successful one and Geoffrey was the one everyone else picked on. When years of suppressed anger, jealousy and frustration finally surfaced, Geoffrey took his revenge by sleeping with Roger's beautiful wife. Was this price enough for all those miserable years of put downs? When Roger turned up dead the police certainly didn't think so.

'[Symons] is in diabolical top form' – *Washington Post*